# The Fool's Journey through the Tarot

# ~ Wands ~

## by Noel Eastwood

### Book 5 The Fool's Journey series

Contact the author, Noel Eastwood:

Email: info@plutoscave.com

Web: http://www.plutoscave.com

Facebook - @PlutosCave

Cover illustration: Peta Fenton

Editor: Kristal, Dan

Tarot Deck: Original Rider-Waite deck (1910)

A special thank you to everyone who assisted me in writing the Fool's Journey series. In particular my brother Mark, my son Steven and his wife, Lorna, who helped me craft the first edition of Follin's Journey. To my generous editors: JoAnn, who gave me so much of her incredible talent and depth of knowledge in the esoteric field; and Kristal, who has been there beside me since the very beginning. To my wife who put up with me disappearing down numerous rabbit holes while I researched and wrote this series. And of course my readers who supported me in giving Follin, Eve and the archetypes their own stories to tell.

~

# Contents

# Author's Preface

Writing this series has been a labour of love as the mysteries of our existence have walked beside me every day of my life. In this final book of the Fool's Journey series, Follin and Eve fulfil their mystic's quest but only after they are faced with life-changing experiences that tests their resolve and their magical powers.

Once again you will meet your favourite characters as they support Follin and his family while also defending the Wands frontiers. Inspired by the esoteric element of fire, the people of the Wands Kingdom demonstrate how to access and harness fire energy using specific meditation forms.

In this final book I wanted to include some of the esoteric systems that I have touched upon throughout this series. You will find elements of Hermeticism, western and Taoist alchemy, shamanism, paganism, Wicca, Druidry, Greek and Celtic mythology, Plato, Jung's Active Imagination, and the magick art of scrying the Tarot archetypes. It was my intention to weave these themes into the story while trying not to interfere with the flow and development of Follin and Eve's journey. Some of the characters use specific Taoist fire meditation forms, these will help you better understand the esoteric element of fire.

I have to admit that this was a hard book to write as I needed to tie off the many loose ends from the previous four books in the series. It was also important that each suit of the Minor and Major Arcana came together in this, the final book.

I can finally confess that in writing this series I have had to live through the themes they presented as I wrote them. For instance, while writing the Pentacles book I was challenged to focus and address issues of the physical and material world: income, health, diet and what to do with myself in retirement. In writing the Swords book I was forced to examine my long-standing writing difficulties, the writing craft itself, and editing, which is my big weakness. The Cups book came at a time when I was driven to face my own inner demons - it sure is funny what comes up when you have time on your hands. In this, my last book of the series, Wands, I have been guided to re-examine my spiritual path that began in 1980. Interestingly I can see that, as a retired psychologist, astrologer, tarotist and Taoist, my own mystic's quest is reflected in Follin's.

The Wands suit highlights the characteristics of the esoteric fire element. These include enthusiasm, imagination, courage, pride, honour, respect, conflict, responsibility, and self-control. These themes are reflected in astrology through the three fire signs, Aries, Leo and Sagittarius; the fire houses, $1^{st}$, $5^{th}$ and $9^{th}$ houses; as well as the fire planets: Mars, Sun and Jupiter.

I shall now leave you to enjoy Follin and Eve's adventures in the Wands Kingdom. I am sure that you will find some useful tips that will guide you along your own mystic's path.

~

Wishing you every success on your own mystic's quest,

Noel Eastwood

Canberra, Australia, January 2022

# **Prologue:** Stealing Fire - a Tale of Magic

It was a cold evening in the Wands Kingdom when Follin arrived home. His Elf Ranger friends were already sitting around the fire in his chambers inside Dragon Mountain Castle. Ziggy, and his adopted brother, Pandjar, rose and embraced Follin. Pandjar's partner and fellow Elf Ranger, Carwen, a dark-haired elf lass, waited politely before kissing Follin lightly on the cheek in greeting.

Pandjar and Carwen had only recently arrived from a patrol on the northern frontier and were looking forward to a warm meal with their friends. The Elf Rangers often accompanied the Wands Fearless and the Pentacles Mountaineer Commandos on their patrols along the borders of the Tarot Empire.

Seated around the blazing fire were Ziggy's wife Sorcha and their two children, Tamotan and Lily. There were also Follin's sister, Theresa, and her husband, Tombei, and their two children Tanika and Atsu. As usual, his parents, the Mage Saoirse and Katlyn, Follin's mother, were also present, lending a hand where they could. It was such a large gathering that they had to bring in the spare table from Follin's alchemy room.

"That cold wind just cuts through my twenty layers of clothing like a knife," announced a shivering Katlyn as she helped serve the evening's meal. "We'll certainly go through some firewood tonight trying to keep everyone warm."

Ziggy looked up from filling his pipe. "All the better to keep the Wildlanders indoors, Katlyn. With luck, this will end their incursions across the borders for a while. We need time to rest up and repair our weapons, bodies and souls."

Follin had always liked Ziggy's brother, Pandjar, a rough yet fascinating character. The Wood Elf warrior was always ready with a joke or an encouraging word. His captivating female companion, Carwen, rarely spoke or engaged in social banter. All the same, like her partner, she was highly respected for her fighting prowess. Follin likened them to a pair of prowling cats, their habits so similar that he caught himself thinking of them as being of one body with two voices.

Follin's seven-year-old twins, Aidan and Fiana, had often asked their parents how Uncle Pandjar got his scars, the three claw marks on his face had always intrigued them. The fact was that even Follin didn't know, he had simply accepted Pandjar's scars for what they were, wounds acquired in battle. It was quite common to see warriors throughout the Tarot Empire, young and old, wear their battle scars with pride.

Pandjar's rugged, cheerful personality was quite different to his brother, Ziggy's quiet, sombre manner. He was tall and well-muscled, even for an Elf Ranger, and a warrior of repute. His reputation for going berserker was often a topic of conversation in the taverns of the frontier Kingdoms. The three livid scars running down his face gave him a fierce, dangerous presence - a man not to be trifled with.

In contrast to her partner's rugged appearance, Carwen had a startling beauty and a self-assurance that caused people to turn and stare. Certainly, most would say that she was attractive, but it was her shrewd intuition and ferocious fighting ability that preceded her. Her slender carriage and stern bearing, like that of her companion, spoke of the hardship they had faced these past months patrolling the Empire's frontiers.

It was after dinner, while sitting around the hearth in Follin's lounge room, that Aidan finally asked the question that had been burning up inside of him.

"Uncle Pandjar, umm..." Aidan paused to look at his father. Follin nodded for him to continue. "Well, I was wondering, how did you get those scars on your face? My Da said you got them fighting in the wars, but Grandpa said you were clawed by a crazed demon. Maybe it was from a dragon, like Nangkari? He's only got one eye, maybe he did it?"

The visiting Elf Rangers looked at each other in surprise, to them the scars were invisible. Regaining his composure, Pandjar smiled at his young host.

"Nay, Aidan, Nangkari is my friend, he wouldn't harm me. I have to admit though, I have been waiting for your father to ask me this same question for many years now, but he just won't. It looks like it's time for me to tell my story."

As he spoke Pandjar unconsciously raised his fingers to trace the scars on his face. "I wear these scars as a reminder," he said as the group drew their woollen rugs closer around their shoulders. "When I was young, I wanted to show everyone that I was tough and brave like my two big brothers, so I embarked on a personal quest into the Hindamar Mountains. I wanted to prove that I was worthy enough to be chosen as one of the famous Elven Rangers. My brothers, Kerrytan and Ziggy, were both warriors of repute, while I was just their weedy little adopted brother. I had something to prove, I wanted to be like them, to earn my place and the respect of my clan."

Ziggy was serving the hot apple pie that Eve and Theresa had made that day, and stopped to put his hand on his younger brother's shoulder.

"Aidan, did you know that Pandjar was adopted by my family when he was little? You see, Pandjar's father was killed in an ambush in the Hindamar Mountains. When his mother heard of her husband's death she pined away and died of a broken heart. So my mother and father agreed that a third son would be good to keep us older boys out of trouble. Kerrytan, our eldest brother, and myself, spent most of our time trying to keep Pandjar out of trouble instead. Our mother's plan worked - in reverse."

"Thank you for butting in big brother. Now let me tell my story," grunted Pandjar. "As you know, our clan was named after Daru, the mother of oaks. She lived on the highest peak of the Hindamar Mountains and was said to be Earth's first-born tree. I wanted to prove my courage and worthiness by bringing a leaf from her tree to my Wood Elf Clan."

Pandjar stopped talking to look at the firelight flickering on the curious faces around him. He accepted Ziggy's offer of tobacco and carefully filled his pipe - the children quietly waited. "I was young and impulsive and had forgotten that there was a tribe of lions who sometimes hunted in that area of the Hindamar Mountains, and they had a reputation for wickedness."

"So, the lions... did they try to eat you?" asked Fiana almost forgetting to breathe in her joy at finally hearing the story of Pandjar's scars. Beside her, Tanika and her little brother Atsu, were silently watching the elf with wide, excited eyes. Elves love to tell stories around the fire at night and this was promising to be a story better than any the children had heard before.

"Certainly they did. In those early days, elf and lion were on speaking terms. We spoke to them and they roared at us," Pandjar joked.

"I thought elves had magic, why didn't your invisibility magic stop the lions trying to eat you?" interrupted Aidan, absently stroking his own face as though he too wore the lion's claw marks.

"In those days lions also had magic. We were much the same in strength, but since then lions have lost theirs. Perhaps Pan took it away from them for abusing his gift, I don't know." Pandjar stopped to relight his pipe. The tobacco was a prized, aromatic leaf from the same Water Elf village that Follin had visited before the twins were born.

Puffing several times at his pipe to form a lion-shaped cloud of smoke above his head, the elf continued his story. "In the early days, there was magic everywhere. We believe that Pan wanted this for all his creatures so that everything on this beautiful planet would be happy, in perfect balance. Sadly, it corrupted many of them instead. The lion tribes formed gangs and fought ferocious battles against each other. They would hunt and devour weaker creatures for their food and pleasure. The elven people eventually gave up trying to be friends with them."

Tamotar called out impatiently, "Hurry up, Uncle Pandjar! Tell Aidan and Fiana how you managed to trick the lions of their meal."

Pandjar's eyes lit up and he all but roared at his nephew. "Am I taking so long that you've lost your manners, young man? But then, I do go on a bit don't I..." The tough warrior's voice softened as he grinned in satisfaction that his story had not lost its power to draw even his nephew to want to listen one more time.

"The mountain was steep and the going was growing more difficult with each step. It was snowing lightly and it was cold, much like it is here tonight." A sudden gust of wind smashed against the window shutters causing the children to grip their blankets tighter as they leaned forward to catch his every word.

"Eventually I reached the final slope that led to the mountain peak and the mother of oaks herself when I saw a band of lions chasing a stag. The stag, Kwadinsa was his name, was a sight to see, he was in the prime of life and I paused to admire his beauty. Alas, I was young, naive and very rash in those days so I thought I might trick the lions of their meal. As the stag raced past, I called to him that I would try to distract the lions. I stood on a tall rock and called to the lions that a troop of elves were hunting the stag. '*Leave the stag alone or we'll shoot our arrows into you instead!*' I shouted." Pandjar winked at the children before resuming.

"That made the lions very angry indeed. Kwadinsa was clever and had been on the run since dawn, leading the lions higher and higher into the mountain peaks trying to exhaust his enemies. Lions don't like the cold and they don't like to climb mountains, it makes them mean and nasty. Distracted by my words they lost sight of the stag which caused them to argue among themselves.

The younger lions growled that they wanted to go back down to the warmer slopes, but their leader forced them to stay. I used my best lion-speak to make them change their minds and go away. Lions are simple creatures and I thought that I was smarter than they were. I tricked the two youngest into turning around but the two eldest lions pricked up their ears when they realised that there was just a single elf voice. You see, a lion can smell an elf a mile away, and that one miserable elf was me. They soon learned that I had no companions to protect me."

"'*Stop arguing!*' cried their leader, '*our prey is now elf, and he is standing right there on top of that rock.*' He roared so loud that I almost fell off the mountain." Pandjar chuckled, his audience now leaning even closer to catch every word of his story. "I knew that if I ran they would easily outrun me and I would soon become their evening meal. Quickly I scanned the rocks around me and found a narrow crack between two large boulders. In the blink of an eye, I had wedged myself as far inside that crevasse as I could."

"*'Get him! He's trying to escape!'* One of the lions called, and, with a rush of muscle and sinew, that darn beast reached his paw in between the rocks and sliced my face open. *'I've got him!'* The lion cried loudly. *'Come, brothers, we've not feasted on elf for a long time. This one is fat and juicy, I can smell it in his blood.'*

"Little did I know that my two older brothers had been following along behind me. Not once did I suspect their presence. I was just a boy and so proud of my brothers. They were masters of evasion and their Elf Ranger training made it impossible for me to notice them. They knew how rash and naive I was and had taken on the role of being my guardians.

"I was terrified, of course. I couldn't magic the lions away, nor could I magic myself deeper into the rocks. I knew that I would die. But just as the four lions started to claw at me again, I heard the cry of a stag, but it sounded strangely familiar. It was my dear brother, Ziggy. He called those lions all sorts of rude names in the stag's tongue. He made fun of their manhood and laughed at their weakness. Lions are proud creatures, even in those days they were prouder than any other creature, except silly me." This made the children chuckle delightedly as each strained to get even closer to their storyteller without actually falling into the blazing hearth itself.

"One by one the lions stopped trying to get at me and they

started arguing with each other again. *'I want the elf hiding in that rock hole! An elf in the claw is worth a dozen stags on the hoof. I say we eat the elf then chase down the stag later!'* said the leader of the lions. *'No!'* cried one of the younger lions. *'I say we take down the stag first, he'll feed us and our pride for a whole week. We'll kill him then come back for the elf, he won't get far with the wounds we've given him.'* That started the four lions arguing all over again.

"Then I heard another voice, it was my other brother, Kerrytan, he was a master mimic and could lion-speak better than any elf. He had listened carefully to their arguing and had learned each of the lions' names. He started saying things to set one against the other. He mimicked their voices and began to tease and insult them until they exploded into violence."

By now everyone was silent and still. The pipes had long gone out but no one had noticed. They were each there, high up in the snow-swept Hindamar Mountains, trapped in a narrow rock crevice, surrounded by four savage lions and the whisperings of Wood elves cleverly mimicking stags and lions.

"I had lost a lot of blood. My face was torn, and my chest bled from the lion's long, sharp claws. My arms and hands were sliced to the bone from trying to fend them off. I knew that I was dying, so, with the last of my strength, I called upon my powers and drew the lion's energy into my own body. Without realising it, I drew their fiery berserker rage into my being as they fought each other outside my tiny rock sanctuary. I drew their life force into my body like a baby suckles milk from its mother's breast. There was no other way for me to stay alive but to imbibe the lion's power - all of it. When a lion is aroused, it becomes pure fire. Those lions were warriors of their tribe, and they had the Flame, just like the Wands people have. That's what kept me alive, and why I am such a, a... why I'm so ferocious in battle. I turn into a wild, berserk lion." Pandjar chuckled and the children could see an elf shape-shifting into a lion in their mind's eye.

"I was weak and had fainted when my brothers finally came to my rescue. As they pulled me free I could see the four lion bodies strewn on the ground. Three had been killed by their own kind and Ziggy finished the last one with his arrows."

All was still, the sound of the pine resin crackling in the fire was all that could be heard. The families gathered together were totally immersed in Pandjar's world beyond time, their breathing almost imperceptible as they waited to hear the ending to the story.

"My brothers stayed with me to tend my wounds, it was six days before I could walk out from among those rocks. Together we climbed the last few paces to the mother of oaks where we each plucked one of the few surviving leaves from her outstretched branches. I found an acorn deep in the snow that had fallen to the ground, one of the few acorns left behind by the Hindamar squirrels, and held it high.

"'*My dear brothers,*' I said, '*I will plant this oak seed in honour of our kinship. I shall tend it for as long as I am alive. It will remind me of my stupidity and of the courage of my brothers.*'" Pandjar stopped speaking to clean and refill his pipe, his mind back on that mountain top.

As Ziggy passed his tobacco pouch to his brother, he said, "Did you know, Aidan, that the tree we sit below in our Daru village, is from the acorn that Pandjar retrieved from the Mother of Oaks? It has survived beyond time to remind us of honour and the bonds of family and friendship."

In the silence, Fiana softly asked, "But what about your brother, Kerrytan, what happened to him?"

Pandjar spoke as he re-lit his pipe with a lighted stick from the fire. "Fiana, my elf-wise lass, there is a hill in the middle of the Forest of Smoke and Fire, there you will find an oak tree that rises above all others. Surrounding this tree is an oak forest, not a big forest but enough to protect a small herd of deer. These are the kin of Kwadinsa, the stag we saved that day on the mountain top. He had returned to the mountain crest and retrieved his own acorn. He planted it to honour us for his rescue. His grave rests beside that of Kerrytan. Sadly, I was not present when Kerrytan died, he was killed in a skirmish with the Wildlanders in that same Forest of Smoke and Fire. Ziggy and I built a stone cairn to mark his grave. Your Aunt Carwen and I plan to visit his and Kwadinsa's graves on our next patrol to the northern frontiers. We had many adventures together, my brothers and I." Pandjar fell silent, staring into the fire, puffing on his pipe. Everyone went quiet for some minutes until the mothers began to stir and prepare the children for bed.

Before moving away from the warmth of the fire, Aidan had one more question that was burning inside of him and needed to be asked.

"Uncle Pandjar, you know how you said that you have lion energy, do you really become a lion when you go berserk?" There came a soft chuckle from the adults.

Turning to look at the youth, Pandjar replied, "Young man, that is a question I ask myself too. When I go into battle, I can feel my fiery lion energy. I become like a wild lion, yes, indeed I do." Aidan could see Carwen smile as she nodded her head in agreement. "But, no one has said that I look like a lion. As you know, the Wands Kingdom is founded on fire energy, and that's what the lion has, fire. I think that's why I love to visit my friends of the Flame here in the Kingdom so much because my type of fire needs fire friends to keep it company."

Pandjar put his hand on his partner's shoulder. "If you want to see another form of fire energy just look at your Aunt Carwen here. Her wolf energy may be a little cooler than the fire of a berserker lion, but when I'm going into battle, I prefer the presence of a fire-being above all others to stand beside me." The pretty elven lass affectionately leaned her head on Pandjar's shoulder.

Sorcha yawned, stretched as she stood then gently took her daughter's hand. Reminding the children to say 'good night' to their guests, she led them towards what had become, on nights like this, the children's communal bedroom.

Mage Saoirse helped his wife, Katlyn, pass steaming cups of spiced mead among the adults quietly warming themselves around the log fire. But Follin wriggled uncomfortably in his seat, he still had questions and didn't know how to ask them without appearing uncouth. Carwen noticed and asked him to speak up.

"Well, I don't want to be rude, but, Pandjar, all your wounds seem to have healed except those scars on your face, so, why do you keep them?"

Pandjar once more lifted his hand to trace the claw marks on his cheek. "I was an excessively proud and impulsive youth. I decided to keep these scars to remind me of my folly that day. It was pride that killed the lions, and it was pride that almost killed me."

~

# Ace of Wands

*the beginning of an exciting adventure.*

The children screamed with delight as they raced into their new home in the Wands Castle. They had been assigned the Master Mage's quarters which had lain derelict, dusty and unused, since the last Wands Mage lived there, and that was almost two hundred years ago. Their chambers had a view along the foothills of Dragon Mountain, home of the dragons of old.

Follin's parents, Katlyn and Mage Saoirse, and his sister, Theresa and her family, lived nearby. After their arrival the families practically lived in each other's homes, Eve said that it was like a family reunion every day.

Their rooms were a mixture of living quarters and alchemist laboratory. A large central kitchen and dining room also served as a meeting room for family gatherings and official business. Fortunately, it was big enough for Follin's extended family to gather of an evening to sing, play, and tell stories around an enormous fireplace. This was where the family spent most of their time, the fireplace provided that homely feel that was a balm to the cold of winter. This was especially so as the days became shorter and colder.

"Ma!" cried seven year old Aidan, throwing his haversack in a corner and grabbing a piece of fruit sitting on the table. "Ma, guess what we did today!"

Eve looked up from the kitchen bench, one hand holding a carrot and the other a small kitchen knife. Following him in through the door was Aidan's twin sister, Fiana, next were their cousins Tanika and Atsu, followed by Ziggy's children, Tamotan and Lily.

"And what did my little prince do at school today then?" Eve called making sure to watch where her children's various belongings ended up as they were left lying around the room.

"We did exercises!" cried Aidan rushing towards the freshly made potato, leek and pepper sandwiches his mother had prepared to feed the starving children. This was a common after-school snack in the Cups Kingdom from whence they had recently arrived.

"And we did a, a, a something like running and jumping and crawling along tree trunks, it was so hard!" interrupted Fiana.

"It's called an 'obstacle course' and it's for training warriors to be strong and agile," Tamotan explained as he reached for a second helping of sandwiches.

"My goodness, it's warriors I have here in my chambers! Brave girls and boys ready to fight the evil from the Wildlands." Eve looked affectionately at the children now feeding themselves and each other in a frenzy of movement. Aidan was slightly taller than his sister, Fiana. Both wore happy smiles that warmed Eve's heart till it almost burst.

"My Da said that the obstacle course here is harder than what the Elf Rangers have for their training, Auntie Eve," added Lily breathlessly.

"And what did you do on your first day at the new school, Lily? Did you run and climb and jump like the others?" Eve often worried that the tiny elf girl would be left out. Lily had witnessed too much sadness in her life, and Eve decided that she needed a guardian auntie who would stand by her.

"Auntie Eve, I tried my best but it was too hard. The teachers let me play on the swings till the others finished their races," replied Lily.

"Well then, little one, you've had the best day ever," announced Eve with an encouraging smile.

"Auntie Eve! Did you know that Tamotan will soon earn his wooden sword?" The twin's cousin, Atsu, was so excited that he almost lost his sandwich to Follin's fae dog, Sox, waiting strategically for the children's scraps to fall to the floor.

"Even though they're new, they'll all get to play games and sing when they do the Moriscan Dancing too. You should come and watch us, Auntie Eve!" squealed Tanika in her unusually high-pitched voice.

The children's first days at school were important, and Eve

decided that she needed to take time off from unpacking their boxes of belongings and go with them in the morning to learn their routines.

It was at this time that Grandma and Grandpa arrived. They had been waiting to greet their grandchildren after their first day at school and wanted to hear their stories. When Mage Saoirse and his family arrived in the Wands Kingdom, Follin's sister, Theresa was in her early school years. They could still remember the excitement of her first day at school.

"And what did our young champions do at school today? Did you run the gauntlet? The river race and the tree climb?" asked Mage Saoirse, 'Grandpa' to his grand-children.

Aidan had by now finished his sandwich and leaped at his grandfather, landing on the old man's chest almost knocking him off his chair.

"I, I, I..." He stuttered trying to speak faster than his brain could keep up. "I won the race across the river, and I swam it all underwater! None of the other kids could stay under long enough to even get half-way across." He beamed with pride. "And Fiana beat all the girls her age too, she stayed under so long the teacher had to dive in to get her out! They thought that she had frozen solid in the cold water."

The twin's cousins, Tanika and Atsu, had made sure to escort the new arrivals on their first day at school. Both of Theresa's children were quiet, serious in manner from their many years of training in the ways of total warfare expected of all who lived in the Wands Kingdom. Their father, Tombei, held a position on the war council and was a master swordsman responsible for training the Wands' Fearless Commando. His physical appearance was uncommon, having arrived as a young man on one of the trading boats from across the seas to the east. His mastery with the katana, a curved sword designed for cutting and slicing rather than stabbing, was beyond any seen in the Wands Kingdom.

The children gave accounts of their days adventures and finally things began to settle down in the household. Fiana's newly acquired kitten, Puss, eventually came out of hiding from under the sofa, while Sox crept carefully between the scampering feet of the children to snaffle up scraps of food dropped on the floor. Molly, the blind elemental introduced to Eve by the High Priestess and The Hierophant, suddenly appeared on Eve's shoulder as the children's wild energy began to dissipate. It was the first of many homecomings after an exciting day at school.

A few days later, while Eve and Follin were meeting with the Wands Royalty and Nangkari, the Wands' one-eyed dragon, the children came bounding inside to pester their afternoon babysitter, a lone and somewhat distraught grandmother.

"Grandma!" called Aidan. Like his twin sister, Fiana, Aidan's light brown hair flashed with sparkles of light as he ran into his grandmother's waiting arms. "Can we go and visit Nangkari now?"

"Heavens and horses, grandson! Didn't I tell ye just yesterday? Nangkari is busy with your Ma and Da? You'll just have to wait till he's free," grunted Katlyn, Follin's mother. Her fingers raked through her grey hair as she held her breath to the count of ten before releasing it.

"But, Grandma! You said we could," added Fiana.

"Galloping ghosts of Grendale's Farm! Not you too!" The elderly lady tried not to smile. She needed her grumpy voice to survive the twin's onslaughts until Eve arrived home. "Do you two nay listen when I speak? As I told you this morning, Nangkari is busy."

The other children had left, having eaten their fill they were escorted to their homes by their parents. Sorcha and Theresa saw that Grandma would have her hands full with Follin's twins and didn't want to impose their own on her for another exhausting afternoon of mayhem. Katlyn led the twins to sit near the warmth of the hearth and sat herself in the leather chair facing them. Sox had already settled himself in front of the warm fire, Puss was curled and asleep beside him on the floor rug.

"But he's a dragon, Grandma," grunted Aidan, climbing precariously along the top of the rickety old sofa.

"And he's a shape-shifter too," added Fiana. "He should just get his business over and done with and then wind time backwards. Grandpa said that a dragon can finish his work before he even starts it." She looked up at her grandmother and giggled, pulled at the ribbon in her long hair and then threw herself into her grandmother's lap.

"Dragons, dungeons and castles! You children will cause me to shape-shift any minute now if you don't stop pestering me."

"But dragons can change time backwards, Nangkari told us so himself," said Aidan, finding the kitten's tail and pulling it. There came a hiss and the kitten disappeared into the alchemy study.

The old woman rubbed at her gnarled fingers and noted how quickly the wind had picked up, it had a chill to it that signaled snow - and she felt it in every bone. The once youthful maiden of the Mystic

Isle, decided that she had put up with enough nonsense from her grandchildren and wondered what she might do to distract them.

"My goodness, 'tis time to prepare dinner and your mother is still not home," she muttered as Fiana grabbed her ribbon and tied it in a complex weave through her grandmother's hair. With an inner sigh Katlyn said, "Perhaps we could play hide and seek?"

"Nah, but we could take Puss with us into Molly's world? She loves it!" exclaimed Aidan now heading towards the alchemy workroom where he had seen the kitten escape to.

"Yes, let's do that! Aidan! Let me hold Puss, she likes to be with me when we visit Molly's home." Fiana tried to grab the wriggling kitten, but her brother held it high in the air out of his sister's reach. Grandma wisely stood and accepted the wriggling cat from a surprised Aidan.

"You can visit the elementals after we have dinner prepared. Right, Aidan, fetch some wood and stoke the fire. Fiana, put the kettle on the stove top, be careful that ye use the wooden stool Argyll made for you. And I don't want either of ye to play with the fire magic Nangkari showed you. The last thing I want is for your mother and father to come home and find two little children burned to a crisp because they didn't listen to their wise grandma."

~

Nangkari's business was with Follin and Eve. They were seated around a large fire with the Wands Knight, Sir Alwyn, the King and Queen of Wands, and Follin's father, the Mage Saoirse. The Emperor, who seemed to spend more time in negotiating with the Wildlanders along the Empire's frontier than at his own castle, had been called out to attend to some issues in the Pentacles Kingdom with Sir Darwyn, the Charioteer, and couldn't attend.

"I know that you have only recently arrived and are still settling into your new home, Follin, but we need you to begin your studies in our Kingdom's fire magic as soon as possible," announced the King. Their meeting place was deep within Dragon Mountain, the den of Nangkari, the last dragon of the Tarot Empire. "We understand that Nangkari, your father, Mage Saoirse, and Sir Alwyn, will be your mentors while in our Kingdom. Your father is the only Fire Mage left in the Tarot Empire. It is an extremely difficult and dangerous quest to become a Fire Mage, and it is even harder to stay alive once initiated. There is a high attrition rate for those who wield the magic of the Wands' Flame."

Nangkari was in his human form, his chair close to the blazing hearth. He was hunched over, smoking his pipe and apparently thinking. There was nothing outstanding about the dragon other than the fact that he had only the one eye, the other socket was severely scarred.

"May I?" asked the dragon politely.

"Certainly, Nangkari," replied the King who had to move his chair a little further back and away from the fire. Where Nangkari loved the heat, no human could handle his idea of 'warm' for long - not even those born and trained to the magic of the Flame.

"For you, Eve, I will leave your training to The Empress and the Angels, the Flame is not for you. You do understand that this is a blessing, do you not?" He turned to look at Follin's wife, his single eye unblinking.

A little flustered and holding back her annoyance, Eve replied. "I'm not quite sure I understand, Nangkari. I did breath work with Hermes, and Hera has taken me to the depths of the earth where the fire energy is hot beyond imagination. So I don't think I need to be spared your knowledge of the Flame."

"These things I know, Priestess Eve. You and Follin were taught the highest of elemental meditations in the Cups Kingdom, were you not?" continued the dragon.

Eve looked questioningly at Follin. When she saw his blank look she turned back to the dragon. "We learned the water meditation of the Cups, if that's what you mean. They all do it in the Cups Kingdom, it isn't a secret. It can't be the most powerful meditation in the world, can it?" she asked in all seriousness, but there was a slight edge of exasperation in her voice.

Nangkari looked at Sao then back to Eve. "Mage Saoirse should have mentioned this fact, since it seems both Hermes and Hera did not. The water meditation is considered the highest form of magic. Did you not travel out of this plane of existence during your Quest of Life? Have you not traveled across time and space with the water breath? Why did no one tell you of its power?" The dragon's voice grew strong with frustration, not quite a shout but it echoed through his chamber.

Mage Saoirse looked at his dragon friend and thought how easily the shape-shifter could mismanage human interactions. At his first meeting with the dragon, he remembered how the beast could barely hold a cordial conversation.

Sao coughed to bring attention to himself, then spoke. "Nangkari, at the time of the Quest of Life no one thought to go beyond the actual experience of the water meditation. We did inform Follin and Eve that it was too powerful even for most of the Cups people. It was very soon after their quest that the High Priestess was attacked by the Wildlander mages. We had no idea what to do until Molly managed to stop the rot caused by their evil spell. Mage Hermes, nearly died trying to find that caterpillar creature that rescued Hera from her entrapment. Then there was Eve's pregnancy and the fear of another Wildlander attack which would be directed at her, the future High Priestess. In addition to this was Ziggy's quest to rescue his wife and children. That was such a rush-about time that no one thought to do more than introduce the water meditation. Afterwards, well, we just forgot. Follin and Eve were left to find out for themselves the power of the water form."

"Harrumph! It seems you humans place a lot of trust in 'finding-out-for-themselves'. That meditation could have crushed your apprentices' future development," came Nangkari's gruff response. He pulled his chair a little closer to the fire and puffed at his pipe as the others waited. The air began to fill with a tranquility that was palpable and the tension in the room eased.

"Nangkari, I love that pipe of yours. One day you must teach my husband how to do that trick, it is so comforting," oozed the Queen. Her smooth charm made Follin almost laugh, and Eve giggled into her hand. Sir Alwyn tipped a salute to his mother and the King winked at her.

In a tone to show that he knew what the Queen was doing, Nangkari continued. "Perhaps I will, perhaps I won't. It depends on my mood," he said dryly.

Sao looked around at the group and took the dragon's response as a hint that he should continue to explain the significance of the fire meditation.

"As you can tell from sitting here in this dragon's furnace, fire can be a difficult master. Once aroused, fire can burn down a village or even the plains of an entire Kingdom. Water, on the other hand, has its own unique dangers, but it is a passive energy. Nangkari wants to remind us that fire is active and extremely dangerous to the uninitiated." Sao paused, waiting for his son and daughter-in-law to respond. "Um, that's a hint."

When Eve remained silent, Follin decided that he should say something. "Yes, we know that water is passive, we've practiced it for years now. Hera taught us how to dissolve into our meditations, it was one of our first lessons. But you wanted to know what we have experienced with fire, so I shall do my best."

Eve watched her husband and noted with pride how much he had changed since his rescue of Sorcha, Ziggy's wife, and their children. Neither Follin nor Ziggy spoke much of what actually happened, but she clearly recognised the leap in confidence that her husband gained that day.

"Fire burns, Master Pew and Mage Hermes have impressed upon me as such. I know from my own experience that fire can be exciting, it enlivens the spirit and drives power into the limbs." Follin put his finger to his chin and thought for a moment. "Many years ago, I used the fire meditation just as my father taught me. I melded with my campfire on my journey through the Major Arcana, I felt consumed with joy. It was one of the most amazing experiences I have ever had. I think it was as powerful as the Cups water meditation, but I don't have enough experience with fire magic to really be the judge of that."

"Priestess Eve, I'd like your informed response please. What has Hera and Hermes taught you of the power of the Flame?" grunted the dragon seemingly absorbed by his pipe and the flickering shadows on his den walls.

"Actually, they didn't really talk much about it at all. The water meditation only came up when we reached the Cups Kingdom. Fire energy was just something that was brushed over, no one ever explained what it did or how to do it. I never really knew enough to even ask about it. Besides, as Sao said, so much happened during our time in the Cups Kingdom that I suppose the two Magician's just forgot..." her voice trailed off as Nangkari turned to look at her with his unblinking eye.

"I know all this, perhaps I should have asked what it was that you wanted from your sojourn through the Wands Kingdom? You, who will one day be High Priestess of the Tarot Empire."

Eve smiled, she was starting to like the Wands' dragon, part wild man and part eccentric, a bit like The Hierophant or even Mage Hermes. "Now that you ask, I want to spend as much time as I can with my children before I am called upon to spend my life serving in the Empire's Sanctuary, that's what I want." Her face was set and even the dragon began to smile, although it was difficult to read his moods as he kept himself so well guarded.

"If that is what you want then, so mote it be. I shall, as I had already decided, mentor Follin. I will be ably assisted by the Fire Mage, Mage Saoirse, and the Force of the Flame, Sir Alwyn." The dragon puffed several times on his pipe before leaning back in his chair and, closing his eye, signaled that their meeting was over.

With a nod from the King the group stood and left the dragon to his den.

~

The next day Follin's training in the way of the Flame began. Many of the preparatory exercises were already embedded in him from his work with Master Pew. From his training in the Pentacles Kingdom, Follin learned that hard work always preceded knowledge and skill. His initiations in the Hindamar Mountains with the earth elementals helped him form a deep, hands-on understanding of the power that can be drawn from the earth's connection with fire.

His training in the Swords Kingdom helped him recognise the importance of study and to seek clarity in all things. The Cups introduced him to a softer, gentler way of managing stress and tension. It also brought him the Dolphin style of fighting that met hardness with softness. When he began quarterstaff training with Sir Alwyn, Follin was told that he must view energy as a dance, a way of finding the pivotal change-point between rock and water. The metaphors of rock, hardness, and water, softness, described the conjunction of fire and water styles. Follin set out immediately to combine the Dolphin water style of fighting he had learned from Sir Rohan, with what he was learning from Sir Alwyn, the way of the Flame.

"I can't get this fire thing sorted out inside my head, Sire. When you show me a kata with the sword or quarterstaff, I automatically begin to soften it into a water kata. I'll make this rock and water thing work though."

"Aye, you're doing fine, lad," the Wands Knight would say, a smile always on his kindly face. "But watch my stick, here, behind your leg," and he would flip Follin into the air with ease. "See? You're too soft, like water, and then, when you try to correct it, you become too hard, like rock. It's all about flowing from one style to the other and then back again. It's like moving in a circle adjusting rock and water as needed. I've seen you do it when you spar, but when you slow down, like now, you lose composure."

Follin nodded trying to understand how he should do just that.

"I'm not saying you're doing things badly, I'm thinking that you need to spend more time in meditation, aye, to build the Flame within."

But Follin wasn't fooled by smooth talk. "I know you're the master of fire magic, Sire, they don't call you the Force of the Flame for nothing. If you don't mind, I think I need you to teach me your personal meditation. That's how I learn, by doing things with those who do it best."

Sir Alwyn looked closely at Follin, grabbed at a rag to wipe the sweat from his brow and said, "Lad, that we shall do. Go now and wash, have a light meal and meet me in my chambers in an hour. I need to consult with my inner self and see what he has to say." He finished with a light chuckle thinking that he had confused his friend. He wasn't to know that Follin knew the inner worlds better than his tutor.

"That I shall, Sire. And I shall enjoy hearing what your inner self has to say," Follin replied as he hurried out of the knight's dojo and headed towards his own chambers. An hour would give him just enough time to clean up, have a meal, and to spend some time with his beloved wife and children.

With Sox at his heel Follin arrived at Sir Alwyn's chambers in time for a warmed brew of honey mead. He sat to gently warm his hands at the knight's fire as he listened to his tutor play on his lute. When Sir Alwyn had finished, Follin joined him in singing a popular Empire ballad of love won and lost. Sox simply curled up as close to the fire as he could get and fell asleep.

"You've a talent for music, Sire. The Pentacles claim to be experts in singing and making music, but I think they may be pipped by the bards of the Wands Kingdom."

"'Tis true, lad," said the Knight. "The Pentacles can sing like a blackbird in the early morn, but it is usually the Wands who compose the tune. They say that it takes a community to craft a great ballad. Swords have the words, Pentacles have the voice, Wands have the creativity, and the Cups give the final product the right tone and emotion. For instance, did you know that our bards have created songs in tribute to your elf friend, Ziggy? He's a hero throughout the Empire."

Follin knew that Ziggy was a brave warrior, he'd even fought beside him, but he hadn't heard any songs made in his honour.

"I'll sing one for you, than we'll get down to business."

Sir Alwyn sang a ballad of friendship and danger, of an adventure that happened more than a thousand years earlier. It told of how Ziggy rescued members of his Daru Clan after they were taken by a rogue dragon. When the knight had finished he stood and placed his lute in another room, well away from the heat of the fire.

"There be nothing worse than to place a lute near the fire, it dries out the timber and that ruins its tone. Then the strings become brittle and they are hard to replace in these troubled times. Always treat your equipment with care, lad, 'tis the small things that count. My lute is my friend, it gets me through the melancholy that creeps upon me like a thief in the night."

"Why melancholy, Sire," asked a curious Follin.

"It is the way of the Wands, a curse in many ways. We live to create, to romance and to give meaning to an otherwise difficult existence. You have seen the Cups hospices and know of their problems first hand. We of the Wands are similarly passionate and have high expectations of life. If we aren't feeling the joy of living, we become vulnerable, a melancholy seeks to invade our spirit." The Wands Knight shook his head. "I think it best that you spend time in our hospices here to see what I'm talking about. I know that Eve is working in several right now. What does she have to say about the peculiarities between Cups and Wands?"

"Eve doesn't say much about her healing work. But she did say that the Wands were passionate, they seek to squeeze every ounce of joy from their day. It seems that unless the Wands people are playing or partying or fighting then they think they aren't living."

"Huh!" Sir Alwyn almost choked on his mead when he heard this. "Oh my! That girl sees too much indeed. I should have paid more attention when Sir Rohan told me of her gifts. Aye, Eve is absolutely correct, we are passionate romantics, and above all naive, we think life is for our pleasure. You know that life is not a hedonistic paradise, it is for living to the full yet with temperance and prudence. These two virtues are frequently absent in my Kingdom. A Wands warrior trains to live their life with no expectation of pleasure, for to have expectations is to incite folly. It is best to expect nothing, then, if you get nothing you can't be upset because you didn't expect anything anyway. If something nice does present itself, then this becomes a bonus and something to rejoice over. Aye, but Wands have huge appetites for happiness. When they let their hair down they will try to squeeze as much joy from life as they can. Yet, when the pleasure is over they fall victim to melancholy. This, my friend, is the challenge of the Wands Kingdom. It is your task to observe our ways and learn, for this is your final elemental lesson before your Magician's initiation."

The two sat quietly in their chairs by the warmth of the knight's hearth, the flames rising with the occasional spark lifting towards the ceiling.

"I will teach you the first lesson of the Flame today," announced the Knight, breaking the cocoon of silence. "You know of the furnace and cauldron just behind the navel, aye?"

"Yes, High Priestess Hera and The Empress taught me centred breathing and circle walking to strengthen it. When I was in the Cups Kingdom I learned to use their water breathing to soften and dissolve myself into its centre. I like it so much that my breathing is almost completely water style." Follin spoke slowly and carefully so that he wouldn't waste the knight's precious time in discovering Follin's strengths and weaknesses.

"Then it is time to introduce you to the Wands fire breathing technique. You will find that the Flame is sheer pleasure, a joy that benumbs the mind. Yet it can burn and make the unwary a creature of destruction. Are you ready for the temptation of the Flame?"

Follin nodded. "Absolutely. Nangkari said that water was the most powerful form of magic so I imagine that the fire breath will be less so... maybe?" He wasn't so sure given the look from his tutor.

"Ha ha!" laughed the Knight. "That is a good answer but quite incorrect. Only those who approach the fire quest through temperance and humility succeed. Many times I have been called to attend our hospices to help treat those burned by awakening their Flame too quickly or incorrectly. Our Cups healers have little experience in treating our brethren who have aroused too much fire. Fire is the nervous system, the raising of kundalini. It can be a deadly exercise to the uninitiated. It is said, '*the novice drowns in the same waters the adept swims in.*'"

"I've heard that saying before, Sire. I think it was in a meditation I did in the Cups Kingdom some years ago. Yes, I've heard it. But if you please, I've not heard it in terms of fire energy."

"This is the first and thus most important lesson in learning to arouse the Flame, so listen carefully. When you awaken kundalini it is to awaken the force of the Flame. An awakening is akin to a wildfire, a fire that can race out of control to burn down whole forests and those within it. Awakening one's Flame is very serious business. The Flame is the process of initiating and controling such an awakening. Those who awaken such a wildfire without knowledge and training are at serious risk of burning their nervous system. Our healers call it 'burnout' or a 'nervous breakdown'. It is unpleasant to witness, my friend. I've seen novices who practiced these exercises beyond their capacity and level of adeptship, and they have suffered. Some recover, but it can take many years of treatment. Those who don't recover live their lives in a state of insufferable debilitation, often so lifeless that to walk down the road takes many days for them to recover."

"I've not heard of this before, Sire, why is awakening the Flame so dangerous?"

"The temptation of the Flame's gifts can push the adept beyond the veil of reality. It lures the gullible and the dolt. As you know, every magical act demands a fee. To wield such power as the Flame is no different."

Follin nodded as he processed the Knight's words. "I sort of understand. Too much of anything can be dangerous."

"Yes, too much fuel in a small fireplace will burn the house down."

"Then my water style is not enough to moderate the Flame when I create it at my centre?"

"Lad, to be honest, your water style is beyond even what I can call upon. I've watched you training with the sword, stick, quarterstaff and bow, you have a style unique in our lands. Both Sir Rohan and myself would struggle to best you in any form of fighting." The Wands Knight quietly considered his next comment. "Water is temperance whereas fire is to arouse passion to its highest level. My task, and that of your father and Nangkari, is to teach you the way of the Flame, and to temper it with your water. You have undertaken the Cups Quest of Life, I haven't had the honour to do that. There will be times when I shall seek your advice." The Knight chuckled when he saw Follin frown. "Fear not, I know what I am doing, and the Flame is a passion you will enjoy once you have learned to bind it with your water."

"That," said Follin, "is what I am here for."

"Then take out the first picture of your Wands lessons, and then we shall begin."

~

# Follin's Meditation - Ace of Wands

*The first image in Follin's collection showed a hand holding a branch emerging from a misty cloud. The branch was covered in small, green leaves. Behind it was a scene of peace and it made him feel excited looking at it. There was a flat grassy plain with a small forest of oaks, beyond that was a snow covered mountain peak and a mountain range further behind it. He longed to roam the plains, the forest and the mountain, they looked vaguely like he was there now and not in the warmth of Sir Alwyn's castle chambers.*

*As soon as he entered his meditation, Follin saw the King and Queen of Wands.*

*"Welcome once again, Follin," said the King, a powerfully built man, red of face and hair with a broad beard that flowed down his chest. "We have the honour of being the tip of the spear in the fight to*

protect our beloved Tarot Empire. We live in a state of total war sparing none but the young, old and infirm. Anyone who can hold a weapon must serve at a moment's notice, for without proper preparation we would buckle under and be swept away by the flood of Wildlanders pressing our borders."

"This is your final lesson in the Tarot Empire," said the Queen with a vibrancy that appeared as bright flashing lights around her. She had a warm, golden aura that flickered like a campfire in the forest at night. "The lesson of the Wands Kingdom is the lesson of the Flame, a fine slave but a cruel master, learn this well and you will earn the appellation of Fire Mage.

Feeling a little nervous that he had brought not just his own family to this dangerous Kingdom, but also those of his elven friend, Ziggy, Follin said, "I've heard of the ongoing skirmishes on the frontiers of your Kingdom, I wish to be of service to you and your people in return. I fear, however, that my family are unprepared for such rigor and may not be able to keep up with your total warfare requirements."

"Total war," regaled the King. "Means everyone must be prepared to fight. Your children, Aidan and Fiana, will train each day with the same joy and passion as their peers. The Wands have a knack for making exercise fun, and I feel that your children are well suited to learn this path of fire. Don't worry about them, go with the flow, like the Strength Lady taught you." The King looked seriously at Follin. "Fire magic will come to you at its own pace, do not try to rush it. As for Eve, she has her own destiny, that as healer. She will be busy enough when winter turns to spring and the fighting on the frontiers begins in *earnest."*

*"Please don't think that your time in our Kingdom is to learn to fight," added the Queen. "Or even to defend our Empire with acts of bravery. That path is for others. Your task is to master the magic of fire. The Flame you seek is your destiny and no other path must you tread while in our Kingdom."*

*As she spoke, she lifted her hands and placed them together, palm facing palm. Separating them slowly there appeared a ball of golden light, an orb so brilliant that Follin had to turn his face away. With a motion of her chin, she sent the glowing orb floating across the table. Follin expected it to be hot, like a flame, but instead it radiated a soft warmth that, when it touched his chest, wrapped him in a radiant joyfulness and a sense of contentment filled his being. With a light jolt the orb firmly entered his chest and Follin emitted a soft cry, almost a sob of pleasure.*

*There came a shuffling sound and Follin turned to see Nangkari sitting by the hearth. "The Flame has many forms, Follin. It can be used to burn, to kill, to inflame the senses and excite desire. For you, the Queen has shown its softer form, love. The love of life and the deep joy of fulfillment. For you it might feel like gratitude, or perhaps a sense of longing for a love you lost long ago. It is your role to learn the many nuances of the Flame and how to manifest them in this world. It is important," the dragon warned, "that you not deviate from our methods as that could prove fatal."*

*As the dragon spoke Mage Hermes appeared. With a surge of affection Follin embraced him.*

*"You made it! How did you do that? I thought your life force was..." Follin stopped speaking knowing that this might cause his mentor some pain.*

*Instead, Hermes smiled in delight. "I've borrowed some of the Empire's force, Hera too."*

*As he spoke, a shadowy form appeared, it was the High Priestess Hera.*

*"I see that you have settled in with your family, Follin. But alas, time passes so quickly." Her voice was soft, fluid to his ears, but her weakness was apparent. "We can't stay long so listen carefully. Due to our weakened state your tuition has been assigned to others. Eve will continue to be tutored by myself when I can, and the three archetypes stationed at the Sanctuary: The Empress, Temperance and the Star Lady."*

*"I remember," said Follin. "You asked me long ago if I would ask*

*Eve to help you protect the Sanctuary. I know that we are both its protectors, one foot in each world, so to speak, but I don't quite understand why Eve isn't going to learn Fire magic, especially since she learned to wield Earth, Air and Water magic so easily."*

*Hera replied. "Eve has a natural aptitude for all four elements so don't worry, she already has Fire magic, but it will manifest in its own time. Her path is internal, yours is external, the physical manifestation of the Sanctuary in the Tarot Empire itself."*

*Nangkari had been listening quietly, his head down so as not to miss the convoluted conversation human's indulged in. He now spoke, "Follin, I trust that you will earn your right to wield the Flame, as you must. Go slowly and gently, learn to walk before you run."*

*As the scene faded it was replaced by that of Sir Alwyn.*

*"Follin, are you ready for your first lesson in the Force of the Flame?" he asked.*

*Follin brightened. "Yes, absolutely."*

*"Enter my being, centre your awareness within the furnace at my navel then follow what I do."*

*At that moment Follin experienced the full Force of the Flame and he knew that this was what he had sought for all his life.*

~

# Two of Wands

While Eve made the most of her time to relish being a mother to her children and enjoy seeing them play with their cousins, Follin was busy learning the lie of the land around Dragon Mountain and the Wands castle that lay snuggled in its foothills. He was ably escorted by Sir Alwyn and the two Wands pages, Page Asha and her partner, Blade. Where Sir Alwyn's beard and hair was a massive flush of red, orange and yellow that sparkled in the sunlight, the two Page's hair shone like flaming beacons. Blade was solidly built whereas Asha was fine-boned, both exhibited well-defined musculature from a lifetime of hard, physical training. Blade explained that every person in the Kingdom was prepared for action at any moment. Although it was uncommon for the Wildlanders to come this close to the Wands castle, a stealth attack or ambush was a constant threat.

The group rode from farm to farm pointing out the vegetable gardens, fruit orchards, vineyards and the herds of horses required for their numerous military patrols. Interspersed at regular intervals were guardhouses with their alert sentries. The group passed several cavalry patrols composed of friendly, but firm-faced men and women, clearly they were warriors not to be trifled with. This was total war and Follin reacquainted himself with the same preparations that he saw in the Pentacles and Swords Kingdoms. He considered how fortunate they were to have been granted time to raise their children in the safety of the Cups Kingdom for their first seven years.

Follin was wise to the nature of warfare, ordinance, supplies, repairs and upkeep from his time with the Swords cavalry and Bowman patrols. His tutoring with The Emperor came in handy, as did his apprenticeship under Master Pew, who never wasted a single grain of charcoal in his smithy. He also knew that running an army and protecting a population the size of the Wands Kingdom, would consume huge volumes of resources.

Sir Alwyn took great pains to educate his ward, he needed Follin up to speed on the situation in his Kingdom as fast as possible. Every question asked was given due consideration.

"We can grow only part of what we require, lad. What you see around us are farms that provide for the castle alone. Simple fare for simple people, the royal court, warriors-in-training and our local patrols. As you have seen we do not indulge in fancy meals or fancy dress, nor even of ceremony, we have no time for that," said a dour Sir Alwyn.

"The people of our Tarot Empire sleep peacefully in their beds at night only because men and women like us stand ready. The Wands protect the northern frontier from the Wildlanders and their miserable, rat-tailed bunch of mages. The Swords have their superb cavalry to patrol the plains to our southeast. Of course, they have their problems too with bands sneaking through the cavalry screens to plunder their farms. The Wildlanders have even been known to evade detection and plunder the Cups villages beyond the Swords River. It's an ongoing battle protecting our communities," offered Page Blade.

"Fortunately, we're well supplied by our cousins in the Pentacles and Cups Kingdoms, bless their souls. They know that without us on twenty-four-hour war footing, there would be no Tarot Empire. If we fall, they fall too," added Page Asha, pulling her horse to stand beside Follin and her Knight. The Pages knew that Follin was far more than a magician's apprentice. The stories they had heard over the past fifteen years attested to the magical powers and maturity of this quiet young man now in their charge.

Follin was lost in thought as he glanced upwards towards the smoke rising from the top of the mountain beside them, Dragon Mountain.

Asha followed his gaze. "That smoke 'tis the dragon's breath the myth-makers say, but really, it's a volcano."

Follin frowned as he looked at Asha. "Did you say 'volcano'?"

"Yes, that's what it's called, why?" she replied.

"My Pentacles apprenticeship was with Master Pew, the Bladesmith. His other apprentice, Justin, saw a volcano in his initiation with the earth spirits. He would be so excited to see a volcano up close like this."

"Master Justin?" queried a bemused Asha. The two Pages shared a glance then laughed.

"Justin's working as our Master Bladesmith right now. We'll take you to see him when we have time," said Blade with a wink to his partner.

Follin's face broke into a smile telegraphing his delight. "Yes, please! He's a dear friend of mine." He paused to savour the moment before continuing. "You know, my children like it here. They get to play with their cousins and they're spoiled by their grandparents, I think I'll like it here too. There's something special about this place that I can't quite put my finger on." As his voice faded, Follin looked around and marvelled at the farmlands scattered between the mountain, the coast and the River of Smoke and Fire. There had been snow the night before and the mountain top was dusted in white, it reminded him of the hair on an old man's head.

Page Blade pulled at his horse's reins and swung around as Sir Alwyn called, "Come on, let's get back to the castle. I want to show Follin our training schools. He'll appreciate our situation all the better for seeing than us talking about it."

On their arrival at the school closest to the castle commons, Follin could see children as young as five years running around swinging sticks at each other. As he got closer, he saw that what he initially thought was a brawl, was in fact a dance, and quite an intricate dance at that. Not only were the children dancing but there were pipers and drummers providing music. Commanding the performance, if that's what it was, stood a slender figure on a raised dais calling the steps.

"That's the school captain, Helminia. Just look at how easily she commands, so majestic. She'll make a leader of one of our Fearless Commando patrols one day," informed Asha pointing to the figure at the front.

"What are they doing? I can see that they're dancing, but what is it with the sticks?" Follin narrowed his gaze trying to sort out the various children and teenagers side-stepping each other, hitting stick against stick and yet not a one got in the other's way.

"It's called Moriscan Dancing, you'll see they have a set pattern to follow. Helminia is calling the dance steps so that no one gets hurt. This is one of our basic fighting strategies, to call a specific formation that will best deal with a skirmish, ambush or a pitched battle. If you watch carefully, you'll see that this is a fighting dance to deal with an ambush on a flat field, like the plains or a dry river bed. It's much easier managing a battle plan when everyone knows what to do, where to move, and importantly, where their partner is standing so they don't strike a friend instead of an enemy," said Blade. "Listen carefully, you will hear her calls and see how everyone moves accordingly. The drummers also have a specific beat for each move and the piper has a specific tune that the children sing to. This is how we train for total war."

"It's a most efficient strategy," added Asha. "See how one line moves to the left and strikes downward and across, while the other line will move to the right to force an opponent into the swinging arc of the first line, clever isn't it?"

"But some of these are only little children, even younger than my own, how do they know what to do so they don't get hurt?" asked Follin, still trying to follow the lines as they formed and broke, only to reform in a different pattern. Throughout the movement, there was the beat of the drum and the music of pipes and the voices of a hundred children singing.

"We're at war, Follin, we have no time for games, and these are not games, though we make it fun," said Blade. "We have competitions too, one school against another." Noticing Follin's look of horror, Blade continued quickly. "No, they don't fight each other, they dance. Some dances will use sticks like this one. That's because there are small children, and a wild swinging stick does little damage to little bones. We've dances designed for open-handed techniques, while others use wooden swords and the quarterstaff, that's for the older children. When they become adolescents, they have to earn the right to use a proper sword. That doesn't happen until they have passed all the tests..." Blade didn't get to finish when Asha stepped in excitedly.

"We have obstacle courses too, for each age group. They have to pass these before they can graduate to the next hardest one. They swim, run, leap and crawl..."

"And they learn how to fight without weapons, open-handed fighting. Their lessons include grappling and throwing, palm strikes, arm and leg locks, punches and kicks. They have to know how to use anything they can get their hands on..."

"Sticks and stones, fists and clawed fingers..."

"Swinging hammers, a pitchfork or a shovel. Our people have no time to choose a suitable weapon in a crisis, so they improvise," added Sir Alwyn leading the group to another section of the school where Follin witnessed a group of teenagers dressed in war paint, battle kit and kilts. He saw that they were helping each other pack their haversacks with water and food, spare weapons and tools for sharpening and repairs. Sir Alwyn explained that the cadets needed to learn how to pack and carry a heavy haversack, as well as to stem a bleeding wound and carry a wounded friend. This was very much a hands-on lesson.

"But they are going to freeze in this cold wind, aren't they?"

asked Follin, unused to the cold he pulled his coat closer around him and slapped his gloved hands together.

Asha answered. "We learn early on how to wield the Flame within. When it gets cold, we awaken our inner fires. That will be a lesson for you while you're here, how to engage the Wands fire magic. Everyone learns it, we have to."

"But all this training and fighting, doesn't it make the children aggressive?" asked Follin watching a particularly violent argument develop between two teenagers who immediately dropped their kits and began wrestling in earnest.

"What? That? No, no, wait and you'll see how our people learn to manage their aggression and not let it get out of hand... just watch."

The two youngsters continued to shout and wrestle, eventually falling to the ground, fighting to gain a hold and lock the limb of their opponent. Nearby stood a single onlooker.

"That's their squad commander. See, now they're shaking hands." Despite Blade's explanation, Follin still had a confused look on his face. "We have a simple rule, once you're bested by your opponent you leave it be, you let the disagreement go. Everyone argues, and teenagers always do or say something that offends another. So they fight, but they fight fairly. Anyone who breaks our rules is dropped down to a lower grade and has to work their way up again. That is extremely humiliating I can tell you. Our rule is to fight fair, with honour and respect, and that's it. We have no need for more rules."

As Follin took it in he could hear the music and drums in the background and noticed that his feet were tapping to its tune.

~

The chill easterly winds from the Hindamar Mountains blew directly towards Dragon Mountain Castle once more. It made for a miserable evening, forcing everyone in the castle to pile logs on their hearths and huddle together around the fire for warmth. To pass the time, the families did what they always did on nights like this: they sang songs, recited poems, and told stories tall and true.

That afternoon the Wood Elves, Ziggy, Sorcha and their two children, along with Theresa and Tombei with their children, arrived at Follin and Eve's chambers. To the parents, it seemed that their children conspired together so that they could all gather at Follin and Eve's rooms for sleepovers. It was just as well they had arrived early because the developing snowstorm soon trapped them inside.

"Uncle Ziggy?" asked Aidan, the eldest of the twins. "Can you tell us Uncle Pandjar's story again, please? The one about how he got his scars." This was a story that grew bigger each day in the youngster's mind.

"Aidan, you've already heard that story, another telling would make it lose its flavour." Ziggy closed his eyes and thought for a moment not wanting to disappoint the child. "I know what, I'll tell you another story. One that will make tonight pass quicker than a shooting star, what do you say to that?"

The light buzz of conversation ceased, and all faces turned to the elf.

"Is it as good as Uncle Pandjar's fight with the lions?" grunted Aidan unconvinced.

"Ha! Of course, young fellow. It's filled with adventure, romance and sacrifice. It's a true story as well, and even my own children haven't heard all of it," Ziggy said as he stood to gather a rug from the pile Eve had placed on a nearby chair. Now that his audience was quietly waiting for him to continue, Ziggy settled in front of the fire and began his story.

"You know how Uncle Pandjar received his scars, well, there are more than mountain lions in our Empire, there are wolves. And on the Mystic Isle live the mightiest of the Wolf Elf Clans." Ziggy lifted the heavy rug from his lap to push a log further into the fire then settled back to continue his tale. "In ancient times there were wolves who spoke, just the same as the mountain lions. There is even one alive today, and that is one of our Elf Rangers, your Auntie Carwen."

"No way!" cried Lily. "Auntie Carwen isn't a wolf at all, she only has that name and comes from the Wolf Clan, that's all."

"Yes, you're right, Auntie Carwen is known by the elves as 'Lone Wolf', but my promise of a good story holds true. So, rug up and huddle around the hearth and I shall fill this cold evening with a story of adventure, romance and sacrifice that will inspire magical dreams tonight." Ziggy's smile was genuine, something he was more comfortable with now that he had his family back in his embrace.

Wanting to add some background to her husband's story, Sorcha turned to Follin and Eve and asked, "Have you ever met any of the Mystic Isle elves?"

Eve looked at Follin before replying. "When I was young, I would go into the forest with my grandparents to find herbs, there we would meet members of the Wolf Elf Clan. They would take us to where we would find the best herbs, but they always made us leave when we'd gathered what we needed and no more. Then they would lead us back out of the forest." Eve paused, put her hand to her chin then continued. "My grandparents said that we should respect the elves because it was their forest, not ours."

Follin added, "When I was a lad, I would see the elves on market day when we traded goods with them. But they were mean, not like here on the mainland. The Fox Clan elves lived near my village and had a bad reputation, they would kill anyone who wandered into their sacred groves. My father always warned us not to go near them. Even a mage is careful around those elves. My father tried to befriend them once, but they wouldn't accept friendship from a human. The Wolf Clan live way up in the northern reaches of the Isle, near Eve's village, they were much nicer."

"Interestingly, Follin, this story includes those very same Fox elves." Ziggy coughed as a plume of smoke escaped the hearth from a savage blast of wind that seemed to be trying to break down their front door. "The King of the Mystic Isle elves, the Fox King, is a vicious and nasty man. His son, Prince Gravus, is even crueller than his father. The Fox Clan's power is in the use of secrecy and cunning, like the fox, and they use it to subdue and dominate their fellow elves. They are the single most powerful clan in the Mystic Isle. There are other, smaller clans, like the Wolf Clan, but the Fox Clan rules them all."

Sorcha took up the story now that she knew where this was heading. "There was a Wolf Elf Princess more beautiful than any other elven girl of the Mystic Isle, and Prince Gravus wanted her for his own..."

Before she could continue, Fiana called out, "Auntie Sorcha, is that Wolf Elf Princess our Auntie Carwen?"

"Yes, Fiana, that is exactly who we're talking about. She was as beautiful then as she is now. But let me get back to the story. Prince Gravus was a spoiled and rotten elf-child who always got what he wanted. The marriage went ahead despite Aunt Carwen and her family's protests. Carwen tried many times to run away but each time she was captured and brought back to the Fox Clan village."

Ziggy was visibly restless. His legs kicked nervously until finally, he couldn't restrain himself.

"Sorry to butt in, Sorcha, but this is the best part! Around this time, me and my brothers, Kerrytan and Pandjar, happened to be looking for elven warriors to join our Elf Rangers. We knew that the elves of the Mystic Isle were brave and vicious fighters so we sailed across to the Mystic Isle to meet them. It was at our meeting in the Fox Clan village that Pandjar cast his eyes upon the fair Princess Carwen and was immediately love-struck. It was soon evident by the foul looks of the men who stood between her and us, that the Princess was their prisoner. We could feel the tension in the air. At that time, we didn't know of the Fox Prince's reputation beyond that of a bold warrior. His cruel nature was evident soon enough.

"We three Wood Elf brothers had a reputation as fierce fighters too and so were invited to feast with the Fox Clan King that night. We felt it strange that as yet, no one had spoken of the Princess. It was as though she was not even there. Her bright eyes and her bold determination to attend the feast told us that she was a true warrior in the mould of her Wolf Clan people. While we were feasting, Prince Gravus stood and announced that any of his people who wished to join our Rangers would be given his blessing to leave with us."

A low sigh escaped Aidan's lips and he whispered, "Oh no. I bet Auntie Carwen wanted to join."

Sorcha smiled and said, "Aidan, Princess Carwen had more than courage and strength, she was of the Wolf Clan, an ancient clan of elves equal to our own Wood and Water clans. Auntie Carwen has the wisdom and instincts of the wolf in her blood too. She stood up at that feast and announced her desire to join the Elf Rangers."

"Aye," chuckled Ziggy. "She was very brave and us three Wood Elves were now very frightened. We didn't travel all that way to end up fighting an entire clan of elves because one strong-willed Princess wanted to escape her cruel husband. When Carwen stood to announce her desire to join us, I saw Pandjar place his hand on his knife hilt, brother Kerrytan saw it too. We both knew that blood would soon be spilled if things got out of hand.

"The Fox Prince was as evil as he was cunning because not a single elf had risen to join the Princess. Princess Carwen stood alone, a lone wolf in all her majesty. Prince Gravus said, '*So, you spoiled child-princess of the Wolf Clan, you wish to join our Elf Rangers here in battle? You forget that your place is beside your Prince, to help me rule my kingdom. But alas, girl, you have less manners than even our Wood Elf visitors.*' It was a rude insult that shocked the other elves at the table. I saw Pandjar sitting very still, his knife was drawn, ready to kill, but it remained hidden by his cloak.

"I knew that Pandjar was waiting to pounce on the Prince but the Prince was too far away and heavily guarded. I looked at my brothers and mind-spoke for them to hold their tongues and their knives. Sometimes it is best to 'not-do' than to rush in. This could disrupt the flow of Tao and change our true destiny. It was a very tense moment. The Fox elves knew that we would fight for our honour and their hands too had dropped to their knife hilts ready to defend their Prince. It was at that moment that the Fox King spoke. He said that as the Princess had decided to join our Rangers then he was bound to honour his son's rash proclamation. He permitted Princess Carwen to leave with us. *'But,'* he said, *'Princess Carwen, you will forever be known as the 'Lone Wolf', an outcast, one who will be slain if you ever return to the Mystic Isle.'*"

Ziggy paused to fill his pipe with tobacco. The children were silent, each seeing the feasting table and the elves with their knives ready in their hands.

"Da, come on, what happened next?" Lily interrupted the silence stating what they all wanted to know.

Ziggy finished tamping the tobacco firmly into the bowl of his pipe. Then, lighting it with a stick from the fire, he eased back in his chair to enjoy the first few puffs of his precious Water Elf tobacco.

"Well, as you can imagine, my little Princess Lily, that was the end of the feast. With sour stomachs, we took our leave and hastened with Auntie Carwen to the coast. It was a long journey, and we knew that we should not dawdle. We ran for two whole days with barely a minute's rest. Several times we met bands of Fox elves and had to fight our way through them. When we arrived at our boat, we were dismayed to see a band of Fox elves running up the sandy beach towards us. We knew that our time was ended and that Prince Gravus would kill us. We were exhausted and we each carried wounds from our fights and had barely eaten since we'd left the elven village.

"Your Uncle Kerrytan was a superb swordsman, he had fought in many battles and was the war chief of our Daru Clan. He saw that the Princess was limping and unable to fight, so he ordered Uncle Pandjar to get her into the boat. Kerrytan knew, as did I, that Pandjar was destined to be with Carwen, and we would do whatever was in our power to protect them both.

"Kerrytan said, '*Little brother, take the Princess to the boat and leave. Don't turn back, just go!*' He didn't wait for Pandjar's refusal but grabbed my arm and together we drew our swords and strode among our enemy. Uncle Pandjar had no choice but to do as Kerrytan commanded, to do otherwise would have meant we would all die, and our sacrifice would be for nothing.

"It was a vicious fight. Twelve against two might seem terrible odds but my brother and I were seasoned warriors. Together we had fought in the Hindamar Mountains, the forests of our Daru lands, and on the plains and foothills of the Wands and Swords Kingdoms. Our Elf Ranger experience held us in good stead. Those Fox elves had been weakened by generations of stealth and cunning rather than raw courage and muscle. It soon became clear to us that they were more exhausted than we were, and that gave us the strength to fight all the harder.

"After cutting our way through the first few fighters we sought their leader, Prince Gravus. But Gravus, the coward, escaped leaving his warriors to keep us from following him. As Kerrytan turned to defend himself against a vicious attack, the Prince took the opportunity to fire an arrow into my brother's back. Although he was able to break the shaft, its poisoned barb slowly drove him to his feet. I had slipped to the ground with a dagger blade in my arm. I tried to rush to protect my dear brother, but alas all I could do was watch him fall..." Here Ziggy's voice softened and finally stopped as he hung his head, reliving that terrible moment.

Sorcha noticed and quickly took up the story. "You see, as Uncle Kerrytan fell, Aunt Carwen saw and cried out. Her arms were strong so she took up the bow that had been hidden in the boat and fired arrows as fast as she could. Uncle Pandjar turned when he heard her cry and that caused his lion's blood to boil in rage. Although not as skilful in weapon play as Uncle Kerrytan, Uncle Pandjar's lion-berserker power made him the most feared of the Elf Rangers. It gave him a strength few warriors could face. Your Aunt Carwen told me later that Uncle Pandjar roared just like a lion as he jumped straight back into the water to slay the last few Fox elves who now sought to cut through Ziggy's guard and kill Uncle Kerrytan. It took three days for the group to sail home to the Water Elf village on the coast. I was there when they arrived, we immediately took them into our home for healing. As you can see, Ziggy recovered but he bears the scar on his arm in recognition of his rescue of the Lone Wolf. Uncle Kerrytan took much longer, the poison had entered his body and it was some months before he was ready to return to his Ranger patrols. Sadly he was lost to us in an ambush in the Forest of Smoke and Fire only a few years later."

Aidan waited politely for a few moments before resuming his questions.

"That's a really good story, but if Uncle Pandjar and Auntie Carwen love each other, why aren't they married?"

"That's not an easy question to answer, Aidan," replied Sorcha. "Auntie Carwen is still a Princess of the Fox Clan. She is still married to Prince Gravus, he has never permitted her to divorce him. Aunt Carwen is honour bound to remain faithful to her sacred vows of betrothal, only upon his death is she free to marry her true love, Uncle Pandjar. You may have noticed that Aunt Carwen is never called by her royal title, Princess. She has forbidden everyone from calling her a Princess ever since she left the Mystic Isle - she left that title behind when she left her cruel husband."

"But couldn't Uncle Pandjar just go and kill Prince Gravus?" asked Fiana.

Sorcha saw that Ziggy was still lost in his own world so she continued her explanations. "Fiana, for some of us, honour can get a little complicated and that means that we shouldn't kill just because we want things our way. An elf's love oath is based on honour, to abandon our honour is to spoil the beauty of our world. They will never wed while Prince Gravus is alive, and they accept that. They cherish their time together with the Rangers knowing that one day fate may unite them as husband and wife. Honour is all we have when life goes against us, remember that my young ones."

The wind picked up and began to howl as though a banshee wailed outside their front door. The window shutters banged but all was quiet within as the children were put to bed. The adults were left to comfortably sit around the glowing fire, silent, thinking of the story of Kerrytan, Pandjar and Carwen, the Lone Wolf.

Follin prepared a jug of warmed gluhwein for his guests. As he poured he mused out loud, "Well, that answers so many questions that have sat at the back of my mind. Carwen is very much a lone wolf and that helps curb Pandjar's restless lion personality."

From the depths of the warm rug wrapped around her, Eve added, "Such a sadness hangs over them, yet when they are together they are so happy. What an incredible story, Ziggy."

"An adventure story, of romance and sacrifice, just as I said it would be," Ziggy said, sipping from his mug of warm spiced wine. "There are tears to be shed this night and I have done so. I still grieve my brother, Kerrytan's passing, the loss of my dear sister Naroo, and the harshness of Carwen and Pandjar's burden. It seems our family has had our share of sadness."

"Although you all had the choice to walk away and abandon Carwen, you didn't," said Follin as he sought to find a moral to the story. "Through your bravery, you gave a wonderful woman freedom, as well as purpose. Carwen is one of the most respected of the Elven Rangers in the Empire. The Wands people love her as much as they do their own elite warriors, the Fearless Commando."

"Yes," replied Ziggy. "But did you see that there were a number of change points in our adventure, any of them could have ended in disaster."

Follin thought for a moment. "The hidden knives at the banquet, yes, they remained hidden allowing the Tao to move the Fox King to send Carwen with you. Then there was the decision to leave immediately so as not to be trapped, I see that. The decision to send Pandjar and Carwen to the boat. There were many change points that could have gone bad instead of good. I see the Tao in action in this story."

"You forgot the only one that was not in our power to orchestrate..."

"Ah, of course, Carwen's cry of horror that brought Pandjar to your rescue," replied Follin.

"It's sometimes the combined series of events that allows the Tao to shift in your favour. This was the lesson of the story, elf-wise, by establishing a series of not-doing the Tao is released to fulfil its purpose. I knew not to interfere, a rash decision would have unsettled our destiny. Our path created a series of change points, and thus is the way of the elves, and in many ways, the Wands."

Follin rubbed his hand over his forehead and grunted. "And here I was enjoying your story for what it was, Ziggy, and now it has turned into a lesson. I think you've spent way too much time with Mage Hermes."

Ziggy pulled his rug tight around himself in preparation for sleeping in front of the fire. "Although I am an elf and not of the Tarot Empire, I too have studied the ways of each Kingdom. They are closely aligned with the Tao in their own, unique manner. The change point is the Tao, that is your lesson to ponder in your meditations tonight."

~

65

# Follin's Meditation - 2 of Wands

*Follin fell asleep as soon as his head hit the pillow. In his dreams he saw an image of a man of authority looking to the horizon, it was the King of Wands. He was holding an orb of the world in one hand, and in his other, he held a staff.*

*"Sire, what do you have to teach me?"*

*The King remained standing and replied, "I have a query of my own that will lead you to your answer. 'What would you do if you believed that you would never be held accountable for your actions?'"*

*Follin was taken aback, this was a strange question indeed.*

*The King continued. "As Ziggy said, the Tao manifests in many ways. In my hand, I hold the power to do great good or great harm. Every decision I make must be measured and examined responsibly. There are only a few simple rules in our Fire Kingdom: firstly, don't indiscriminately squash those who stand between you and your goal, they too have their reasons and purpose in this life. Secondly, consider what guides your decisions: before you act, ask yourself, 'are my motives pure?'"*

*Turning to Follin, the King handed him the orb representing the world. Follin could feel the orb's power, exciting and arousing.*

*'This makes me melancholic and sad,' Follin thought. 'There is so much evil that has been done by good people giving in to the demands and lies of corrupt leaders. Those leaders live by a creed of lust, greed, and total disinterest in the well being of those they are responsible for. The King is different, he is steadfast, not to be swayed, he takes his*

*position as ruler seriously. He knows that the well being of every person in his Kingdom relies on the decisions he makes.'*

*The King said, "A fire's instinct is to consume all before it. This fire is both physical and metaphysical. One's lusts, once ignited, can arouse the best and worst in any of us, this is especially so for the exuberant and excitable Wands." The King, accepting the orb from Follin's hands, returned his gaze to the beautiful landscape before them.*

*"Before I go, may I ask some questions?"*

*"Certainly," replied the King.*

*"I've heard the term Force of the Flame used quite a few times, and I know that this is Sir Alwyn's title. But I am unsure of what it means."*

*"Then let me put your mind at ease. The Wands Kingdom is based on the fire element, myself and my Queen make fire energy available to all of our citizens. It is up to their personal values, attitudes and dedication to their training, to be able to access it properly. Fire can be a nuisance, it makes people angry, impulsive, irresponsible and hyperactive. The Flame is the manifestation of fire within the recipient's body. When they have learned how to manage this Flame they have developed the Force. The term Force means that the practitioner is an adept who uses the Flame responsibly."*

*"Does that mean the Force of the Flame is the practical application of fire energy?"*

*"Yes, Sir Alwyn uses this Force responsibly, in all that he does. His ability to command fire energy is almost as good as Nangkari the dragon, myself and the Queen."*

"My next question is about the story Ziggy told us this evening. He said that the Wands' change point is related to the Tao, can you please explain this to me?"

"In many ways, the Wands change point is the balance of water and fire. This is often described as hardness of rock versus softness of water. By acting responsibly and engaging the not-doing of the Strength Lady, the Tao, you can find the balance or change point between the two opposites. This can tip destiny in your favour."

Follin wrote up his journal then fell asleep, wondering if he would act responsibly if he had the Force of the Flame at his disposal.

~

# Three of Wands

*wanderer, travel, trade, the mystic's journey, strategic thinking,*

*responsible decisions.*

Follin and Ziggy's families easily assimilated themselves into the community of the Wands Kingdom. Sorcha and Eve were asked to join the Wool Weavers and the Bean Burners, two of the many women's groups that helped bond and hold the Wands community together. Eve knew that she only had a limited time to enjoy herself as a mother and left no day empty in her desire to be part of her children's upbringing. All too soon she would be called upon to leave her family to become the High Priestess of the Tarot Empire.

The twins were kept busy with their schooling, and each

afternoon they participated in games and competitions as part of the training necessary for a Kingdom at war. Every activity was directed in some way in training for the survival of their community.

As Eve and Sorcha arrived with their children at the school one morning, they met Carwen waiting for them at the school entrance.

"Good morning, I've been waiting for you," Carwen announced, her bright smile betraying that something exciting was on offer.

"We see you, Carwen, and it looks like you have something interesting for us, yes?" answered Eve.

The Elf Ranger affectionately ruffled the children's hair as they called goodbye to their mothers before racing off to play with their friends in the schoolyard.

"I certainly do have something interesting for you. Today is market day at the Royal Exchange. It's in the main section of the market square, only a short walk from here. Would you care to see it?"

"Royal Exchange? What could that be I wonder..." Sorcha frowned trying to decide if this was something she should know about.

"It's where the Empire's merchants and intelligentsia gather when the big ships come in. It's packed with food stalls, entertainment and loads of shopping. The trading ships that sail beyond our shores stop here on their way to the Sword and Cups Kingdoms. For many of them, this is their first stop which means the collectors and sellers have first pick of whatever the adventurers have brought back with them. It could be a strange-looking bird or a flower, delicious exotic fruits, the horn of a unicorn, or some odd-looking coins from a far-off place."

"Ooh, yes please! Lead on, dear girl!" Eve took Sorcha's and

Carwen's proffered arms and the three walked briskly towards the Wands' Royal Exchange.

Carwen paused as they came to the busy central lane lined by an avenue of bare cherry trees. It reminded Eve of an honour guard, sentinels set to guard a sacred passage.

"This is Cherry Tree Lane, you should see it in the spring with all its blossoms, it is so beautiful. It's where the wealthy folk live. Either they live here or they rent rooms for their practice. There are a lot of traders from the Pentacles, Cups and Swords Kingdoms who have residences here too. They try to get to the ships first so they can buy goods and curios for the various collectors around the Empire. Look, there's the Swords group now. They've already been to the wharves where the ships dock by the looks of it, see, they have an entourage of loaded wagons and hand carts." Carwen's step grew faster causing Eve and Sorcha to hurry along behind her. Heads turned to stare at the three spirited women heading briskly towards the line of carriers.

"Come on, let's look at what curios they've got inside those hand carts!" cried the Elf Ranger lass.

Coming abreast of the hand carts, the girls slowed to walk alongside a young man who, with a bright smile, drew back the covering to reveal a set of golden statues, no doubt of some foreign gods, kings or queens.

"Look 'ere m'ladies, some beautiful statues from way beyond our shores to the east. A pretty penny that will bring for the master, I'd say."

"Oh my, what amazing artwork!" gushed Eve as she reached over to stroke the smooth, golden statues. "I bet the Pentacles merchants pushed your Swords masters hard. They love a bargain, and any artwork that they might be able to copy would be worth a small fortune to them."

"Aye, indeed. We got there just ahead of them, m'lady," replied the young man gladly matching his pace with the three attentive women. "The adventurer who secured these statues is a local lad, most of them come from the Wands Kingdom, you know. They go places no one else would ever dare go. This fellow is one of our preferred collectors, he always gives us first refusal, that's 'cause he gets a handsome kickback from us, he does. Those crazy Wands collectors love danger. Some end up wealthy and bring their exotic women folk back to the Kingdoms. Some, though, stay and raise their families in the lands where these ships trade, and some end up leaving their bones to dry in the sun. 'Tis a dangerous business this collecting, it certainly is, m'ladies."

Eve's eyes grew larger as Carwen escorted them beyond the file of hand carts and into the market square. The Royal Exchange was an enormous courtyard surrounded by cafes that sold the rare brew she loved so much - coffee. There were dining rooms where the well-to-do would entertain their business acquaintances, clothing stores, stores filled with household goods and bric-a-brac, rare spices, and artworks of all descriptions. But what drew her attention and curiosity was the naturalist's displays. Lined up on long trestles were pinned butterflies, the colours superior to anything she had seen, even in the Mystic Isle. There were tusks and horns from strange animals, potted exotic plants, odd-shaped fruits and tubers, statues of foreign gods and goddesses, there was so much for her to see that she felt dizzy.

"Hey! Over here!" came a friendly cry. As Eve turned, she saw Page Asha waving to them. "I've saved a table for us! Hurry, before someone tries to take it!"

Settling into their seats the newcomers were introduced to a menu that would tempt even the King and Queen of the Pentacles Kingdom. There were several varieties of coffee, a half dozen types of tea, cakes, pastries, soups, pies, cookies and biscuits, it was more deliciously diverse than anything Eve had seen in all four Kingdoms.

"My goodness! There is so much variety and their names so strange, I don't know what to order," she exclaimed.

"Yes, indeed, make sure you try their amazing custard and strawberry tarts," gushed Asha. "When the ships come in, they bring things from far and wide. One day I'd love to go and see what treasures lie beyond our shores. Hey, we should come here next week, they're putting on a play: 'The Pilgrim and the Pardoner'. It's about greed, trickery, and moral justice, you'll love it! Afterwards, they hold the Tea Ceremony. Did you know that Tombei introduced it? He said that his people use it to embrace the universe within."

Asha paused to take a breath. "I love it here at the exchange. I could spend all day just watching the merchants, bankers, and court officials, huddled together making secret plans for their business projects. See those investors over there," the young Page pointed with her chin so as not to draw attention. "Well, they're talking with Mr Darkener, he has a patent for an invention that pumps water uphill. He demonstrated it a few weeks ago and everyone in the Kingdom went crazy! Imagine having water running up into our castle, all the way to the top? No more carrying buckets up and down stairs. How amazing would that be!"

Carwen added, "Mr Darkener isn't a Wands resident either. He arrived here last year from somewhere over the seas in one of the Cups ships."

Asha quickly continued. "The Emperor encourages new ideas, skills and inventions from all over the world. It keeps us strong. We have partnerships with just about everyone, even with some of the Wildlander villages. That's why our Emperor is so busy travelling all over the place. He takes his Swords negotiators and Pentacles merchants with him to promote our Empire and forge alliances with foreign kingdoms. It's these strong bonds that help us keep our finger on the pulse of their politics so that our little Tarot Empire can survive into the future."

"Did you know, Eve, that your brother-in-law, Tombei, arrived in one of those overseas ships? His swordsmanship was so masterful that Sir Alwyn invited him to train our Fearless Commando," offered Carwen, finally managing to get another word in edge-ways. "He met Theresa through Sao, your father-in-law. He decided to stay once his contract expired. I've trained with Tombei myself, he's an incredible swordsman. I doubt even Alwyn would best him with the sword alone." As an afterthought she added, "Of course, Alwyn would win if he used his Force of the Flame."

"And," Asha quickly inserted herself back into the conversation. "Did you know that our Swords universities have made us the centre of the intellectual universe too? People come from all corners of the world to study in our Empire. And those..." she pointed with her chin again. "Those are the King's investigators. They find the best opportunities and minds then connect them with our Swords and Pentacles masters."

The girls hung arm in arm for the rest of the day, slowly exploring all that the Royal Exchange had to offer. They met people who kindly contributed their knowledge of the collections on their tables, or of the goods they had retrieved from the ships and now had on display.

*'This has to be one of the most enjoyable days I've had in ages,'* Eve thought as they headed back towards the schoolyard to pick up the children.

~

Sir Darwyn was needed by his Emperor and had to pass the responsibility of caring for his charges over to the Wands Kingdom. With his chariot he was kept busy accompanying The Emperor on his journeys around the Empire and beyond. Sir Darwyn was comforted in the knowledge that Follin and his family were guarded by his friends. It was impossible to separate Follin from Ziggy these days, and with his elf friend came Pandjar and Carwen, all three members of the famed Elf Rangers.

The previous summer had seen the Black Plague return to the regions north of the Wands Kingdom, taking one in five of everyone it touched. The Emperor took pains to travel with Sir Darwyn to as many of the ravaged Wildlander villages as he could. They distributed Mage Hermes' herbal preparations, produced in volume by the apothecaries of the Pentacles Kingdom, to every village they visited.

To assist in these humanitarian trips, The Emperor asked Londar, the Hindamar Mountain Highlands lad, captured by the Swords cavalry some ten or more years earlier, to accompany him. This proved to be one of the best decisions he made during this time. Londar had grown into a man of note. Not only could he fight as hard as any Wildlander Browncap from his Highlands home, but he had the skills of the Swords negotiators to assist him in convincing his people of The Emperor's good intentions.

The Emperor knew that by providing medical support to these far-flung villages he helped save lives and prevent the spread of the plague. This gave him leverage in his negotiations for peace with these hard-living Wildlanders. With Mage Hermes unable to attend these excursions, Londar and Sir Darwyn's presence gave him companionship as well as a sounding board in his negotiations with the many village leaders. It was the Wildlander Mages Guild that was the cause of their enmity, and The Emperor made every effort to end this conflict. These trips allowed him to see first-hand the living conditions of the Wildlander's, and to gauge their willingness to stand up to these rogue mages.

~

Although Follin was invited to join many of the men's groups, he was advised to hold off until he had completed his fire training. His friendship with members of the Fearless Commando provided him with the opportunity to continue his training in swordsmanship and archery. He also enjoyed learning the way of the quarterstaff, the traditional Wands weapon.

Follin appreciated how thoroughly the path of the Flame was embedded in the Wands way of life. Every activity required some form of energy breathing.

The sword was easily his favourite weapon, but he had little sparring opportunity as Master Pew's sword destroyed even the best-made swords of the Wands commando. Once his elemental-forged sword was in his hand it became a whirling scythe, a blade that seemed to cut and stab at will. His Dolphin Clan fighting style learned from Sir Rohan of the Cups Kingdom, combined with his Pan-like intuitive fighting ability, allowed him to exploit the weakness in a foe's aura. His reputation rose to new heights as he defeated all his opponents, even against the best of the Wands Kingdom. It was a brave man who offered to spar with Follin, and then only when he used his wooden training sword.

After a while, it was the quarterstaff that Follin became particularly fond of. It presented a challenge as it forced him to learn how to blend both fire and water techniques. The quarterstaff required a subtle fire-style form but he found that his body would always default to a water-style movement instead.

Each day Follin also made time to train with the Elf Rangers in activities that they described as 'guerrilla fighting'. He had no idea what a 'guerrilla' was, but the elves seemed to know. The Rangers took him on long walks into the woodlands around the castle to refine his skills. He already had a sixth sense for the forest around him, and at times, even the elves were astonished at his ability to bend the forest elementals to his will.

Follin's skill in using the Flame increased rapidly. Many times he was stopped on his way home and congratulated on his skill by those who had watched him train.

~

During one of his meditations, High Priestess Hera and Mage Hermes informed Follin that Mage Armitar was no longer capable of manifesting in physical form since he was attacked by Sox. However, he remained in contact with the rogue Mages Guild and was a danger to anyone who ventured into the worlds beyond the physical plane. This news frightened everyone, so it was decided that Sox, and Eve's blind elemental, Molly, should accompany the twins every day until Mage Armitar was sent beyond the Shadowlands for good.

Given the incessant curiosity of the twins, Follin took pains to impress upon Sox to remain with them at all times. Not only would they wander off around the castle and the surrounding commons, but they would disappear into the astral planes to play with the fae and elementals. Despite Eve and Follin's warnings that Mage Armitar was particularly powerful in this realm, the twins were so apt at moving back and forth that nothing would stop them.

"Sox, my lad, it is up to you, your fae friends, and Molly, to keep an eye on them," Follin would say each morning before heading out for training. "If anything happens come straight to me and Eve, got it?" And each morning Sox would give a light bark as if to say, *Don't worry, Molly and I can handle anything.*

~

The Old Smokey Inn was one of the more popular Wands

communal meeting places. Members of the commando and retired warriors would frequently drop in for a pint of ale, a meal, and a good conversation to ward off those darker moments that plagued many of the warriors who suffered from post-traumatic stress. One day, Follin and his father, the Mage Saoirse, stopped there for lunch and found Nangkari in his human form, sitting at his favourite table by the fireplace.

As soon as they sat down, Nangkari started talking, as was his way when he had something to say. "Follin, today I shall tell you the story of how I met your father, and how he came to earn the title of Dragon Mage."

Mage Saoirse grunted and stood up, he really didn't want to hear that particular story. The mage strode to the bar to order a jug of brown ale and two plates of Follin's favourite lentil and leek pie for their lunch.

"Lentils and leeks again? I don't quite understand your vegetarian tastes, Follin," announced Nangkari as their steaming meals were placed before them. In the middle of the table was a plate piled high with roasted potatoes. The innkeeper made it a habit to always bring a plate of Nangkari's favourite dish whenever he visited. Follin suspected that might be because the dragon's presence always attracted visitors to his inn.

"I love vegetables, all kinds of vegetables, Nangkari," replied Follin. "My time on the road with the Major Arcana taught me that eating simple foods was good for my purse and my body - and I never got sick. Besides, when Eve and I lived in the Cups Kingdom we ate mostly vegetables there too. Page Jon explained that their Water Elf blood and their sensitivity to suffering made it painful for them to kill. That's why they don't serve in the military, they heal but don't fight. Killing makes them go crazy. So now I just love me lentils, leeks 'n 'taters, just like you do."

Nangkari nodded his head. "Taters, everyone loves 'taters. I think there are more 'tater growers in the Kingdom of Fire than there are ants. It's lucky for you folk that there is only one little dragon here in the Kingdom, and he shape-shifts to avoid eating them. Mind, I've eaten many a man in my day, it's what dragons do, but I'd be rather embarrassed if I accidentally ate one of my friends. Dragons go a bit crazy when they get hungry and can easily fail to discriminate friend from food."

Mage Saoirse and Follin smiled at the dragon's comment. They knew that in the past the Tarot Empire had been home to more than a dozen dragons and that Nangkari belonged to a large family. Sadly, they had all but disappeared leaving this single, one-eyed dragon to live out his days alone.

"Nay, not alone, not when I have friends like you, Hermes and your Da."

Follin almost leapt from his chair, he didn't know that dragons could read minds.

"Aye, that we do, and more," came Nangkari's dry response.

"I'm having trouble working you out. A dragon who is a fire adept, shape-shifts, eats potatoes so he doesn't have to eat his friends, and he also reads minds. What else do you do?" asked Follin trying to mimic the same flat, dry tone the dragon used.

"You know that dragons are also Time Masters. I know Sao spoke to you about that, I heard him."

"Yes, we spoke about your peculiarity with time, but it doesn't mean that I understand you."

"Hmm, time for us is like sand. You can shape it, dig a hole in it, even move it to another place. As a mage in training, you know that everything has a fee attached. Magic is not free, it demands payment, be that years of training, the draining of your life-force, and in some cases, as is happening to your teachers, Hermes and Hera, it can cost you your life."

"Yes, I know a little of the cost. So, do you still time travel?" Follin was fascinated with where the conversation was leading.

"I don't need to. In my younger days I did, a little, but if I were to be totally honest I would say that my interest in time travel was never strong, it is overrated. I much prefer living in the moment. It gives me great satisfaction to deal with the consequences of my actions, while humans simply squeal and squawk over the injustice of it."

"You prefer consequences? I don't understand..." Follin suddenly noticed his pie and quickly began eating, it was soon followed by a mouthful of brown ale. He relished both his meal and the conversation with a being older than anyone, perhaps as old as Pan himself.

"Ah, the folly of humans, to think that you can run away from your mistakes without restitution. To do this for eternity makes one fake, a shadow of what you are meant to be. There is no character development in the failure to confront painful experiences. One who avoids one's consequences becomes a predator, a pariah of self and others, loathsome to the eye and heart. I am as old as you believe me to be and have seen this statement to be true. Hearken my words, human, and live an eventful life. Take time to reflect upon your experiences, for an unexamined life is not worth living."

Mage Saoirse looked at Follin and nodded his head, but Follin wasn't convinced.

"Nangkari, did you not try to avoid the consequences of your mistakes when you were young?" he asked.

"My life is long and yet I can go back now and relive my mistakes to soften their blow. I have done so, to my every mistake, to my every failure, they are all lessons I have had to learn from. I did this by returning to every painful experience, nurturing my younger self, to bring him wisdom and comfort. I recommend it..." Nangkari thought for a moment before declaring, "Well now, this is interesting indeed. I am seldom surprised by a human, but I see that you already do this, you call it... let me see..."

"It's called 'rescuing the inner child'. I learned how to do it on my Major Arcana journey, in my Hermit's cottage. I would be a mindless ninny by now if I didn't practice rescuing myself from all of my stupid and mindless acts, the times I was unjustly punished and beaten, and the times I failed to act when I should have," added Follin quietly. He knew that what he said would upset his father who wasn't there when his son needed him the most.

"Yes, I can see it now, a powerful practice indeed. So, it was the Hermit's cottage and the Strength Lady. Wait, I also see The Hierophant and Darwyn, they assisted you too, they are all good friends of mine.

You have had some wonderful masters of life to lead you along the mystic's path." With his single eye, Nangkari looked steadily into Follin's, something he rarely did. The dragon disliked looking within a human's soul, too often he was disappointed to find them vague, apathetic and selfish. "Hmm, I see it is time I told you the story of how I met your father. It is a gruesome tale, I warn you, and it was the last time I stretched time."

Follin looked at his father wondering why he hadn't told him this story himself.

Mage Saoirse returned his gaze. "I know what you're thinking, son, but it is the dragon's way. Nangkari thinks I'm not smart enough to tell it on my own. There's a possibility that I would be tempted to censor some of the madcap things I've done along the path of the Dragon Mage."

Follin looked into the dragon's unblinking eye. This was going to be an interesting story indeed, he thought.

"I'm ready, but first I must order another jug of this fine ale... Nangkari, hold that thought!" Follin jumped up and walked briskly to the bar. He was soon back with their refreshments.

"Listen well, Follin, for this is a tale of good fortune, courage and folly, of wisdom gained and innocence lost." Thus began Nangkari, last dragon of the Tarot Empire. "Your father spent a short time studying fire magic with the Wands, picking up bits and pieces where he could, but there had not been a Fire Mage in the Tarot Empire for more than a century, so what he learned was only part of what he desired. He sought to speak with the Wands King and Queen, but they refused to teach him. They said that their elemental magic was too powerful for a novice mage. Sao decided that he should talk to us, the dragons of Dragon Mountain. At that time some of my family were still living in the Wands Kingdom. When he approached us, we rebuked him saying that humans don't live long enough to properly learn the magic of the dragon's Flame.

"Undeterred, Sao left the Tarot Empire and travelled across the treeless steppes in the northern Outlands. A barren, frozen region no dragon would consider worth visiting. The people living there were wild, wilder than any known to us scaled creatures. Their sorcerers drew upon the magic of animals, the weather spirits, and the cycles of nature."

Mage Saoirse quickly added for Follin's benefit. "In those lands, a mage is called a 'shaman'."

"Yes, I believe so," continued the dragon. "These shaman are powerful, they knew more of fire magic than what Sao could learn in the Tarot Empire. He stayed with them for some years. This was while he was still a headstrong youth who knew no better than to go head-first into the jaws of danger.

"The shamanic path is hard, so hard that Sao was frequently tempted to run away, but his pride kept him there. In their shamanic circles he heard whisperings that it was possible to steal a dragon's magic. The day eventually came when his mentor told him that he must leave. Sao was not an Outlander, he belonged to no tribe. Fearing that he could turn his magic against them if he learned the deepest secrets of the shamanic path, the tribesmen sent him away."

Again, Sao interrupted. "Nangkari makes it sound like I was not valued, but the truth is, the tribesmen and women were kindly, but frightened. My magic was different to theirs and so their shaman asked me to leave for my own safety."

"Harrumph!" grunted the dragon trying his best to craft the story in a manner that would conform to a normal human conversation. "Yes, and thus Sao left the shamanic circle and went to live in the Hindamar Mountains where he stayed for some years with the hermits and seers of the Wildlanders."

"That's where I met a wagon worker named Frailbones. He was living among the Wildlanders, the Browncap and Bluebeard tribes of the Hindamar Mountain Highlands. It is also where I met that scoundrel, Mage Armitar," added Sao.

"Thank you, now let me continue... where was I... oh, yes, it gets cold in the mountains. In following the hermit's path of the highlands, Sao decided on a solitary meditation retreat and found a cave for his practice. Like a fool, he had nothing more than his cloak for warmth. Fearing that he would freeze to death, it finally dawned on him that he should use his shamanic training to create an inner flame. In desperation, he began slow, centred breathing, and soon fell asleep. When he awoke the following morning, he found that he was aflame with power. The ice that had formed inside the cave over centuries had melted and his wet cloak was dry."

Once again Sao became animated and joined Nangkari in telling the story. "That was one of the most amazing experiences of my life, Follin. As the saying goes, '*necessity is the mother of invention.*'"

"Indeed," continued the dragon dryly. "Over the next few months, your father spent most of each day in meditation to arouse his Flame. This is what magicians call 'internal alchemy', a means to create the Elixir of Life, a very advanced practice for a human."

The dragon interrupted his explanation to sip at his ale and enjoy some roasted potatoes. This gave Mage Saoirse the opportunity to add a little background to the story.

"As you know, internal alchemy is the mixing of the finer essences of the four elements. It is something that a magician learns at the height of their training. The Tarot Empire Mages have all but died out. Besides myself, only Mage Hermes and a few Swords wing-mages, have survived. The last Fire Mage of the Wands Kingdom passed away more than a century ago. My shaman mentors of the north refused to take me further for fear that I would challenge them and steal their secrets. I felt lost, alone and abandoned, yet my hunger was insatiable. At the time of this story, I had but a rudimentary understanding of internal alchemy but no mentor who would take me to the highest levels of initiation. That was when I decided that I would do it myself."

"Harrumph!" Nangkari grunted before taking up where he had left off. "As you say, my friend. Now let's get back to my tale. Your father found that he could leave his body sitting in the cave while his dream body went to the stars and back. On one of his journeys he met a dragon also on the astral plains, that dragon was Nangkari, who is me. I was amazed that a mere human could do such a thing so I invited him to visit me in my Dragon Mountain home."

Nangkari stopped talking and turned to Sao, and waited. Mage

Saoirse picked up the story thread and continued.

"Son, to my aged ears this story ends on a horrid note. I was the most stupid mage on the planet, I still am sometimes," he added with a chuckle. "I walked across the mountains in the middle of winter with nothing but my cloak and sandals. I knew no cold. I felt nothing but an elation so high that I sang every song I knew until my voice grew hoarse. I was experienced in the hallucinogenic plants of the shamans and knew that I had gone beyond even the heights I experienced with my shaman mentor.

"I decided to take a detour to visit the Forest of Smoke and Fire on the frontier and pay my respects at Kerrytan's cairn. The forest takes its name from the countless coal seams deep within those hills, some of which had been burning for many centuries." Mage Saoirse stopped for a moment, his face creased as he decided how best to continue his story.

"Son, I must confess my folly. Having worked the fire within my belly to dispel the cold, I had the deluded thought that I could enter the caverns where the coal seams burned. I thought that I had control of fire magic and that I would be protected from the flames within those hills. That way I would earn respect from the dragons of Dragon Mountain and they would teach me their secrets. To my absolute horror, I was not immune to fire. Had Nangkari not sensed what I planned to do and rushed from his den, I would have just been another puff of smoke rising above the forest trees."

Nangkari took up the story. "Such is the folly of humans. I saw his plan one evening in my dreams and when I awoke I sensed that he had gone into the flaming caverns. That was one of the few times I travelled outside of time and arrived at the moment Sao placed his feet on those white-hot coals. His feet were instantly incinerated. I bore him back to our family den and there we treated him. Alas, your father carries the scars of his folly, but he also earned our respect. As he recovered I undertook to train him in the dragon style of fire magic."

Follin's eyes widened and he stared at his father. "Da, is that why you would never tell us how you got those burns on your legs? You always said that one day, when we were older, you would tell us. Ha, and I thought that I was the only family member blessed with an abundance of folly." Follin smiled but his father remained silent.

"Son," said his father softly. "I have never been so frightened in all my life than I was that day. I could feel my feet melting, I mean it, truly they had begun to melt by the time Nangkari got to me. I thought that I would die a most horrid death. I was saved by Nangkari's family. They caused my feet to regenerate and then taught me how to keep the energy flowing until I had regrown each of my toes. I still have nightmares, oh yes, and I still wake in the middle of the night to reach down and make sure my toes are still with me."

Follin didn't smile when he saw how serious his father was, so he changed the subject a little. "Da, remember that fire exercise you told me about when I was a child and we were camping in the forest? I did it on my Major Arcana sojourn, it made me feel fantastic. I sort of know what you mean, the power of the Flame is seductive. Now I have your experience to show me that sometimes what one feels in spirit is not always what one would feel in the physical plane."

Mage Saoirse grunted soberly, "Exactly."

"Your journey into the magic of the Flame has begun, Follin," said the dragon lifting a roasted potato to his lips. "I wanted you to hear this story so that you wouldn't do anything as foolish as your Da. Now let's eat, drink and laugh, these stories of the past make me hungry, and thirsty," Nangkari said as he took up his mug of ale.

~

# Follin's Meditation - 3 of Wands

*The image Follin scryed that night was of a man looking upon a number of sailing ships. He was dressed in robes, perhaps he was a merchant watching his trading ships setting out for distant shores. Or perhaps they were returning with goods and skilled people.*

*Follin engaged with the man in his meditation. "Sir, what is it that you seek to teach me?"*

*The man looked at Follin and said, "I have many plans, many possibilities. I wish to do the right thing by myself, my family and ultimately my Kingdom. To do so I must make wise decisions that benefit us all. We plant the seeds of our destiny years in advance, we nurture the first green shoots and watch them grow. Some die, some grow crooked, but only a few will bear fruit worthy of our attention. To live in these times we must be patient, diligent and vigilant. Sometimes it only takes a single mistake, a single poor choice or a single misplaced trust and our Kingdom could fall."*

*"Is this about decision making?"*

*"Yes, making the correct choice requires consideration, proper research of the pros and cons of each option available. A decision that may impact the welfare of others needs careful consideration."*

*"And how should I make good decisions?"*

*"That, Follin, is why you have journeyed through each Kingdom of the Tarot Empire. When you accept the position of Magician you will have a foundation of empathy, courage and wisdom to know how and when to act and when to wait."*

*Follin quietly considered the man's answer.*

*"Yes, I understand that, but sometimes there will be no time for reflection. I might need to make a snap decision, what do I do then?"*

*"Most certainly you will sometimes be called upon to give an immediate response. This is why your training has been focused on making your spirit pure - so that a situation like that never really arises," was the man's reply.*

*As he spoke Follin noticed that the man, whom he thought was just a mirror to his inner self, began to take the form of his master, Mage Hermes.*

*"Master!" cried Follin affectionately. Hermes was pale, even more so in the dim vision of Follin's meditation.*

*"I see that the Flame is already burning within you," declared Master Hermes. "The lesson of the Wands is the responsible use of the Flame. Learn to dance with its change point, to balance fire with water, and you will see that the ships you put to sea will return with riches beyond your imagination."*

~

# Four of Wands

*celebration, united purpose, structure, stability, family, community effort.*

The Winter Solstice was Market Day, and the castle common was abuzz with people, entertainment, food, and drink. Every three months teams from each school would compete in a variety of events for prizes handed out by the King and Queen. This was an opportunity for the youngsters to display their martial arts skills.

The Wands villagers used this as an excuse to show off their prized beasts, homemade preserves, wines, ale, pastries and cakes, and assorted artwork and craft wares. The competition was fierce and the prizes were many. The local taverns and boarding rooms were always booked out a year ahead, while their wagons, donkeys, horses and oxen were in high demand on these special occasions.

As Follin and his family strolled around the packed common, they were treated to music and performances, puppet shows, maypole and ribbon dances, displays of tapestry, clothing, basket weaving as well as games of strength and prowess. The weather that day was mild for midwinter and the snow underfoot remained firm.

Another section of the common held the naturalist's displays with artifacts and other wonders from all over the Empire and beyond. Their tables were loaded with strange-looking stuffed animals, dried herbs and spices, fossils, crystals and gemstones. Businessmen and merchants from each Kingdom competed to buy, sell and trade their ideas, inventions and machines.

Those arriving from distant villages would spend three or four days enjoying the opportunity to meet old friends, to party, gamble, and to romance new-found loves. To add spice to their celebration, the King and Queen gave their own Force of the Flame display, and that meant there would be fireworks of a rare kind.

Follin was especially excited because he had received a message from his friend Argyll who would be entering his artwork in the woodcarver's competition. Justin was also there giving a display in bladesmithing.

Follin's dear friend, Justin, had earned his place in the Blacksmith's Guild as a full Master Bladesmith. After completing his apprenticeship under Master Pew, and then several years to fulfil his journeyman duties, Justin had set up his smithy in one of the pretty seaside villages on the east coast of the Wands Kingdom. It was said that Justin's skill was so highly regarded that he had been approached to relocate his smithy in kingdoms way beyond the borders of the Tarot Empire.

Argyll was happy to stay working at his carpentry and wood carving craft south of Dragon Mountain Castle. He had a staff of three carpenters and his carvings were a common sight throughout the Empire. Follin was proud of his friends and excited that he finally had time to catch up with them.

"Eve, look! It's Argyll and his woodwork stall! Come on, let's drop in and say hello."

The twins were enthralled with the markets and its displays. Not only were there various exotic meals to be had at the food stalls, but there were fruits on sticks wrapped in toffee which they demanded their parents buy.

"I see you, Argyll!" called Follin on reaching the woodcarver's stall. It was only mid-morning yet the market was packed with people. The sounds of children laughing, friends calling to each other across packed tables, sellers bandying their goods, entertainers singing and playing instruments - everyone was suffused with the warmth of friendship.

"Follin!" replied Argyll, looking up as he carefully rolled a large barrel of apple cider into his tent. It was in payment for a carved statue of a flying dragon with a deer in his claws. This, Argyll pointed out to its new owner, represented the Wands very own dragon, Nangkari, in his prime.

The two met between swarms of people and hugged in friendship. Eventually, Eve made it through the throng with the children who squealed in delight at seeing their Uncle Argyll.

"Where's your little elemental? Is it in your canvas tent, Uncle Argyll? I can't see anywhere she could safely make a nest... it's just too small," cried Fiana looking about for a tree that may be hiding Argyll's woodwork elemental. When they had visited in the past the woodcarver always made a point to call his elemental to come out and play with Molly, Sox and the children.

"Alas, my dear Fiana, 'tis way too far from home for her. If I brought her here, she would sulk and refuse to help me with my work as punishment. You know how shy she is."

"Aye, that's true," replied Eve, catching Argyll's wink. "Elementals are so shy, and besides she might get lost in the crowd."

"So, will you be competing in any of the games today?" asked Argyll, bending down so that the children could hear him above the noise of the crowd.

"Nah," said Fiana smoothly. "It's too cold for them to hold swimming competitions, but if they did we'd win every single one, wouldn't we Aidan?"

"You bet! Fiana can swim faster and stay underwater longer than anyone in the castle, even me!" He was clearly proud of his sister.

"And I bet you don't even have to breathe when you get out of the water." Argyll smiled knowing that these two children could breathe underwater almost indefinitely.

"The Cups kids can do it too, but Aidan and I can do it better even than them," Fiana replied proudly.

"What I want to see is the King and Queen's fire displays," added Eve. "I heard that their command of the Flame is as good as Nangkari's."

Follin looked at his wife and smiled. "I'm not so sure of that, Eve. Nangkari was born to the Flame before time began. The Wands Royal family are newly awakened elementals and command fire, but they had to learn to wield the Flame in their human form. It's not easy, you know."

"Huh! So you say, smarty-pants." Eve lifted her head and smiled at Follin's serious look. "Stop showing off, Follin. Just because you learn directly from the dragon-man and Sir Alwyn, doesn't mean you know everything about fire and Flame."

At that moment they heard a familiar voice calling, it was Carwen and Pandjar, accompanied by Ziggy and his family.

Argyll smiled, he had formed a close bond with Follin's elven friends over the years and was delighted to see them.

"Well, who should I see in this mad throng of people but the brave Prince Tamotar and Princess Lily of the Wood Elves!" Argyll always made a point to engage with Ziggy's children. He had learned of their experiences at the hands of Mage Armitar and their seclusion in the cave. There they had spent many years hiding from the evil that was waiting for them outside.

"Uncle Argyll!" the children cried and raced to leap into his arms.

"So, did you make it into any of the teams for today's competition?" he asked, gently putting them down before his back gave way.

"Aye, I'm competing in the open Moriscan Dance with the sword and then again with the quarterstaff!" announced Tamotar.

"And I'm in the junior Ribbon Dance team, and the quarterstaff team too," said Lily just as proudly.

After they had seen most of the sights, Carwen took the children to join Katlyn, Theresa and Mage Saoirse in the community kitchen. There they would help serve meals to the villagers who couldn't afford the expensive dishes sold at most of the Pentacles and Cups stalls.

After some searching, Follin finally found Justin on the edge of the common working at a makeshift dragon-forge bellowing a cloud of smoke. Justin stood at the front of a group of men from one of the ocean-going ships there for the express purpose of seeing a Master Bladesmith at work. They hoped to entice him to return to their kingdoms when the markets were over.

"Justin!" called Follin as he approached. At hearing his name, Justin suddenly stopped speaking to leap through the crowd and grasp his old friend in a bear hug.

"Follin! I am so pleased you could make it!" he laughed. "I really need someone to help pump the bellows."

That evening Justin and his family arrived at Follin's chambers for dinner and a sleepover. Once again, the lounge room was a packed affair with the elves, Follin's parents and his sister Theresa and her family. Despite his usually introverted manner, Justin was the centre of attention that evening.

"The Alchemists Guild, well actually, it's not really an accredited guild within the Empire... but it's all the rage here in the Wands

Kingdom. I tell you it's the bride's knickers..." Justin winked at the giggling children. "Oh my goodness, I've got Master Pew's manners I have. But really, we've got so many odd-bods in our membership like cooks, candlestick makers, master mariners, geographers, soap boilers, muskmelon men, metallurgists, brewers and distillers, an arrow fletcher, even a few school teachers. Hey, did you know that some kingdoms employ alchemists to make gold to pay off their debts?"

"What do the other guilds think about this? I bet the Barber-Surgeon's Guild is outraged that the alchemists are so popular. Besides, is alchemy really a science?" asked Follin.

"Of course it is, it's one of the natural sciences, besides, what is science but observation and the testing of one's hypothesis? This 'science' lark is overrated I tell you." Justin was having a grand time.

Mage Saoirse decided to join the conversation. Stretching his hand towards Ziggy's offered tobacco pouch he said, "Don't forget, alchemy has two pathways, internal and external. An alchemist seeks to turn base metals and other substances into gold, that's external alchemy, and what a mystic seeks in their practice is internal alchemy."

"Sao, in my country we practice what you call 'internal alchemy'," added Tombei, Theresa's husband. "I'm wondering, is this form of alchemy something only mages know?"

Mage Saoirse considered the question. "Hmm, come to think of it, I see no reason why mages should be the only ones who would know of these things, Tombei. In my studies with the outlander shamans, they knew more about internal alchemy than many in the kingdoms I've visited. They treat magic as part of life. In fact, even the children use specific meditations to summon animals to their spears during the hunt."

"We have no alchemy in our world. We just do it, we don't bother wasting time trying to understand it," said Ziggy, sending a series of smoke rings above his head. He chuckled delightedly when the children poked their fingers through them.

Follin was ready to re-enter the conversation. "I think I understand what Justin is getting at. We have a magical system where internal alchemy is the norm for most of us in this room. There is a different form of alchemy used by the healers of the Cups Kingdom. Then there's the inner alchemy of the magician and shaman. In the Cups and Wands Kingdoms, this would be called the Quest of Life and the Force of the Flame. The external form of transforming raw ores into gold and other essential elements must have some validity... surely? Otherwise, no one would have joined Justin's guild."

"It's not my guild, Follin," said Justin firmly. "I'm just a member. What I love is how some of those people have discovered various new chemical compounds which they extract from different ores. I have access to them through my membership and that gives me an edge in my smithing. What me and my elemental can do is truly incredible with these extra resources."

"So that's why you have been head-hunted by those kingdoms across the seas?" asked a curious Eve.

"Yes, I suppose it has something to do with it. Since joining the Alchemist's Guild my weapons have become far superior to my competitors. There are many physical qualities that my elemental has been able to imbue into my weapons and tools with the new chemical compounds the alchemists have developed." Justin put his hand to his chin and thought for a moment before proceeding. "Most of the guild's members are totally fixated on making gold. Their chemical experiments are designed to make what they call the Philosopher's Stone. This magical stone is supposed to turn base metals into gold and produce health and longevity. I don't bother with that, but I must say that the apparatus these alchemists have developed are extraordinary. They use their instruments to create wondrous compounds. For instance, they can distil the fragrance of a rose that can be sold to the highest bidder. To capture the scent of a rose, my friends," and he looked around to include everyone. "That is true magic!"

"I think I know what you mean, Justin," commented Mage Saoirse. "Those of us who adhere to the practice of internal alchemy, use this to purify one's spirit in preparation for transformation and enlightenment. We would call this creating the Elixir of Life. I imagine that this elixir is similar to the alchemist's Philosopher's Stone but for different purposes."

"What healers and mages do, and what an alchemist working at a forge, still or a workbench does, is to create something unique," added Follin. "But trying to create gold, now that is strange indeed."

"If I wanted gold for my princess, I would wait at the wharves for the next ship from Daejima, they are the preeminent gold traders of our region. If I wanted to harness this Elixir of Life, say for a duel, I would seek it at my hara, what you call your navel chakra. One is external gold, while the other is internal gold. Both are of great value in their own way." Tombei was well-travelled and clearly knew more than most in the Wands Kingdom on the topic of internal and external forms of the martial arts.

"If we are talking about gold as an internal form, then would healing be one of its manifestations?" Sorcha asked.

"Aye, that is a good question," said Mage Saoirse. "We could say that a healer's gold is his or her life force. That skill is gold to someone with a sick child, a wound or an illness. Gold can be a word that describes a value, that value being the power of wealth, the power of owning property or servants, or the power of saving a life."

The conversation shifted to Justin's experiences as a journeyman. He explained that to complete his apprenticeship and be accepted into the smithing guild, a tradesman was required to travel and practice according to the style and needs of each Kingdom in the Empire. Their conversation continued long into the night.

The next day Eve was up early to do her rounds in the hospital. She was a highly regarded healer, often her very presence seemed to bring healing to the sick. She would enter a light trance to connect with her patient then consult with the healers on what approach to take be it herbals, manipulation, or hands-on energy work. Eve wanted to complete her rounds early so that she could return to the markets before it grew dark.

On this day the King and Queen of Wands were to hand out the awards for the competitions and would then display their own prowess in Fire Magic. As evening approached, people began to gravitate towards the Monarch's podium. There were many hundreds of villagers and visitors from other regions and countries. The atmosphere was electric and the crowd restless.

Late that afternoon the King and Queen arrived to present their awards. As each proud recipient received their gifts the crowd applauded with growing enthusiasm and excitement. Just as the last recipient walked off the podium there came a buzz from among the crowd as a warm, sensual energy permeated the air. The performance the people had been waiting for was about to begin.

Once a year, at the Winter Solstice, the King and Queen would give a demonstration of their command of the Force of the Flame. Although everyone in the Wands Kingdom understood fire magic, only those few who studied it under the mentorship of a master, had the ability to wield such power. This evening was an opportunity for the Monarchs to demonstrate that they still had the ability to hold their own against the enormous odds they faced on the frontier of the Tarot Empire.

"Rarely do we speak of our Wands' magic, for it is not words that hold back the hordes of our enemies but the strength of our community. Tonight you will witness the power of the Wands Flame, that which lies at our foundation as a Kingdom and that which keeps us safe," announced the King before resuming his seat to give way to his Queen.

"Dear people, we act when action is required, that is the Wands way. In these dark days we must show our force, the Force of the Flame. Unfortunately, Sir Alwyn is busy commanding our forces to the east and so cannot be here to demonstrate with us. Tonight your King and I shall do our best to make up for his absence."

As she spoke the Queen began to glow, a golden globe of light appeared above her head and she slowly rose into the air. As though held by a giant's hand she floated above the crowd, her radiant aura passed among the people, each receiving a blessing of the Wands' Flame. Her radiance was so bright that most could not bear to look at her, their cries of amazement cut through the chill in the growing darkness.

As the Queen slowly returned to her seat, the King stood and suddenly shot straight up into the air. Higher and higher he went until he appeared as a bolt of lightning. There came a crack of thunder from above the crowd that shook the ground. More cries, many of fear, echoed amongst the crowd. The King glowed as bright as the sun itself, slowly spiralling downwards to stop only metres above the crowd. He opened his arms as if to embrace his subjects and bathed everyone in an electrifying golden light.

"My people, your dedication to each other has always kept us a tight, loving community. With so many hands turned against us by the rogue mages of the Wildlanders, my Queen and I often struggle to provide for everyone in our beloved Kingdom. We would like to acknowledge that it is you who have stood firm to keep our Kingdom safe, not us." The King paused for a brief moment. "Would you now please open your hearts to receive our blessing." As he spoke the Queen lifted out of her chair and floated to be beside her partner. As they came together they created a dome of golden light to encompass the crowd.

"Open your hearts, feel our joy and our love. May our gift of the Flame enter and heal your soul. Take this gift and give it freely to those who are not able to be present tonight: the sick, the sad, and the lonely." The royal couple glowed so brightly that everyone below was forced to close their eyes. Each revelled in the sensation of the Flame as the people stood, reaching their hands into the air, sparks flying from their fingertips. Some swooned and dropped to their knees in joy, some began to laugh, while others cried with relief as they unleashed the burden of trauma and suffering from their soul.

The Flame remained glowing for several minutes before darkness claimed the evening and the people slowly, joyfully, returned to their homes. For the newcomers, the muted sounds of conversation and a glowing aura around each person was an amazing sight they would never forget.

~

# Follin's Meditation - 4 of Wands

*Follin could see two young women dancing around four standing quarterstaff bedecked in flowers and vines. Behind them was a small gathering of people, they appeared relaxed, enjoying each other's company. This was a celebration of sorts, and soon he was mesmerised by the girls' display of joyful abandon.*

*Before he could speak with the girls, Follin spied Mage Hermes standing to one side, watching him.*

*"Follin, I feel the warm glow of happiness in my soul watching these girls dancing and singing, what do you feel?" the Magician asked.*

*"I feel happiness too but there is more to this image than just joy, is there not?"*

*"I too can see beyond the raw energy that emanates from this image. Can you describe it?" inquired the Mage.*

*Follin sought an answer to his mentor's question. "There must be something that has brought about this celebration. It can't just be a spontaneous party or something like that, there must be something that preceded it."*

*Mage Hermes narrowed his eyes as he watched Follin process the image in his mind. When Follin looked up he noticed how aged his master had become. Where rose coloured cheeks once held Mage Hermes smile in place, there now sat wrinkles showing the tired muscles in his master's face. A sense of sadness threatened to overwhelm him, but he pulled himself back and focused on Hermes' question.*

*"Examining these images is like telling a story," answered Follin.*

*"There is always a before and an after, but I don't have access to these, not yet."* He frowned, just like his master had. *"I know, the clue is in the behaviour of the actors in the image. These girls are joyous, yes, and they are carefree. There is no evidence of danger nor of coercion, they are free to act in a spontaneous manner flowing with the energy around them..."*

Before Follin could continue the Mage said, *"Remember, these are Wands girls, they represent the Flame. Perhaps that will help you in deciphering this image."*

*"Yes, I was about to say something like that,"* Follin was following a process of elimination, just as he had been taught in the Swords Kingdom. *"Fire arises from within, I know it can consume as much as it excites. These girls are excited, they are freely expressing the raw energy of the Flame yet not inhibited by it. This is basically a joyful, carefree image of freedom, no attachments, just happiness. Something has happened that made them spontaneously happy."*

*"Yes, but...?"*

Follin smiled. *"But there doesn't need to be a trigger. This image shows that sometimes the best thing to do is feel the Flame within and let it flow. In this case, it is joyful abandon."*

*"And those four staff, what of they?"*

Follin slowed his mind, he had to now backtrack and process the foreground.

*"I see it, Mage Hermes, I see the staff as implements or an extension of the Flame. The Wands play with the sticks in their Moriscan dancing, they are always training, singing, and dancing, it's part of their*

daily routines in preparation for war. The number four is like a table, four legs hold it firmly to the ground, which makes it hard to tip over. The four staff and the joyful girls show that when we allow the Flame to flow in its own way, without trying to control it or push it, then we are stable. Wands people can become too enthusiastic, too aroused. If they suppress their fiery urges they might corrupt it and become frustrated and violent. Perhaps this is an image that says we should feel the force of the Flame and acknowledge it. To allow it to flow safely, stable and safe like a four-legged table."

"So what has your time in the hospitals and conversations with Eve shown you? I understand that she has described her experiences patching up the wounded and injured Wands who have let their Flame control their decisions. How dies this inform the lesson of the Wands in situations like that of the image in front of you?"

"Eve told me stories of how the younger Wands compete to outdo each other, pushing too hard to become the best. Many of them end up in the emergency ward with broken arms and sore heads. When the Flame is doused, when a Wands feels despondent and depressed, they push harder trying to feel better. They get drunk, do stupid and dangerous things and get into fights." At that moment Follin turned away from watching the girls dancing and asked his mentor. "But this causes me some confusion. Don't they allow their Flame to flow like the girls here have done?"

Mage Hermes nodded in understanding. "Yes, they allow it to flow, but they have a bitterness, an unresolved longing within. A pure heart flows easily. One who has trained with intent and discipline to control their Flame will also celebrate as these girls do. Those who have earned the true expression of the Wands Flame do not end up in hospital with broken heads and a damaged reputation. Those girls are young, it's not easy for youths to allow their Flame to flow as it needs. However, these girls are Wands girls, they have disciplined their minds and the fire within.

"Here is your lesson, Follin. It is necessary for one on the mystic's path to discipline oneself in every way to truly allow the Force of the Flame to forge its own path. Allowing the Flame to move of its own accord is frightening for many of us, particularly in the Cups Kingdom where passion precedes acts of revenge and jealousy abounds."

Follin nodded. "Yes, I see that now. But the Cups use water meditation, surely they can control their fire energy too?"

"Nay, water energy is already flowing, it can quench, and it can lead the adept of water to places of incredible beauty. But those with an excess of fire energy must temper their Flame for it will turn the water element into steam, and as we all know, steam gives a nasty burn."

"But," continued Follin. "I've mastered water but I'm not a master of fire, how do I control this steam that threatens to burn me?"

Mage Hermes stared at Follin and said softly, "Follin, it is not in your nature to indulge in your fire energy. You have always been blessed by the element of water. For you, and some others, it is easy to moderate your Flame. Those of the Wands, and many of the other Kingdoms, their self-control is limited and when the Flame ignites it is best to stand back."

"But..." Follin got no further.

*"The lesson for this image is that the training of one's self-control through specific meditation techniques, allows one to harness the Flame without effort. Look at those girls, they don't need to control themselves at all. Why? Because they already have control, through their training they have earned the right to release their Flame in this manner. The mystic, too, seeks to unite both water and fire within their being as these girls have done. One day soon, during your initiation I suspect, you will find out what I mean. Now go to sleep, it is almost morning."*

*When he awoke Follin wrote up his meditation in his journal. He then understood that the girls' celebration was mirrored in the display of the Force of the Flame by the Wands Monarchs the night before.*

~

# Five of Wands

*competition, inspired chaos, play, conflict, rivalry, argument,*

*commitment, standing strong against adversity.*

A few weeks after the Winter Solstice celebrations, a band of Fox elves ambushed an Elf Ranger patrol in the foothills of the Hindamar Mountains. This was a short-range patrol of a small band of Rangers led by Carwen, the Lone Wolf. A loner by name and by nature, she refused to stay cooped up in the castle and would often volunteer to lead these small patrols. At other times she would simply disappear for weeks at a time.

"Carwen only had time to show me what happened before the Fox's hid her from my clear-sight," cried Pandjar, his face creased in anguish as he restlessly paced the floor. "The patrol was only meant to be a short trip to restock the supplies in one of our caves, but the Fox Clan ambushed them and they've taken Carwen prisoner. We've got to hurry before they make their way back to the Mystic Isle."

"Damn those blackguard rogues! Wildlanders and Fox elves, curse them all!" growled the grey-haired, old warrior, Captain Nilyard, commander of the Wands Home Guard, as he escorted Follin, Ziggy and Pandjar into the castle's Great Hall.

"I'm sorry but we've no spare troops," announced the King. "Alwyn and Blade are with our reserves managing a disturbance in the Forest of Smoke and Fire. You're all we have to pursue these rebel elves." The King of Wands had few options. "Captain Nilyard, please prepare our guests for their patrol. Those Fox elves are like the wind, make haste and bring back our Lone Wolf and her Rangers."

"Sire, we shall," said Ziggy, pulling Pandjar towards the door. At that moment Page Asha ran into the room.

"I've just spoken with the Queen, she said that you need to leave right now, no second must be wasted..." she stopped speaking when she saw that the group were already preparing to leave. "Oh, I'll see that the horses are made ready and rations prepared."

Follin slipped into action mode, collecting his sword, bow and quarterstaff from their resting place by the door. Having said a rushed good-bye to Eve, he joined Ziggy and Pandjar as they hurriedly planned their trek to where Carwen's Elf Ranger patrol was last known to be.

"Sox? What about Sox?" called Asha as she led Follin's horse out of the stable.

Follin shook his head. "Asha, I'm not comfortable with this situation, not at all." After some moments of thought, Follin had his answer. "I need to leave Sox here to protect my family."

Pandjar impatiently kicked at the snow on the ground waiting to lead his brother and Follin towards the foothills of the Hindamar Mountains. He was worried, Carwen would have mind-talked him if she could, but he had not heard a word from her since her patrol was ambushed. He and Ziggy had tried to communicate with her, only to come up against a wall of silence - the Fox elves had cunningly disrupted all communication using their powerful cloaking spells.

By late afternoon it began to grow bitterly cold, soon it would be nightfall when the temperatures would drop well below freezing.

"We'll stop here, this overhang should give us a little protection and that stand of trees should have wood to give us fire for warmth and cooking. Hurry now, the horses need rubbing down, feeding, and covering," Ziggy commanded as he leapt off his horse and began removing its heavy supply packs.

The cold was bad, so bad that it stung Follin's fingers when he removed his gloves. Each of the group had their training to fall back on except Follin, he was still acclimatised to the warmth of the Cups' sunshine. Only with great effort was he able to conjure a semblance of the inner flame that he had trained daily to acquire. Recognising that he needed help to stay warm that night, Follin politely asked if he could sleep between the two elves.

Ziggy smiled as he replied. "Don't be embarrassed, Follin. It's standard practice for members of the commando to share their body

warmth on patrol. There's also a little trick we use when it's this cold."
Ziggy pulled his leather jacket aside to reveal a tightly woven cloth, six
inches wide, wrapped around his midsection. "See this, it is of very fine
wool. We wrap it around our waist to hold in the warmth of our navel
chakra. It will keep you warm even on the coldest nights." Ziggy
unwrapped his woollen sash and handed it to his friend.

That night the sash and the warmth of his friends beside him,
kept Follin comfortably warm. Unfortunately, none of them could keep
the horses warm for any length of time. When Ziggy and Pandjar
checked their mounts in the morning it was decided to send the horses
home.

"We've no choice," announced Pandjar. "These neddies won't last
long in this cold. Look at them, they've only recently returned from one
of the northern patrols and they haven't fully recovered."

"I'll not ride a horse that is unwell. I didn't need a horse on my
Major Arcana trek all those years ago. I didn't need one in the climb up
into the Hindamar Mountain with Master Pew either. I have two good
legs my father always called 'Shank's Ponies', they served me well in the
past and they'll serve me well now." Follin began unpacking his gear
from his horse's bags to fill his haversack.

"My only concern, Follin, is how to get the horses back home
safely," grunted Ziggy. "Any ideas gentlemen?"

Pandjar was distracted but came back to the conversation when
he heard the worried tone in his brother's voice.

"We have no time to take them home, I say we leave them to find
their own way back." He looked impatiently at Follin. "Elf-wise, can you

mind-talk a horse?"

Follin almost broke out laughing but saw the seriousness in his friend's eyes. "No, but I can call on Sox to lead them home."

"Good," was Pandjar's gruff reply as he packed his haversack before extinguishing their breakfast fire.

It hadn't snowed in the twenty-four hours since they had departed, which allowed them to pick up Carwen and her patrol's tracks.

"Look," whispered Ziggy, stopping suddenly and pointing. The snow had been kicked about to reveal a patch of browned grass, torn as though from a scuffle. "They were in a fight, and here, they've dropped this cloth." He picked it up to examine before handing it to his brother.

"That's from Carwen's vest. She tore it off so we would find it," said Pandjar, his breath forming a cloud around him in the chill air.

"And here, Tentor and Agran, Carwen's lead scouts." Ziggy bent to examine the arrows embedded in their friend's bodies. "These arrows, they are of the Fox Clan."

The band gathered around three more frozen bodies of their colleagues. Their faces darkened to see their friends so casually discarded without effort to bury them. This was a tragedy that none had wished to see, but it was not unexpected.

"Look, over there, they have Bluebeard markings," announced Ziggy pointing out several shallow graves a little further from the track. It was with sadness that they arranged the bodies of their comrades ready for their return.

"That be that then," was all Ziggy could say, it was enough. They knew the fate of their friend's souls, they would not have the pleasure of returning to this world, ever.

The group resumed their trek among the low foothills. The mighty Hindamar Mountains on their left rose upwards as they drew further west towards the coast. They recognised that the Fox elves had powerful cloaking spells, but mostly they were bothered that they could not mind-talk Carwen.

They had little choice but to follow what they believed to be the Fox elf's tracks which ran along a rough path heading westwards. This was the most probable path the kidnappers would have taken to get to the coast and their home on the Mystic isle.

By the second day, Follin began to tire. His training shoes were totally unsuited for mountain treking. He'd forgotten to change into his mountain boots before setting off on their rescue. The boots of the Elf Rangers, Mountaineers and Fearless Commandos were tough, thickened by layers of wool and leather to keep out the sharp stones, cold and ice of the mountains. That evening after their meal, Ziggy called Follin to him.

"I noticed that you've been limping. Let me see those shoes of yours."

"Aye, those were made for dancing around with a quarterstaff on nice, soft grass, not for climbing mountains," grunted Pandjar unable to hide his frustration.

While Follin held his feet to the fire to dry out, the two elves examined the holes in his shoes.

Ziggy shook his head. "Follin, we can't take you any further. These are useless for a mountain patrol. Another day along this path and we'll need to carry you."

Pandjar let out a deep sigh. "If your feet be too raw I can take you back..." he didn't finish. Pandjar was torn, he didn't want to abandon his lover's rescue but he also had a duty to protect Follin, the future Magician of the Tarot Empire.

"Nay, you're needed here, Pandjar. I can make my own way back, there are no enemies between here and the castle." Follin was bitterly disappointed in himself and refused to slow his friends any more than he already had.

The two elves silently watched as Follin replaced his worn shoes and, having finished their meal, they packed their cooking gear into their bags and prepared for sleep. They would be up just after midnight. No one spoke, there was no call to waste more words on an issue that was already settled.

That night Follin spoke with his mentor, Mage Hermes, and discussed the problem. It was of such importance that he had planned to follow his father's example and fill the holes with grass and bark until his shoes fell apart, then he would bind his feet with cloth until that wore out, then finally he would walk barefoot.

"Follin, as amazing a cobbler as you may be, grass, bark and cloth, a walking shoe doth not make." Hermes stifled a laugh as he continued. "Why did no one think to borrow a pair of Elf Ranger mountaineer boots? Those elven warriors no longer have need of them, nor would they be disinclined to see you borrow them to complete such a worthy mission."

In his next meditation, Follin sought his wife. Eve sent her love and the twins' joy warmed his heart.

"Da, have you found Auntie Carwen yet?" asked Fiana, the sleep heavy in her voice.

"Darling, we have her tracks in our eyes every second of our trek," he replied as he held tight to the warm feeling of love that Eve sent to help him sleep.

"Hey, Da, Asha said Sox brought your horses home. You should have asked Fiana and me to get them. Sox would have looked after us," was Aidan's simple input. Follin was silently pleased that his children were not worried about his absence.

He slept until the midnight wake-up call and bid his friends good fortune. He told them of his plan to take a pair of the Ranger's boots but they didn't see a reason for him to bother.

"Our Ranger brothers would be honoured, Follin, but there is little chance of you catching up with us. You should make haste to the castle and prepare to meet us on our return with some food, we'll be needing it by then," said Ziggy.

They were fatigued from the relentless cold and the frustration of not being able to contact Carwen. It looked as though the Fox band were travelling as fast as they were and had no intention of slowing. The impenetrable cloaking spell caused the two Wood elves to wonder exactly where the Fox elves were heading. It was clear that they knew they were being pursued.

"This patrol is dangerous and it might end badly. Your magician's head is much too precious. Go home, elf-wise, we have experience in pursuits of this kind." Pandjar grabbed at his haversack, lifting it onto his shoulders he was ready to continue their pursuit.

Ziggy walked around the fire to embrace his friend. His smile was warm but Follin could sense that hope appeared to have left their little group behind on the cold slopes of the mountain.

Finally, Pandjar's frustration broke and his inner lion roared. "Those cut-throats have fouled my vision! Carwen can't contact me and I can't locate her! The scoundrels have thrown a mist over my eyes so thick that I can't even see if they are on this mountain or the next!"

Ziggy stood beside his brother and touched his shoulder. The lion berserker slowly faded from his brother's face. For a brief moment, Pandjar looked like a lost little boy, but it quickly disappeared leaving Follin uncertain if he had seen it at all. The rugged Ranger grunted, impatient to get back to following what few tracks they could see - or imagined.

"Carwen is a crafty Wolf Elf. This is not the first time she has had to fight off the warriors of the Fox Clan, nor of the Wildlanders. She has the cunning and the willfulness of the wolf, so don't worry," called Ziggy over his shoulder as the two elves set off at a slow jog along the faint track that led deep into the snow-covered hills.

In desperate need to save his feet from further trauma, Follin found that he could ignite the Flame at his navel chakra. By directing it beyond his body he ran so that his feet barely touched the ground. Within a few minutes of arriving at the scene of the ambush he found what he was looking for. Pulling at the dry bushes he built a small fire to warm the thick leather boots so that he could remove them from the frozen feet of the elven warrior.

"Thank you, friend. I know you to be Karadar, keeper of bees in your Water village. I am saddened by your passing and it is with gratitude that I accept your gift. I shall use these well, have no fear of that."

Curling himself around the fire, Follin, in his warm, well-soled boots, fell fast asleep not waking until late afternoon.

~

Unbeknownst to the rescue party, the Fox elves had fallen afoul of their Bluebeard companions.

"I'm fed up with you lot telling us what to do!" howled Ostick, leader of the Bluebeard escort party. "It's always *'you do this, you do that!'* One more precious word from you lot and I'll stick this blade up 'yer gizzard!"

Fifteen Fox elves and nine Bluebeards were settled around a small fire in a low, snow-covered gully warming their meals. They had started out with equal numbers, but what grace they had for each other was long gone.

"You've our gold in your wallet so don't think that you haven't been handsomely paid, Ostick. And don't forget, it was us that saved you when you befouled our ambush. It was your own foolishness that got your men killed, you trumped-up highlander buffoon," retorted Gilbert, the elf captain, his face tight in the cold morning air.

The Bluebeard leader laughed in derision. "You think you saved us? Don't make me spit in your face! We saved your stinking hides and lost six good men doing it! If it wasn't for my spearmen your lads would

119

be frozen corpses by now."

The enmity between the two groups had been festering beneath the surface from the start of their patrol. The Fox elves needed the Bluebeards as their ticket to walk freely through the Wildlander villages without fear of reprisal. Without their Bluebeard guides, they would have been tracked down and hunted by every Hindamar Highlander from the moment they set foot on their lands. There was no friendship nor bond of goodwill between the Mystic Isle elf and Wildlander. The Wildlander's natural distrust of the Mystic Isle elves had made every moment together a festering ordeal.

Carwen, the Lone Wolf, had commanded a small band of Elf Rangers to drop off supplies in the Hindamar Highlands. The Fox elves and their Bluebeard guides had carefully stalked them for several days. The Fox elf magic of invisibility and confusion made it a simple ambush and all but the Wolf Princess had fallen. The losses to the ambush party were but the six Bluebeard warriors who had rushed the Rangers a fraction too early.

"My men have held to their end of the bargain, but one more stinking word from you and we'll walk. You can find your own way home!" barked Ostick through a mouthful of venison from a deer they had taken the day before.

Gilbert, an honest if not polite Fox elf, was furious.

"My Prince has paid good money for your services so you'll do as you're told, Ostick, and do it willingly."

"Willingly? You think I fear you and your glorified elven friends? I've seen better swordsmen in a village pigpen!" replied the Bluebeard leader spraying pieces of his meal as he spoke.

"I'm warning you, one more word and I'll stick my boot so far up your rump that you'll be chewing my toenails for a week," Gilbert replied, dropping his hand to the sword at his waist. The others around the fire immediately shifted their stance, several dropping their plates to reach for their weapons.

Ostick grunted in disbelief and spat the rest of his meal onto the snow. With a roar, he stood and reached for his spear, only to crash headfirst into the fire, an arrow through his neck. There was a sudden melee of arms, legs, swords, knives and spears. Weapons flashed and men screamed in anger and agony in the misty gloom until all was silent. Twelve Fox elves stood over the nine Bluebeard bodies, their heaving chests added their frosted breath to the smoke and mist of their campsite.

The smell of sizzling flesh filled the air but no one moved, something was amiss. To their horror, the prisoner, Princess Carwen, was nowhere to be seen.

"I don't believe it!" howled Gilbert in frustration. "We've come all this way through hostile territory, useless cast-off guides, and now this stupid dolt has caused us to lose our cargo!"

Simon, Gilbert's second in command, swiftly circled their camp scanning the ground for signs of their prisoner's escape. The morning mist was as thick as soup and any signs on the ground would be difficult for even a sharp-eyed elf to see.

"I see no tracks, that bird has flown, Gilbert. We've no choice but to stop our cloaking spell so that we can locate the Lone Wolf. It'll mean that the Rangers tracking us will have full vision again, but it can't be helped."

"Blast those Bluebeard vermin," grunted Gilbert, his mind racing. "Right, pack up, we've tracking to do. Those Wood Elf Rangers will soon find us. We must hurry."

~

Carwen sat quietly observing the growing frustrations of her captors and their Bluebeard guides. She had made it a point to add her comments of discontent at every opportunity in an effort to stir up trouble. She complained to her fellow elves of the Wildlander's body odour and bad habits, and she poisoned the minds of the Bluebeards by complaining of the elf's rude treatment and condescending attitude towards them.

"Those Fox elves treat you like you're their slaves, like children. You should stand up for yourselves. Without you, they wouldn't have made it this far. They should be grateful, instead they insult you," the Lone Wolf whispered.

It was her words that triggered the opportunity she needed to escape. Glancing behind her, she saw the blood flying from the severed head of a Bluebeard spearman and knew that she had but moments to take herself as far from this place as she could. Thick mist or no, those elves could track a feather on the wind.

One skill Carwen had in abundance was that of the wolf. By embedding herself into the wolf form she could run leaving barely a footprint in the snow. With discomfort from her frozen, bound hands, she raced across the snow towards her now deceased Ranger patrol.

There she would find a blade to cut her bonds. Her Fox elf captors had starved and ill treated her, and now she wanted weapons to kill, and food to sustain her rage.

~

Follin woke to the bright afternoon sunshine with a smile. He had a fine pair of boots, only slightly worn, and his belly was full. He packed his bowl into his haversack, swung his sword to the small of his back so that he could travel without it tripping him up in the snow, and set off at a fast jog to be with his friends.

The two Wood elves, unaware of the events down below, had been following a cleverly laid false trail sending them deep into the mountain ranges. The cunning of a Fox elf knows no bounds and even Ziggy and Pandjar, experienced Elf Rangers, were caught in the web woven by their enemy's spell.

The Fox elf's magic was now totally focused on locating Carwen and preventing her from communicating with Pandjar and Ziggy. She sensed that her canny captors had turned their cloaking spell and melded it with her aura. Try as she may, she was unable to cast it off.

"Gravus, you and your warriors will pay for this," she whispered as she loped lightly over the snow. "When I get back to my fallen Rangers I'll have what I need to kill you and your henchmen."

Not far from his campfire, Follin paused, his senses told him that someone was approaching, fast. With practised ease, he strung his bow and knocked an arrow ready to meet whatever was out there in the rising mist.

Carwen was uncertain of the aura she sensed ahead of her. It was mingled with that of her partner, Pandjar and his brother, Ziggy. She slowed her pace and, pursing her blue lips together, she blew a note to announce her presence.

"Carwen?" cried Follin, lowering his bow.

"Yes, it's me," came Carwen's weak reply. The effects of exhaustion was clear, she could barely speak as she stumbled into Follin's waiting arms. "Cut my bonds, my hands are like ice crystals."

As Follin held his friend tight to his chest he could sense her exhausted state. Bringing his life force into his centre he sent a blast of fire energy into the core of her body.

"I've got you, Carwen, now hold still while I cut these bonds. Then we'll go back to the Ranger camp and light a fire. There's food there and weapons..."

"Just cut the rope, Follin, before my hands drop off."

Follin smiled to himself, this was so like the Lone Wolf, direct and to the point. He slid his knife between her hands and cut the bonds.

"They're like blocks of ice. Let me put some life back into them." He held Carwen's frozen hands between his own allowing his fire energy to warm them. "They're swollen too, that's not good," he muttered as he used his breath to direct more healing energy into her hands.

Carwen didn't argue, the pain was initially unbearable but within a few moments, she closed her eyes and sighed, she felt safe with Follin beside her.

"Where's Pandjar and Ziggy? I can detect their scent, but they are gone from here, why?"

Follin looked at Carwen's exhausted eyes. "We have been tracking you since we found out you were taken. I had to come back to borrow one of your patrolman's boots. I honoured him in our traditional way." Follin shuffled a little uncomfortably, taking from the dead was frowned upon in some cultures.

Carwen looked down at Follin's boots. "Good, they'll help you take down our Fox enemy. It is an honour you bestow upon Karadar's soul."

The two suddenly stopped talking as the sound of voices floated to their ears.

"Fox, I can smell their filth!" Carwen whispered and her body stiffened.

"They're close, Carwen. I can see them forming in the mist beyond. They know we are here."

"Then we fight." Carwen reached for her sword but there was nothing by her side. "Follin, I need a weapon."

Follin swore softly, something he never did, but right now he was in a quandary. "Damn it! I have a bow, knife, sword and quarterstaff, what is your strength?"

Carwen's clear eyes stared at her rescuer. "Elf-wise, I'm not trained in quarterstaff and my bow arm is too stiff to pull. But, I am a master of the sword and knife. If it is your wish, I shall take the magical sword you offer. I feel that it will be a foolish blunder for me to wield anything else this day."

The voices of the Fox elves drew closer, they had their prey surrounded. When they saw Follin as their prisoner's lone defender the elves laughed and jeered.

"Ah, yes, my sword, it is my treasure, but today you shall wield it to honour my master and myself. Have no fear, Carwen, I have mastery of the quarterstaff and bow. Let us finish this and avenge your Ranger friends." Follin drew his sword and passed it to the Lone Wolf. He knew that today blood would flow at its touch. Quickly changing his mindset he forced a smile knowing that his quarterstaff prowess would soon be put to the test.

With a spark of belief that they may succeed, Carwen accepted Follin's sword from his hand, and, to Follin's surprise, she bowed to him as she stood. The Lone Wolf stiffened momentarily as the power of Follin's sword entered her body.

"Elf-wise, this is a powerful sword indeed. I sense the elemental's hand as well as Master Pew's and your own. Let's show these scoundrels how we fight in the Wands Kingdom," she hissed.

Though still weak from her treatment at the hands of her captors, Carwen turned to face the enemy, her sword held on-guard above her shoulder. As she calmed her breath she synchronised her breath with Follin's. To her surprise she felt the sword respond, it triggered her own wolf energy and power surged into her limbs. It was not enough, she knew, but she smiled knowing that to die fighting was an honourable death indeed.

"Lone Wolf," Follin grinned. "All will be fine this day. My sword is with my trusted sister, my bow is in my hands, and my quarterstaff is ready. I sense order in the universe and this is how things should be."

Follin had spoken without thinking, his mind no longer functioning in its usual linear manner. He could see the entire battlefield as though it was a field of play. He could sense the mood, strength and weakness of each combatant. Every move he would take was etched in his mind ready to be played out.

Shifting his mind to his bow, gifted by the Swords Bowman, he rapid-fired three arrows, each hitting its mark in the rising mist.

"I see you, Follin," Carwen whispered, her fingers flexing around the grip of the sword handle.

In shocked surprise, Gilbert blinked several times as he saw his men drop, and immediately swung into action.

"Kill the bowman but spare the princess!"

Carwen met them with the blade of her sword and the force of her wolf spirit. Her body had yet to recover but her rage was strong. Follin was in a space that he would later recall as much like Pan's touch at the rescue of Sorcha and the two children near Naroo's resting place.

As he drew his bow, Follin drew the Flame deep into his body. With each release, he sensed and guided the arrows to his selected target. He then dropped his bow and hefted his quarterstaff into a swinging arc above his head to strike the five arrows that winged their way at him in retaliation. He easily smacked them out of the air. Then, twisting Dolphin style, he sprang forward to take down the two closest elf warriors before they could move to defend themselves.

By now the others had joined the fight. Follin saw Carwen defending herself against three elves. As though in slow motion he spun himself on the balls of his feet and knocked one of the closest elves senseless to the ground. He was circle walking, the skill he learned so long ago from The Empress and refined by his training with Ziggy and the Cups Knight, Sir Rohan. Twisting sideways to dodge a swinging sword blade he jabbed the elf in the solar plexus forcing him to pull away from the fight. In this fashion, Follin felt the force of his fire energy, the Flame, pushing him, generating greater magnitudes of force with every move.

The press of the enemy was more intense, violent and coordinated than what he had experienced before, even with the Wands weapons masters. Sensing the Wands change point forming, he immediately melded his Dolphin style with that of the Flame. The twisting, spinning thrusts, parries and jabs of his staff were mixed with palm and elbow strikes, leg locks and kicks. Each Fox elf that was unwise enough to approach was summarily knocked either unconscious or immobilised and unable to continue the fight.

"Enough!" came a sharp command from the Fox captain. "Step back, all of you, this is getting us nowhere!"

Immediately the remaining elves removed themselves from the fray and stood on-guard in a circle around Follin and Carwen. Their heavy breathing created a cloud of frost in the air around the two defenders.

Follin was unscathed, his face flushed with an inner glow. Certainly, he felt challenged, the skill of the Fox elves was at a level beyond even what he had experienced in sparing with the best of the Wands warriors. But then, a dozen desperate elves would always prove more challenging than single combat, he reasoned.

He looked at his companion, Carwen was kneeling on the ground, her face contorted in pain and exhaustion. Blood was smeared across her face as she tried to stem the flow from a deep wound to her neck.

"What do you want, Fox?" called Follin. He was ready to continue at the slightest suggestion of deception. "I will take you all down, you can't win." He quickly scanned those elves lying on the ground in pain unable to rejoin the fight.

"I see that you will not relinquish our prisoner. I also acknowledge that we may have trouble besting you. But first, let me introduce myself. My name is Gilbert of the Fox Clan, first bodyguard of Gravus, Prince of the Mystic Isle. I am honoured to bear witness to your skill, but I am curious, what is your name."

"I am but a fool from the village of Saoirse," came Follin's curt reply. He was still aroused in body and mind and wanted to continue the fight. He truly felt that he was only just starting to warm up.

"Step aside, Staff Master of the Mystic Isle who calls himself a fool. Princess Carwen is the wife of our Prince. She is honour bound to return to her husband and we have pledged to bring her home. This is not your fight, sir, let us take her and we each retain our honour," announced Gilbert.

"You are mistaken, Gilbert of the Fox Clan, this is my fight. I understand that your King has pledged to kill the Lone Wolf the moment she sets foot on your soil. It is you who must stand down and leave. If it is your wish I will escort you through the highlands to the coast for these are evil times and the Highlanders don't take kindly to trespassers." Follin spoke with a directness he'd not felt before, and he liked it.

"Nay, fool, I regret that we cannot do that. You must step aside or we will be forced to kill you. The Princess is nigh dead on her feet as you can see. Leave her with us and I promise that she will not be harmed. You have my honour and my word on this." Gilbert knew that the cloaking spell was no longer active and the two Wood Elf Rangers were no doubt racing to Carwen's rescue. He was desperate, and now this upstart with no name or lineage had spoiled his plans.

"I don't wish to dishonour your pledge to your Prince, but I must decline." Follin instinctively moved to stand between Carwen and the captain, when, in a flash of movement, he was forced into the defence of his companion.

"Then die you must!" grunted the elf captain hefting his blade at his enemy.

Follin swung his quarterstaff in an arc above his head to meet the swinging blade of the Fox captain. Gilbert's sword came down right at the centre of Follin's quarterstaff with such force that both sword and staff shattered. Gilbert staggered backwards in shock, his arm benumbed. Follin recovered a split second faster to reach down and grasp his sword that had dropped from Carwen's bloodied fingers. Immediately a familiar sensation burst into his limbs and he felt the full power of his blade surge into him.

"You scab-backed villain!" Follin cried as he swung into the same pattern of assault that he had started, Dolphin style with its core of fire.

With Master Pew's sword in his hand, Follin struck at Gilbert, smacking the flat of his blade across the top of the elf's head dropping him senseless to the ground. In the next moment, he had trapped the leg of an attacking elf and forced the hilt of his sword into the man's midsection paralysing him. Follin followed this with a punch of fire energy that caused a third elf to collapse in agony. The last elf was dispatched with similar skill and ease.

Pausing to take in the now quiet battle scene, Follin heard a voice. At first, it was tiny, as though from a great distance. Then it became annoying, causing him to turn to catch the words.

"What?" he asked absently as he scanned the area for any elf that he may have left standing.

"Follin, it is over," whispered Carwen at his feet. "I have Pandjar's mind-talk, he will be here within the hour. You must tie these men up and I must heal before I bleed to death."

At the sound of her voice, Follin turned to stare at his companion. Carwen had not risen from her position on the ground. Her hand had slipped as she struggled to keep it tight on the sword cut to her neck. The wound was deep and blood seeped brightly from between her fingers. Although undefeated in battle, assisted by Master Pew's elemental magic, without Master Lexus' scabbard, Carwen remained susceptible to injury. Once more, Follin acted instinctively.

"Hold still, Carwen, let me see to your wound." It was deep and he knew that it would prove fatal if he didn't act quickly. Sticking the tip of his sword into the snow beside him, he put his right hand over Carwen's wound. Moving his left hand to the centre of her chest he felt for the Lone Wolf's internal Flame, it was weak. In that shocking moment of realisation at how dangerously close she was to death, Follin quickly built a searing heat within his body.

Follin's navel centre was still roaring from the fight, so he quickly formed the cauldron around his furnace as he had been taught. With three rapid breaths he created a pearl of fire, a condensed form of energy so powerful that it felt like a drop of white-hot iron burning in the centre of his abdomen. Closing his eyes he breathed deeply into his centre, took the pearl and forced it into the palm of his right hand to seal Carwen's wound.

"Argh!" Carwen's sudden cry sounded both of pain and bliss, then she collapsed unconscious to the ground.

Follin looked at the result of his healing. Lifting his hand he saw that the wound was sealed and had stopped bleeding. The Lone Wolf was out of danger, she had enough life force in her heart centre to carry her through for the next few crucial hours. He felt tired but shrugged it off as he bent over his haversack to grab the cloth that he used to bind his meals. This was a habit from his days wandering the countryside in the Major Arcana. He gently bandaged Carwen's wound and wrapped her in one of the Fox elf's fur coats.

The groans from the wounded Fox elves caused him to pull himself out of his thoughts and back into the world. Without a second thought he stood and began the task of tying his prisoner's hands and feet in preparation for his friend's arrival.

"What will you do to us?" asked Simon, his chest and ribs bruised making it difficult for him to breathe.

"If you give me your word of honour that you will go straight home to your clan, I shall release you."

Follin had removed the elves' weapons and placed them in a pile and began readying to light a fire. He closed his eyes and extended his hand towards the tinder that he had placed on the cleared ground. With several deep breaths he forced his Flame into the pile. With a startled gasp from the elves around him, it burst into flame.

"Who by the thunder gods are you?" asked a voice from the circle of prisoners.

"He's a magician, a Wands Fire Mage for sure, no others can make fire without flame," came Gilbert's pain-wracked voice.

"I'm just a foolish wanderer from the Mystic Isle," Follin replied. He looked at his handiwork and smiled. This was the first time he had attempted lighting a fire with his Flame, and it felt wonderful.

"I've never seen a trick like that before," came another voice from among the prisoners.

"It's no trick, Listan, it's elemental magic, they call it the Flame within. This fellow from the Mystic Isle is no simple trickster. No one has bested me in a fight before, certainly no human." Addressing Follin directly, Captain Gilbert asked, "Master of the Staff and Flame, who are you?"

Follin turned to look at his audience and replied, "My name is Follin, and as I said, I am a fool from the Mystic Isle."

"You're no fool," grunted a hardened Fox warrior. The elf gently touched his swollen cheek with one hand while trying to flex the fingers of the other. "I've not seen fighting like that 'afore neither. I know that style though, I've seen it..." he thought for a moment. "Dolphin style of the Cups Kingdom, that's what it is."

"Aye, but that punch of energy that knocked Velkar to the ground, that's the Wands Flame. Poor Velkar, he's still unconscious."

"Master Follin, will Velkar recover?" asked a young elf looking at his friend lying unconscious on the ground beside him.

Follin leaned over the fallen elf and felt for his life force. It was strong.

"Your friend is asleep. Leave him, he will be fine when he wakes."

"Why are you letting us live? We've killed your Ranger friends and your Wood elf escort will be here soon, they will most certainly want revenge." Captain Gilbert had lost to this young master, but he held out hope to return to his clan and family.

"Captain, I believe you have honour, enough at least, to keep your word to refrain from harming anyone on your journey home. It will be dangerous and I have left you your knives for protection."

"But there are Wildlanders who will find our tracks and seek to kill us, and there are lions and wolves in these mountains. You should have saved us at least one bow," moaned one of the Fox elves nursing a broken rib.

"I expect your Wood elf friends will want us dead too," another elf complained as he nursed a dislocated shoulder.

"Perhaps you should have thought of these things before you massacred my Ranger friends," stated Follin as he pushed the elves' weapons into the fire which would twist them out of shape, rendering them useless.

It was at this time that Carwen woke and sat up. She looked around at the group of swollen faces, bruised and broken limbs of her would-be captors.

"Follin," she whispered. "What's happening?"

Captain Gilbert answered her in the elven tongue. "Your champion has bested us, we of the royal guard. You are the luckiest princess and we the most miserable of elves. Go in peace Princess Carwen, Lone Wolf, may we never meet again."

Follin turned to question what Gilbert had said but at that moment he saw Pandjar and Ziggy racing towards them across the snow.

Pandjar scanned the group before dropping to one knee to inspect his lover.

"Carwen, are you well? Let me see that wound..." he lifted Follin's bandage, and, after some prodding, was satisfied that his partner was out of danger. Turning to the prisoners he said, "Gilbert, you scoundrel, I should kill you and your filth right now, but you are Follin's prisoners and it is up to him to decide your fate."

Ziggy wasn't so easy to convince.

"Gilbert, you and your men owe those elves a life for your cowardly slaughter." He pointed in the direction of the fallen Rangers. "I would slay you right now and send you to serve their needs for eternity."

"Nay, Ziggy, nay, they are my prisoners. They have given their word to return home, in peace, and I will honour mine. When this one awakes they shall be on their way. Our mission is done. Albeit sadness grips our hearts at the loss of our friends."

"I am unhappy with your decision, Follin, but they are your prisoners and your oath to them is mine." Ziggy bent over the Fox captain and spoke in the elven tongue. "Gilbert, I know thee. If I or any of my Rangers see your face again, in peace or war, you will find yourself on the ground just as still and cold as those you murdered." He stood and walked away.

~

# Follin's Meditation - 5 of Wands

*The image Follin examined was one of a group of people fighting. It could be the Wands performing their Moriscan dance, or perhaps it was a proper fight, he couldn't tell. Entering the image in his meditative state he stood to one side watching as he tried to figure it out.*

*"Follin," spoke a voice beside him. "As you know from experience, conflict is part of human nature. Humans are competitive creatures, like all of nature they strive to survive yet sometimes that leads to conflict."*

*Follin nodded as he recognised that it was Nangkari speaking to him. "Is that the meaning of this image then?" he asked.*

*"Certainly, a simple image has a simple meaning. Conflict is not always violent, sometimes it is competitive, fun, but it must be seen in context of what occurred beforehand."*

*"This could be a game, like the Wands games that they use in training?"*

*"Perhaps," was the dragon's reply.*

*"But isn't that what I really should be learning here? I mean, if I am to learn the meaning of the Wands' condition, their characteristics and what they stand for, shouldn't I know what this image represents?"*

*"Do you know what happened five minutes ago, before this image arose? Do you know what is in the minds of the participants here? Do you presume to know everything?"*

*"No, I can only see what I see, I don't have the trick of time travel. But it bothers me, this is either a fight or a game, I can't tell the difference."*

*"Even a Master Mage has no knowledge of that, you ask too much of yourself." The dragon's voice was soft.*

*"Nangkari, I've never seen you in your dragon form. Would you do me the honour? Please?" he asked.*

*Nangkari suddenly laughed, one of those rare moments of passion that dragons appeared to have lost thousands of years ago.*

*"I don't believe that you have, but I will demand a boon from you in return."*

*"A boon? What could I ever give a dragon that he doesn't already have or can't command for himself? But ask away, I am your servant."*

*Nangkari lifted his eyebrows as he smiled, much as a human would in a display of delight or satisfaction.*

*"Follin, the boon I ask of thee is to accept a gift that will provide a greater understanding of this image you struggle to understand. It is a gift of enormous value, one that a magician would die for."*

*"Ha!" laughed Follin almost too loudly. "Now you've got me! What is it, come on Nangkari, you can't dangle this carrot in front of me, what is the boon you ask?"*

*Nangkari was no longer smiling, his face had softened, and he almost had the look of a child seeking approval for a work he had made for his teacher.*

*"Please accept the gift of my form. I have decided that it is time I had some fun. Of course, I have the Wands Royal family, they are pleasant, but elementals are not my type. I have your father and the Tarot archetypes, and while they are dear friends, they are not like you. In you, I feel a camaraderie of my own kind."*

*Follin was taken aback but quickly replied, "If that is it, then I accept."*

*"That is the answer I expected," Nangkari said with growing enthusiasm. "The image you are scrying is to remind us that conflict can be healthy competition, or it can be an expression of aggression, revenge, or for keeping others from harming those we love. You know this conflict as does your father, both of you have fought to protect those close to your hearts. But do not be afraid of conflict, it is sometimes necessary. Now meld with me and we shall find another way to understand the meaning of this image."*

*Just as he had experienced with the god Pan, Follin felt himself within the dragon's enormous, muscled body.*

*In his head, Follin heard Nangkari's voice. "Now fly!"*

*Immediately Follin felt his arms become wings and his dragon's tail empowered his movements. The twisting of his body helped him hold his direction as he powered above the Dragon Mountain Castle and sought to fly towards the Hindamar Mountain ranges to the west.*

*"This is something I've never felt before. I can feel a power within me, what is it?" asked Follin.*

*"That is dragon power!" laughed Nangkari in delight.*

*They flew in exhilarated silence through the evening clouds, sometimes high then to suddenly swoop low to glide above the treetops. Over time Follin felt a fatigue he had never known before. A fatigue that seeped into his bones and then into his soul.*

*"Nangkari, I am so tired. I'm afraid I'm about to fall out of the sky... help me," Follin sighed. In fact, he felt that he had already begun*

*to collapse within.*

*"No, I'm not going to help you. You said that you wanted to know the meaning of the image and so I am giving you another interpretation. If you can tell me what that is I shall help you," was the dragon's response.*

*Follin felt himself almost cry out in terror - he really was falling now, straight down.*

*"You'd better hurry because the ground is coming up to meet you rather fast."*

*"I..." WHAM! The pain was horrific. Follin felt his bones snapping, puncturing his organs and his life force quickly slipped from him along with the blood spilled on the ground beneath.*

*"Well, I did warn you that you were getting very close to the ground."*

*Suddenly they were back in the skies above. It was evening and they flew just below the clouds. Follin felt the fatigue in his limbs and his heart was cold.*

*"What happened? I just died, didn't I?" he asked.*

*"Yes, in a way you did, or rather, I did, it is my body after all."*

*"Oh, so you time-travelled backwards?"*

*"Yes, I did. I suggest that you think a little quicker this time."*

*"Oh, no! I'm trying but I can't stay up here, my wings won't flap anymore. I'm exhausted, and I can't think like this..." WHAM! The pain, oh the pain. Follin felt himself slamming through the pine trees to finally smash into the ground.*

*Again he was back in the air, his face cold from the icy air blowing off the Hindamar Mountains. His limbs already turning into lumps of frozen flesh.*

*"Nangkari, I'm falling but I can't do anything about it... what is this lesson?" he asked knowing full well what was about to happen.*

*"I know!" WHAM!*

*"Too late my friend. And if you don't hurry up with your answer you know what will happen." They were back in the skies above the mountains and Nangkari's voice echoed his delight. The dragon hadn't had so much fun in centuries.*

*"I know the answer, Nangkari! It's determination, commitment, and giving everything to a dedicated purpose. That's what this image also says!" cried Follin in desperation. He was so shaken by the violence of hitting the ground that he did not want a repeat experience.*

*"Well done. Mind you, I would have liked one more dive but alas, it seems that you have had enough. Yes, the image shows determination, but why?"*

*"No, no more questions!" Follin immediately felt his wings stiffen and his head bent towards the earth. "That's not fair!"*

*"Well, what is the answer, quickly now!"*

*"I, umm, in times of immediate danger one must give everything in a fight to protect those they love. A fight to the death, to give less is to court failure!" screamed Follin just as he was about to slam into the ground.*

*Nangkari took control of his body and Follin, to his enormous relief, became a passenger.*

*"Yes, now you will never forget this lesson. If you believe that*

*something is worth fighting for, you will give your all. In the Wands Kingdom every person, be they a labourer on a farm, a servant in the village tavern, a sweeper of the training grounds, and every member of the commando, knows this lesson. And now you do too."*

*Follin struggled to stop shaking as they settled into the steady rhythm of flight.*

*"Nangkari, so this is the gift you have for me?" asked Follin, completely exhausted.*

*"My gift is one of knowledge, and knowledge earned is knowledge kept. This, my friend, is the lesson of the Kingdom of Fire!"*

~

# Six of Wands

*victory, triumph, pride, attention-seeking, accomplishment, recognition for a job well-done, respect the dead and honour the living.*

Eve called to Follin on her return from the hospital that afternoon, "Hey, guess what!"

Follin was in a state of contentment. The fire warmed his feet while he examined his walking shoes to see if he could repair the gaping holes in them. The twins were with their cousins at Auntie Theresa's cottage for the afternoon, and he and Eve had some free time to be with each other for a change.

"I don't know, why not tell me?" he replied, bending to scratch Sox under the chin just the way his dog liked it. Sox was taking some well-deserved time-out from watching the twins, it was Molly's turn.

"Well, since you don't seem to care," Eve huffed. "I'm now head of the Royal Wands Hospital. And, I've got a dozen or more student healers under me and nearly a hundred beds."

That news made Follin look up and pay attention.

"That's a well-earned reward for our High Priestess in waiting," he said with a big grin on his face.

Eve laughed, throwing herself onto the couch beside Follin. "I've spent all day organising new staff rosters and rearranging the beds in the wards. Did you know that Sir Rohan helped set up this hospital? That's my big news, so, what have you been doing?"

"Me? Well, let me see... a couple of days ago I rescued a fair maiden from a band of marauding Fox elves hell-bent on kidnapping and murdering her. Yesterday I spent all day in bed asleep, and today I spent time with Nangkari perfecting my breath of the Flame. He said that I need to hold it in my navel for a full ten minutes before I graduate, but it burns when I try to do it that long. To make matters worse, it makes me fall asleep. Nangkari said that I did it instinctively when forced to fight the Fox Elves, but I now need to learn how to do it consciously."

"I was thinking that I could fall fast asleep myself, right now after my busy day. But here is my poor dear husband, who has had such a tough time playing with his friends." Eve thought for a moment. "Hey, did I remind you to make sure your grimoire is up to date? Hera mentioned that we both needed to display our grimoires and magician's tools at our initiation."

Follin looked at Eve inquisitively. "Grimoire? You mean my journals?"

"Yes, where you write down your spells and dreams and meditations and things, didn't Mage Hermes tell you?"

"No, he's not said much about my initiation. I'm not sure he wants to think of it, it means the end of his time here." Follin paused. "It makes me sad thinking about it. But yes, I'm up to date with my grimoire. In fact, I've a dozen stored away in my chest from all the years I've trained in magic."

Eve leaned forward to examine the holes in Follin's shoes before dropping her head into his lap. Yawning loudly she reached up to stroke his face and said, "I'm going to catch a few minutes shut-eye. Wake me when we need to pick up the twins."

~

Aunt Theresa was struggling with her own problems. It seemed that every time Follin's twins visited, she had her hands full keeping them from taking Tanika and Atsu into the astral planes to play with Sox and Molly's friends.

"But we love it, Ma, come on, we'll be back by dinner time," argued Tanika. "Molly will be there and she always makes sure we're safe. And Aidan and Fiana, they know everything. And you should see where the elementals live, it's amazing. There are tunnels filled with animals and insects that live in the ground, Molly has so many magical friends." In her mid teens, Tanika was soon to enter her first year of cadetship to become an officer in the Fearless Commando. She was one of the bright stars of her clan. The daughter of the famous swordsman,

Tombei, Tanika's skill in all martial arts placed her in a class of her own. Her younger brother, Atsu, wasn't far behind her in skill or determination.

Theresa was never sure how to treat her brother's children. The twins were too precocious for her uncomplicated, old country manner. Having survived the hardship of her childhood in Saoirse village, and then a rushed relocation to the Wands Kingdom, she longed for simplicity in all things. Her husband, Tombei, never pressured her to be like the other city girls. He loved that she approached each day with the single desire to keep things simple. Theresa, the love of Tombei's life, was one of the few women in the castle that preferred home to the excitement freely available in the Wands castle. That was why he stayed in the Wands Kingdom once his contract with the King had run to completion. Tombei, the renowned warrior, loved his family with a passion.

"Sweetheart," called Tombei from the bathroom where he had been soaking after a day of training. "I'll be out in a minute and then I can take them to the obstacle course."

Theresa sighed with relief. She had always prided herself on being a good mother to her children - until Follin and his family arrived, that is. Now she felt as though she was just a bundle of nerves. If it wasn't for her mother dropping in as often as she could to help, she believed she would have gone mad.

"Yes, thank you. Ma and Da are bringing Nangkari over for dinner so I need to get the potatoes on as soon as possible, they take ages to cook." She giggled, a sound that was always a delight to the loving ears of her husband. "Nangkari said that if I didn't put a plate of potatoes out for him, he might have to eat our children instead."

Tombei laughed as he stood and reached for a towel. "I tell you what. Don't bake any potatoes and see if Nangkari would accept Follin's twins instead. I think that's a fair trade."

"Hey!" came a familiar voice at the front door. "I heard that!" called Follin as he raced into the kitchen to hug his little sister. "I'll trade a bowl of your tomato, onion and garlic pasta for the twins, they are driving us nuts. I tell you, all they want to do is fight with their sticks all day long. Then they want to go for a swim in the fish ponds of the Keep, and if they can't do that they want to take Sox and Molly into the castle halls to look for ghosts and secret passageways. I tell you..."

It was decided that Tombei and Follin would take the children to play on the obstacle course while Eve helped Theresa prepare their dinner. Eve had to convince the children that they had annoyed Molly and Sox enough. Indeed, the earth elemental and the fae dog were content to warm themselves beside the fire.

At the evening dinner, Aidan, ever the curious one, was seated beside Nangkari and, as usual, he had a question he was dying to ask the dragon. At last, Eve put him at ease.

"Nangkari, if you don't mind, Aidan has been dying to know how you lost your eye. Can you please put him out of his misery?" she said.

Nangkari stopped eating, his fork with its skewed potato, halfway to his mouth.

"Harrumph!" he grunted loudly to show that he was annoyed at the interruption to his feasting. "Hmm, let me see, so you want to know why this old dragon only has one eye? Well, my little friend, we dragons are violent creatures. There was a time when we killed to live, and we lived to kill. But it's a simple story, I lost my eye in a fight with another of the draig folk. I was young, foolish, and trying to impress a pretty young lady dragon. But that was a long time ago, back in the days when all creatures fought for supremacy. These days I follow the Tao, the way of not-doing, it's easier."

Not satisfied with his answer, Aidan asked, "How come you didn't go back in time and change it so you won the fight and didn't lose your eye?"

"Nay, that would have been disrespectful to my opponent. He earned the right to say he bested me. Why would I take that away from him? Nay, little one, I would never do that."

"But don't you miss having both eyes?" Aidan wouldn't let go, he wanted to know everything.

"Miss my eye? No, not at all. I see the truth better without eyes. That fight helped me understand the way of the Tao, and one day you too will know the Tao as I do. But, I must warn you not to seek it, for in its seeking you will find nothing. The Tao cannot be found by looking, little one."

Aidan turned and looked at his father, who turned to look at Mage Saoirse.

Mage Saoirse decided that it was up to him to help his grandson. "Nangkari, I think the boy has no idea what you're talking about. Can you simplify it for him?"

"Humans!" announced Nangkari, sweeping his gaze around the

room to embrace them all. "I must ask pardon of the elves here, for they alone will ken what I mean."

"Aye, Nangkari, we ken thee," agreed Pandjar. He looked at Carwen, she had a smile on her face clearly enjoying the dragon's manner. Despite her recent ordeal with the Fox elves, Carwen wanted to be with family that night. Her neck still throbbed but the energy pearl Follin embedded into her wound was still pulsing, its healing powers unabated. Eve said that its healing should continue for another day or two.

"But how do I practice the Tao?" asked Aidan, waiting for his moment of enlightenment with great expectation.

"The word 'Tao' means 'the way' or 'the path'. I was told by the Strength Lady that this is best interpreted as 'to do', which means that you do the Tao rather than think about it. One simple 'doing' exercise is your centred walking. You can use it when you practice your Moriscan dance steps with stick and quarterstaff. But," continued Follin, "you will find that you are walking your path when you practice your water meditation from the Cups Kingdom. I know of no other way unless Nangkari can enlighten us?"

Aidan thought for a moment, he was now more confused than enlightened and began to lose interest. "But, Nangkari, if I lost my eyes will I still see like you do?" he asked, his eyes brightened now that he was back to his original question.

The shape-shifting dragon, however, was of a mind that the answer had already been given. All he wanted was to get back to his feasting.

"Little one, in the tragic world of humans, you will need both your eyes wide open. But when you are one with the Tao, you will see everything in its true light with your eyes closed tight."

~

The following day Follin was invited to witness a squad of junior officer cadets prepare for their graduation into the Fearless Commando. Instead, he saw what appeared to be a vicious all-in brawl.

*'This looks pretty serious,'* he thought. *'That one has a nasty bruise on his cheek and there's another bleeding from a cut to her mouth... I think I should do something to stop this.'* Follin took a step towards the group but was brought up short by a shout from behind him.

"Hold, you don't need to interfere."

Follin turned to see Sir Alwyn striding towards him.

In bewilderment, he replied, "But they're going to kill each other."

Sir Alwyn stared at Follin for a moment before answering. "Patience. Although they are fighting, there is more to this than meets the eye."

Follin felt a fluttering pain in his chest as he saw a staff strike one of the girls solidly on the shoulder. Another of the group struggled to stand after being tripped and flung heavily to the ground.

"Hold!" came a voice from within the group. "It's time to stop." It was Rhianna, one of the senior commando instructors. At her call, Follin realised that they were training, but it certainly was realistic.

"Senior Instructor Rhianna!" called Sir Alwyn. "May I introduce you to Follin, our apprentice Mage."

The woman was past her prime yet her thick, golden hair proudly shone from beneath her woollen cap. As she stood respectfully before them, her aura was so powerful that it almost pushed Follin over.

"Welcome, Master, I hope you enjoyed our performance," she said, delighted with Follin's expression of awe.

"Yes, thank you. I was quite convinced though, that this was a proper fight. I can see a fair bit of blood and some bruises among your cadets, I was about to step in and stop it."

Rhianna turned to look at Sir Alwyn, her eyes widened. "Step in and stop us? Why would he do that?"

"He's still learning the many ways we train our commando," said the Knight.

At that Rhianna smiled and nodded her understanding. "I've heard good things about you and your wife, Priestess Eve. You're from the Mystic Isle, are you not?" she asked comfortably.

"Yes," mumbled Follin. "Eve and I are islanders, yes, but we've spent many years now in the Tarot Empire learning the ways of each Kingdom."

"Then you have the Empire's elemental magic to draw upon?" Rhianna looked directly into Follin's eyes, her engaging expression caused Follin to feel slightly flustered.

"Yes, I know some magic of the Kingdoms. But please don't think I'm a master of any of them. Eve, she knows much more than I do. She's a healer, her knowledge is extensive. All I know is how to fight."

That was definitely the wrong thing to say to a Wands commando. Rhianna immediately spun around to face her commander.

"Sire, may I match Master Follin with the quarterstaff?" Rhianna asked, her grin was way too broad for Follin's comfort.

"Aye," replied Sir Alwyn, a look of delight clear on his face. "Yes, you can match him, but best him? Nay, he's a master of the elements."

Follin looked from Rhianna to Sir Alwyn, he wasn't keen on a duel with this powerful woman, not at all. Rhianna immediately swung around and bowed low to Follin.

"Master Follin, would you give me the honour of sparring with you? I wish to know what these other elemental styles have to offer that might be anywhere near as good as our Force of the Flame."

"I've, ah, actually, I've not learned any other style but that of water and only some of fire," he muttered.

"Oh, come on now, Follin, that is simply not true. You learned patience and confidence as well as strength and endurance in your Pentacles sojourn. The Swords taught you to draw a bow and to process strategically without wasting time in thinking. And Cups, well, you learned the Dolphin style directly from Sir Rohan himself. And as for the fire element, you beat the Fox elf patrol single-handedly, ending the fight with a blast of fire energy," announced Sir Alwyn, placing his hands firmly on his hips.

Rhianna continued to stare at Follin. "Master, I would be honoured if you would demonstrate your skills to me..." she paused for a moment before smoothly adding, "Or perhaps I can demonstrate my skills to you?" She lifted her quarterstaff from its resting place at her side and adopted a defensive posture.

Follin looked at Sir Alwyn who casually handed him his own quarterstaff, then nodded for them to begin.

The two sparred carefully for a few minutes, testing each other's defences. Follin immediately recognised that Rhianna was a formidable warrior in her own right, and why she was one of the senior instructors of the combined schools of the castle precincts. She pushed Follin on several occasions causing him to draw upon his Dolphin style to good effect. Rhianna stumbled several times when he casually parried or slipped aside from her swinging staff. The group of trainee cadets stood watching silently, amazed at the ease with which Follin countered their instructor's growing flurry of assaults.

Rhianna grew increasingly confident, sensing that Follin could defend but was incapable of attack. His Dolphin style was impossible to break through using standard quarterstaff tactics, so she decided that a full-on fire-style assault would break the stalemate.

It happened as the hardened warrior charged Follin with a yell attempting to panic him. This was a simple technique used to frighten an opponent into making an error. Follin reacted instinctively. Having no time to produce a defensive move, he dropped to one knee, drew the Flame into his heart chakra, and, holding his left palm facing Rhianna, he pulsed a bolt of energy that sent her flying backwards several meters. She landed flat on her back and lay still, making no movement at all.

Horrified at what he had done, Follin raced over to her prostrate form on the ground. As he bent to examine his sparring partner for injuries, he stopped and looked quizzically at her.

"Rhianna, you're smiling. Are you all right?" he asked as he reached out his hand to lift her upright.

Brushing the snow from her clothing she suddenly leaned forward into Follin's chest and kissed him. In shock, Follin tried to pull away but she grabbed and held him tight against her body.

"Well now you two, that was a wonderful demonstration of fire and water style fighting. Now if you could just find the time to join us over here," called Sir Alwyn laughing at Rhianna's reaction.

"I, I... I'm sorry Master Follin. I don't know what got into me!" Rhianna was clearly horrified. She pulled away and ran - straight into the waiting arms of the Wands Knight.

When the group had settled down and the chatter subsided, the Knight called everyone to attention.

"Sire, if I may ask, how did the Mage do that? He sent Rhianna flying!" asked one of the cadets.

Another added, "And why did she kiss him? Surely she would have wanted to hit him instead?"

"Cadets, you have witnessed a rare display of water style fighting used against a fire style attack. Senior Instructor Rhianna is good, very good, but she has no experience against Dolphin style fighting. Follin is a master of the water style, I've not seen better."

"But, Sire, the thing he did, with his hand. He, like, pushed a bolt of energy at Senior Instructor Rhianna and knocked her backwards." This came from Ewan, one of the more promising cadets who would be promoted as soon as his training was complete.

"And then she kissed him? Come on, Sire, what really happened?" cried another with laughter in her voice.

"Instructor Rhianna never kissed me when I knocked her over," called another of the cadets which caused a flurry of chuckles.

"Right, come to order... cadets - attention!" Senior Instructor Rhianna had regained her composure and was back in control. These were her cadets and she was responsible for their conduct before their superior, and that superior was a Royal no less.

Twelve pairs of feet snapped together, quarterstaff butts slammed into the ground beside them. Faces stiffened and eyes focused directly to the front.

"Cadets, at ease!" came the Senior Instructor's order, and the squad eased their stance. Rhianna now turned and addressed her Knight.

"No excuses, Sire, my mistake. These ruffians have forgotten their manners for which I shall address as soon as we finish here. I will put myself on a charge of misdemeanour as well."

"No, you won't, Rhianna. You will stand at ease with your cadets and listen while I explain what just happened. It is I who should be on a charge for not preparing you, but I had no idea that Master Follin could use the Force of the Flame with such finesse."

Heads turned slightly and eyes looked from side to side as the cadets engaged their colleagues in anticipation of their Knight's explanation.

"The Dolphin style of fighting is circular, parry, or block, with an immediate return strike or thrust to a vulnerable point in the body. It is completely reflexive. You know this but not to the depth Master Follin does. Fire, which we saw at the end of this combat, is the application of force to drive through an enemy's defences. Follin did not use the full power of his Flame until the very end of combat, but only when Rhianna gave him no room to manoeuvre. It was a masterful assault by Rhianna and one that in normal combat would have won her the match. Alas, Follin instinctively drew upon the Flame and sent a bolt of energy at Rhianna's body causing her to explode backwards."

"Sire, if I may ask a question?" came a voice from among the cadets.

"Certainly, Cadet Ewan," replied the Knight.

"Why didn't Rhianna die?" That caused a few snorts and chuckles from the cadets.

"Good question. Master Follin somehow controlled the Force of the Flame. He drew his power into his centre and directed a moderated pulse by putting forward his free hand, palm facing his opponent. The pulse was but a fraction of the force he could have used. If he had connected with her using his fist or pointed fingers at a vulnerable point on Senior Instructor Rhianna's torso or head, then it could have been much more serious."

"So, he held back and only used part of the Flame?"

"Exactly," replied the Knight.

"But, Sire, that still doesn't explain why she kissed him," said the same voice.

"The pulse of the Flame was soft, as soft as a kiss, yet look how far it knocked your instructor. It triggered an explosion in her heart centre opening her up to a moment of nirvana, of bliss. Senior Instructor Rhianna responded instinctively to a pulse of energy to the heart chakra. I would not recommend you do this in combat with the Wildlanders though. Instead of sitting up and giving you a kiss, they would no doubt want to hit you."

Follin had been listening with interest. "Sir Alwyn, actually, I tempered my pulse of the Flame with my heart centre and automatically directed it at the Captain's heart centre so as not to hurt her." Turning to Rhianna he said, "I think that's why you felt so... amorous." A broad smile slowly blossomed across his face.

As Senior Instructor of the academy's Cadet Officers, Rhianna decided that it was time she explained what she had experienced in her own words.

"May I explain what it felt like, Sire?" she asked, her face struggling to hide her embarrassment.

"Of course, I'm as curious as everyone else," replied the Knight.

Rhianna forced a smile, a tight, flushed smile. "It hit me right at the moment I ignited my own Flame. I empowered my Force into a peak of power and lunged with my staff. I intended to smash through Master Follin's defences. It was right at that moment that I felt myself flying through the air. I hit the ground but I didn't feel anything but sheer bliss. For the following few seconds, I had no control over my actions." Turning to Follin she said, "I am truly sorry, Master Follin, but it's true, I couldn't control myself. At that moment my heart was aflame. I was so overwhelmed with a sense of love that I just had to... kiss you."

"What did it feel like really? Come on, Senior Instructor Rhianna, no holding back!" laughed Ewan. Sir Alwyn chuckled with the others.

"Well... I mean... no!" laughed the cadet's instructor, joining in the fun. "That's something you will have to find out for yourself, Ewan. I'm not saying any more!"

Turning to face Follin, Rhianna stood with her staff butt planted firmly on the ground and bowed low.

"Master Follin, thank you for your demonstration. I know the way of the Flame from many years of training and it can be devastating when wielded by a Master such as yourself. But your Dolphin Style is," she sought for a suitable word. "It is impossible to describe, I couldn't even touch you."

Officer cadet, Ewan, called again, "Permission to speak? Master Follin, was that what you did when you fought those Fox elves to rescue the Lone Wolf?"

"Yes! Please tell us!" cried another cadet. "We heard that you fought a patrol of elite elf warriors and defeated them without a scratch."

It was an eventful morning but Sir Alwyn finally called an end to their visit. Leaving the satisfied cadets to their training, Sir Alwyn led Follin towards the Old Smokey Inn to debrief.

"Sire, what is the lesson for me here? I'm surely at a loss."

"Sometimes what we think we see is not what is really happening. When you arrived you witnessed the cadets fighting. There was anger and there was aggression, but it was tempered. These cadet officers will soon join our Fearless Commando on patrol before they earn their commissions. One day they will be called upon to fight for their lives and those of their comrades. I wanted you to see just how serious we in the Wands Kingdom take our training."

"This was a proper fight?"

"Indeed, it wasn't play-acting. I was pleased that you agreed to demonstrate your Dolphin style too. You showed our cadets that the water style can defeat a foe without any harm to their opponent. In fact, it becomes a fight of no-fight, the way of the Strength Lady, of the Tao. And, by the way, our cadets were captivated by your description of the fight with the Fox elves. They will never forget today's lessons."

"Thank you, it was a pleasure to be with such an enthusiastic audience. But, just to get this straight, was the lesson for the cadets about how the Flame doesn't always have to hurt your opponent?"

"You've got it, but only an adept has that skill and these cadets have many years training of the Flame ahead of them. I was most pleased that they were able to witness such an adept today," replied Sir Alwyn.

~

# Follin's Meditation - 6 of Wands

*The image shows a man on horseback parading through the streets displaying a wreath of triumph. 'This is a parade of honour,' thought Follin. He walked along beside the man on the horse to experience the ecstatic displays of the folk watching the parade. After some minutes he decided to call out to the man on the horse.*

*"Hey, sir, do you have time to speak with me?" he yelled trying to be heard above the noise of the crowd.*

*The man looked down, leapt off his horse and in one bound grasped Follin by the hand.*

*"Well, hello, Follin, of course I have time for the hero of the Flame. This triumph is all about you, didn't you know that?"*

*Follin took a step backwards in surprise. "What? No, what do you mean?"*

*"Your control of the Flame, sir, you have proven that you can command our Kingdom's element, fire," the man replied.*

*"Me? No, no, I haven't learned near enough to consider myself a fire adept. Maybe I can control a little of the Flame within, but command that power, no, no..."*

*"This is my fault, I've confused you. Let me explain. In the Kingdom of Fire, one must undergo a series of trials to control the Flame. You have made a critical breakthrough, you have used the Flame in a safe and controlled manner. This is what we are celebrating. Soon you will be tested one more time, and that will confirm you as a Fire Adept and become our Fire Mage."*

"And what sort of trial is that?" Follin asked.

"Your mentors haven't introduced you to the next stage of your journey? Then I shall not preempt them. Just let me say that you have achieved a high honour, this triumph is yours to enjoy. Look, there's the Old Smokey Inn at the end of this avenue. Come, let me introduce you to another of their specialties: curried potato, refried beans and spinach pie, you'll love it."

~

# Seven of Wands

*confrontation, defence, moral high ground, readiness, courage, I will retreat no more, enemy at our gates.*

A messenger arrived at the castle announcing that a band of Cindermen, one of the Wildlander tribes north of the Forest of Smoke and Fire, was ravaging and plundering the farms along the Wands' east coast. Despite it still being winter, when skirmishes were few and far between, there had been an overwhelming number of recent requests for support from around the Wands Kingdom. This left the castle precinct with less than a company of commandos available for the defence of the farmlands.

A scratch squad of thirty warriors was all Sir Alwyn could put together at a moment's notice. To boost their numbers, Ewan, barely eighteen years old, one of the newly graduated cadet officers, was invited to join them. His older sister, Mahina, only recently commissioned into the Fearless Commando, was included in the reserve platoon. Thrown together was a mixture of retired and battle-weary commandos, a sprinkling of youths like Ewan, and a handful of regulars barely recovered from their wounds.

Sir Alwyn knew how vulnerable his patrol was, but the Cindermen had violated the peace-pact that allowed both sides to bring in the harvest. They had a treaty to cease all warlike actions until the crops had been sown the following spring. This had been agreed upon by the tribes north of the frontiers with The Emperor many years ago.

Upon meeting their enemy, Sir Alwyn's patrol was soon fighting a withdrawal against a much superior force. Hoping to slow the Cindermen's savage attacks on their villages and farms, the commando sought to draw them into the myriad of winding gullies and hills that led deep into the Forest of Smoke and Fire. It was fortunate that, although cold winds blew down from the Hindamar Mountains, the forest rarely saw snow.

In a desperate attempt to escape, the survivors fled into a narrow gully which they soon found blocked by a recent rockfall. It brought them to a sudden halt. It was late afternoon, and they were exhausted. The patrol had been on the run for almost a week in their efforts to avoid being wiped out by the superior numbers of their enemy. Sir Alwyn called his commando to rest in the narrow gully. The air was still and the temperature cool as the surviving warriors crouched beside their leader to consider their options.

"Sire?" grunted Nilyard, the aged Captain of the Home Guard as he crouched in an attempt to ease his aching back. "I think this be it. We make a stand, come what may. The lads be drained of fire-spirit from all this runnin' and fightin'. And your fire-gift to keep us going, I fear, has done you almost to death itself."

The laboured breathing of their comrades was enough to remind them that their fate was all but sealed. Their patrol to hinder the movement of these Wildlanders in their north-eastern frontier had come to an end.

"Lads, I'm sorry," was all the Wands Knight could mutter, his breath sounding like a rasp on a blunt plough shear.

Each warrior knew the score. They had outfought the Cindermen at every contact, but what had once been a patrol of thirty now numbered eight. They tended to their injuries as they sat waiting for their leader to decide their fate. The sound of soft voices brought Sir Alwyn back to full consciousness as the two rear scouts came running towards them in haste.

"Sire, the Cindermen be but an hour behind. They picked up our tracks earlier this morning," panted young Ewan.

"We wanted to send an arrow or two into them, but we followed your orders and came straight back," added Mahina, Ewan's older sister. "'Twas a pity though, one or two less might have made..." her voice went silent when she saw the rockfall blocking their escape. "That be what I think it be?" Her low groan brought a few tired heads up and one or two curses from the older men.

"It seems that our runnin' has now come to an end," grunted Captain Nilyard, helping the scouts to the last of his water. "Take a knee and rest a mite. We'll no doubt have action 'afore the sun drops below the gully lip."

"Call in the flank guards, it's no use wasting energy trying to find a way to climb that rockfall." Sir Alwyn spoke softly, his voice almost a whisper.

Captain Nilyard looked at his corporal and nodded. The stocky, sandy-haired young man trotted off to bring in the men seeking a way around the landslide blocking their escape.

"As you see there's no retreat, we must stand and face our enemy and bring this running to an end." Sir Alwyn slowly looked around at his commando as he addressed them. "We don't want to slip on our own blood, so we will fight in bare feet. As this will be our last battle we'll honour our ancestors by wearing our clan's kilt, and carry our traditional weapon, the quarterstaff. That's good enough to accompany us on our journey to the Shadowlands. We don't want to upset the Cindermen and put on too good a show now, do we lads?" There came a few stoic chuckles.

The Wands Knight leaned on his captain's shoulder. All the same, he swayed a little and immediately several friendly hands reached out to steady him.

"Thank you, but I must prepare myself to face that scab-backed spider, Mage Festra." He looked at his commando, they had sacrificed their warm beds, their lovers, and their hot meals to be with him, knowing that they may not return. "Nilyard, my dear old friend, help me sit beside that bush. Have the lads take their meal, and drink what's left of the water." Turning awkwardly to his commando he said, "It's time for you to make peace within your soul. Know that although I am a little broken in body I can still awaken the Flame to share with you."

"Sire, we be prepared, you know. We all expected that this might end bad like," said one of the aged veterans.

"Aye, Sire, we done this 'afore... but we be afeared you might not be able to tap into Kingdom's Flame," croaked another, a stained bandage crisscrossing his ribs.

"Shut up you dolt!" snapped a weary warrior beside him. "Sire knows what he's doin'. Fire magic be his thing, not thou's."

"I don't know about you lot," grunted one of the veterans. "But I'm so hungry I could eat a horse, then chase down its rider for dessert." There were a few dry chuckles from his friends at the old soldier's joke.

"Hey, settle down everyone, Sir Alwyn needs a bit o' quiet now. Get yourselves fed and prepare thy personal gear in a pile over against yon rock," said Captain Nilyard, before helping the much loved Wands Knight to the only standing bush not flattened by the rockfall.

The patrol members grunted in resignation as they removed their haversacks to make their preparations. Each warrior stripped off their jackets and removed their sandals. They were now clad in their traditional battle dress, the kilt, each clan proudly displayed in its particular colours and weave. Their most precious items were placed inside their haversack, alongside their personal belongings they placed their bow, arrows, swords and spears.

The sun was nearing the end of its journey towards the crest of the gully to the west as Sir Alwyn prepared himself for the coming fight. Turning his face to the setting sun he sucked its light into his heart and navel chakras with a sudden indrawn breath. The blast of fire that ripped into him felt as though a raw, white-hot brand had stabbed him. To the Knight, it was sheer ecstasy. He repeated this twice more, each time holding the Flame inside his body, forcing its heat deep into his organs, limbs and muscles.

'*I must try for one more breath. I'll need it to fight Mage Festra.*' The Wands Knight put his mind into the flaming cauldron that sat just behind his navel. He grimaced as he once more sucked the flames of the dying sun into his navel centre to condense it into the white pearl of the Flame. It pained but it also sent spasms of ecstasy through his body.

More, he needed more! An inaudible scream began to build in his chest as he panted, each pant sending slivers of fire into his hands and feet. This was a most dangerous endeavour and one that only the Wands Royals could perform safely. The Knight felt a scream rip through his chest as he managed to draw that final breath before a shuddering spasm forced him into oblivion.

While Sir Alwyn was struggling to empower himself with the Flame, Mahina was seated beside her brother, Ewan, trying to comfort him.

"Breathe, Ewan, breathe. Come on, you know the drill, breathe into your centre, it'll disperse the gloom." She touched her brother's shoulder gently to show that she was there for him. Ewan began to sob softly and that brought the attention of the others who were quietly preparing themselves in their own way.

"Hey," said Mahina in her effort to comfort her brother. "Remember your commando initiation?"

Ewan nodded woodenly. "Aye, four weapons and four opponents for each. It was murder. It took me a week to recover."

"I remember my own, first the open hand, that was hard enough. Then there was the sword, then the quarterstaff, and finally the bow. I never made it to the bow, my arms were like porridge, my legs so bruised I could barely stand. And I had that broken finger and a black eye, remember? You're one of the few who has ever made it to the bow." Mahina put her hand on her brother's shoulder once more.

Ewan gave a wan smile. "Aye, I heard most never get to the bow. I suppose we're a tough bunch, us Fearless Commandos."

Captain Nilyard had been watching, knowing that this would probably happen. He was fond of the siblings, the youngest of the patrol, called up early because of this latest series of attacks on the coastal villages. He knew their parents, kindly farm-folk, they would sadly grieve the loss of their children. He came to sit beside Ewan and put his arm around the boy's shoulder, much as an uncle would his nephew.

"Lad, you be chosen for this patrol because you were top of your class. Your feat of arms has helped us make it this far, I'm proud of thee. Take heart, you fight with heroes, us all be heroes today." Nilyard almost laughed, he knew how hollow his words must sound. How does one soothe the fears of a youth facing death, he asked himself.

"I'm not so afraid of dying, Captain, but I want to be with my mother and father." Ewan almost broke at this and stopped to choke back his sobs. "I just want this to stop so I can go home," was all he could say.

Nilyard, the hardened warrior who had devoted his life to safeguard those he loved, bent his head, and shed his own tears, unafraid that the others would see him. It was a time to cry, to acknowledge the sorrow lying in one's heart.

"Captain," said Mahina softly, a little embarrassed that she had to interrupt the moment when those who face death seek to make peace with themselves. "Captain Nilyard, the Cindermen, they approach."

Nilyard shook his head a little to dispel the tears on his cheeks. He stood and held out his hand for Ewan to take.

"Ewan, are you ready to join me, Sir Alwyn, and your comrades-at-arms?"

Ewan looked at his captain's tear-streaked face, and at that moment he found the strength to accept his fate. Wiping the back of his hand across his eyes he took a few deep breaths then reached up to grab Nilyard's hand.

"Aye, I'm ready," he said shakily. "Fear not that I will let my comrades down, I'm staunch." The two stared at each other, an acknowledgment of truth passed between them, and they joined the others in their final preparations.

Gripping their quarterstaff in their right hands the commandos gathered silently around Captain Nilyard. The warriors turned at their captain's command to face the setting sun. As initiates of the Wands fire magic, they drew their fire breath down to their navel chakra and filled their body with the sun's last rays of light.

With an acknowledged look at his friends and then to the youngest of their group, Ewan and Mahina, Captain Nilyard began the Wands' Death Song. In a soft, low voice he began to sing, the others joining in.


*I look at the clouds as I walk, behold, they are on fire.*

*It fills my heart with joy, though I know I will not see tomorrow.*

*I look at the clouds as I walk, alas, a warrior does not cry.*

*My tears must not fall, to blur the path I take.*

*I look at the clouds as I walk, and hold my family deep within my heart.*

*The cries of battle grow louder, the spirits of my ancestors draw near.*

*I look at the clouds as I walk, soon I shall roam among them.*

*Hark! I hear the call to join my comrades, I surrender to my fate.*


As the song finished and the voices subsided into silence, Sir Alwyn opened his eyes.

"It is almost time to stand-to-arms and perform the haka."

"I'll lead if you like, Sire. No sense in draining more of your power. You'll need it for the fight," offered Captain Nilyard. Throughout their rushed escape, Sir Alwyn had made his fire energy available to keep his commando's spirits high. Doing so had drained him almost beyond his capacity to recover, and this worried his old companion.

"My dear friend, this is my swan-song," Sir Alwyn smiled. "You wouldn't take that from me, would you?"

"Alas, if it be your wish to lead us in our battle cry, it is your right. Lead us, Sire."

The warriors had prepared themselves, briskly rubbing oil into their limbs and stretching their aching and exhausted muscles. Busy as they were, they didn't miss the exchange between their two leaders. As initiates of the Flame, they too could tap into the Wands fire, to a degree, but after many days of running and fighting, any semblance of recovery was beyond them.

With the sounds of the approaching Cindermen in his ears, Sir Alwyn closed his eyes and took a slow breath, sending his mind deep into the centre of his being.

"Ah, it is there, I feel it!" he cried loud enough for all to hear. His commando looked at each other and smiles broke across their faces to dispel their frowns. With a final shout, a clap of thunder rendered the air, and each member of the patrol felt a sharp burning sensation at the centre of their body.

"Mahina!" cried Ewan. "I can feel it!"

Mahina laughed. "You and I together. We'll stand shoulder to shoulder in this fight. Now stand still while I rub oil into your limbs. We don't want some nasty Cindermen throwing you to the ground and lizard-sticking you, do we."

~

"They be entering yon blind gully, Captain Tarzis. They've not known of the landslide, there be no way out, not without wings." At eighteen years of age, Harald was considered the best of the Cindermen scouts. His youthful band, village friends all, sat at their captain's fire and accepted the food and water offered. They were parched and half-starved having followed the footprints of their enemy these past few days without respite.

"Are their numbers the same?" demanded the young mage leaning over the small band at the fire like a starved scarecrow.

"Sir Alwyn leads but a handful, most are wounded. They have the fire force to feed them though, no one else could run like they do with the wounds they carry," answered Jarack, his surly answer showed his disgust at the mage's rude manners. He turned his face away so the mage wouldn't see him, then passed his hands over his eyes to protect himself from the mage's evil eye.

Sander spoke quickly, trying to cover his friend's reaction. "The Fearless support their wounded, their footprints show they are beyond exhausted, easy pickings I reckon, Mage Festra."

"Ha!" exclaimed the mage, his youthful voice all but breaking into a squeak in his enthusiasm for revenge against their legendary foe. "Charge them now! Before they realise they've walked into a trap!"

"Nay, mage, we know where they are and they cannot escape. We'll rest some and prepare in our traditional manner, and we'll only take those fit to fight, no others." Captain Tarzis' voice was firm and authoritative. He would not let this upstart of a mage bleed his beloved tribesmen to fulfil his lust for revenge.

The thin, weasel-faced mage blanched at the authority of the Cindermen leader's reply. Tarzis saw the look of rage in the mage's eyes and continued unabashed.

"Festra," Tarzis deliberately left the mage's appellation off. "It's a mage's role to use the soft hand of persuasion to direct his people. Us soldiers should be allowed to do what we do best, and that is kill our enemy." Noting the defiant scowl in the young mage's eyes, Tarzis stood and drew himself up to his full height. "You shall remain with the wounded and ponder the wisdom of your order's teachings, little man."

Sander punched Jarack in the arm, making sure that the mage didn't see him. They both had to restrain themselves from giggling at the despised mage's rebuke.

Captain Tarzis, the Cindermen war chief, called over his shoulder at his second in command, ignoring the glowering mage beside him. "Levert, when you have the men ready, we be leaving to do the dirty work of the mage's council."

"Tarzis, you swine! I'll make you regret this. Try to stop me and I shall be forced to infect your gizzard with yellow pus." Despite his youth, a mage of Festra's high degree could easily kill. Tarzis had seen Festra do just that in a moment of rage only a few days earlier.

"Alas," grunted the Cindermen leader. "If you wish to join us then you may, but you will not interfere with my leadership. Another loss to these Wands rascals and it will be on your head, and you alone will be answerable to the Mage Council, not I."

Within the hour, sixty Cindermen warriors began the short march to the blocked gully to meet their foe.

~

"They be on their way, Sire!" cried the scout as Sir Alwyn silently gazed at the pile of haversacks, spears, swords, vests, sandals, and other paraphernalia of the Wands warriors.

"Cindermen be damned!" grunted one of the Fearless. "They suck on us like a leech."

"Aye," called another voice. "But if I die, I wish it to be at the hands of these, they be the best I've fought, and I've fought a few."

"Hundred fifty Cindermen to take down thirty Wands? That ain't bad odds to start with..."

"Can't keep runnin' 'n fightin' like this, 'tis time to step upon Dame Fortuna's spinning wheel."

Sir Alwyn's calming voice interrupted them as Captain Nilyard briskly rubbed oil into his limbs in preparation for the fight. "We tried to do the impossible, but Dame Fortuna indeed has spun her wheel." He looked around and spied a clearing that backed against the rocky gully wall. "That's the place we will make our stand."

"It's how we die that lingers in an enemy's mind," called one of the commandos.

"It's how they kill us is what lingers in ours!" grunted another to a few soft chuckles.

"The Cindermen will deliver our belongings to the closest village," announced Nilyard, ignoring his men's banter. "They be our enemy, but they be honest."

"Not them scoundrel mages! I don't trust that Festra to honour the dead," said one of the commandos, laying his beloved spear and wallet neatly on the growing pile.

"Or the living!" answered another, to muffled grunts from a few of the patrol.

Ewan looked up as though just waking and called, "Sire, why don't

us archers knock a few of the Cindermen down before they get to us."
Some of the commando stopped what they were doing to listen to their
Knight's answer.

Sir Alwyn ran his hand through his red beard and closed his eyes
for a moment. No one saw the tears threatening to form at the corner
of his eyes.

"Ewan, you and your sister are the youngest Fearless on this
patrol, a reward for your dedication and courage. If it were in my power,
I would send you home to your mother on one of those Swords wings,
but I can't and it sorrows me to fail you this day." The red-haired knight
got no further as several voices called out.

"Sire! Thee nay failed us. We be the ones what failed you!" called
one of the warriors.

"Ye gave us the honour of serving our Kingdom, to protect
families and friends. If today be our last, then let us take up our
quarterstaff and fight!" cried Captain Nilyard removing his archer's wrist
guard to lovingly lay it beside his bow and quiver. Grasping his well-
worn staff he swung it in an arc over his head. "Come on, there be
Cindermen heads waiting for me to crack open!" There was a cold grin
on his face that caused Ewan to smile as he struggled to control his
nervousness.

"Aye, we are Wands, born and bred to fight," Sir Alwyn answered
Ewan at last. He too had stripped to the waist and held his staff firmly in
his hand. "This wand is our standard, the weapon of our Kingdom. Since
childhood we have learned the Moriscan dance, we lived and loved with
our staff by our sides. I will die with my staff in my hands, and I shall

carry it into the next world when I pass from this one."

"If that be our way, Sire, then I be there to stand beside thee," came Ewan's reply. He gripped his staff and, swinging it above his head, slammed its butt into the ground at his feet.

Mahina looked at her brother, then Sir Alwyn. "Aye, and I too stand beside thee, Sire!"

In silence, the warriors finished their preparations and took up their staff to stand with their brothers-in-arms in preparation for their battle-cry, the haka. They could now see their enemy approaching through the low scrubby bush at their front.

~

While still an apprentice of the Wildlander Mages Guild, Festra distinguished himself by the ease with which he dominated others. Mage Armitar had noted Festra's use of the voice and took him on as his apprentice. He taught the youth how to enhance his natural talent to control the minds of men. This led to his being placed in command of the wild Cindermen villagers north of the Tarot Empire, a command he relished, like his mentor, with psychopathic glee.

Mage Festra stood at the front of those he controlled, a mixture of archers, spearmen and swordsmen. Gathered before them were the last of the Wands patrol, stripped to the waist, each with their traditional quarterstaff in hand. Mahina, the only female of the troop, wore her kilt and a tartan sash covering her breasts, a splash of colour on her tanned skin.

The Cindermen outnumbered their enemy almost ten to one, yet Mage Festra had worked himself into a rage. The chase had cost him half his warriors and had wasted a precious week of plundering the lightly defended Wands villages along the eastern seaboard. Despite their overwhelming numbers, the mage knew that his warriors were terrified of their enemy. In his desperation to kill Sir Alwyn, he would need to enliven his voice to the best of his ability and arouse his men to do his bidding. He knew that he would become famous as the slayer of the champion of the Wands Kingdom if he was successful this day.

The Mage studied his men, each shivered in fear at the sight of the oiled, bare-chested warriors before them. The Wands commando stood silent, resolute, many wore scars of battle that stood out like medals of honour. They were a sight to instil fear in anyone such was their fierce, proud bearing. Their leader, the famous Sir Alwyn, stood as steady as a rock, surrounded by a radiant aura of gold. They were arrayed in a line with Sir Alwyn in front, one hand held his staff, its butt firmly planted on the ground, his other rested on his hip as though he had all the time in the world to dispatch his enemy.

*'I lead a company of cowards, cowards all of you,'* Mage Festra muttered to himself in disgust as he noted the miserable faces of his warriors, bunched together in small groups, shivering in fear.

Turning to his Cindermen warriors the mage spoke loudly, the craft of his guild on his lips. "My beloved men, most feared warriors of the Wildlands, listen to my words. Today we make history, and your names will live forever in the songs of the bards of our people." The Cindermen, mesmerised by the fearful apparition of the Wands warriors in front of them, slowly brought their attention to their mage. His voice felt like a healing balm on a stinging wound.

"We shall easily dispatch these barbarians to the Shadowlands. These are but ruffians who steal our food, kill our livestock, our wives, and our children. For their greed and blood lust, we shall avenge our people this day. We will kill them and the vilest of them all, Sir Alwyn!"

Tarzis, the Cindermen leader, stood beside the mage at the front of his men. Awakening from the spell of the Mage's honeyed voice, he pushed Festra to the side with his powerful arm. Turning to his men he said angrily, "Listen not to this mealy-mouthed mage, he seeks to dishonour us all..." but before he could finish, Mage Festra had recovered and pulled the Cindermen captain around to face him.

"You will obey me!" the mage screamed. Losing control, he grabbed at the captain's arm and tried to throw the big man to the ground.

"Nay, viperous leech!" cried Tarzis. "Ye shall shut thy miserable mouth-hole! We be Cindermen and we honour the Wands in this, their last stand." He pushed the mage so hard that the slim youth crashed heavily to the ground. Mage Festra lay still, his face a mask of rage that slowly calmed to a slit-eyed cunning.

Addressing the Wands Knight, Tarzis called, "It be your day to die, Alwyn, but know that we will respect you in death. You have led us a merry dance and cost us many lives, some of those be my kin and fire-friends. Say thy piece now, for it is thy destiny to look to the shadowy clouds above." The big man paused, "because that is where we be sending thee!"

Sir Alwyn breathed deeply, beside him stood Captain Nilyard who had been by his side for over forty years.

"Captain Tarzis," answered Sir Alwyn. "We shall stand and fight this day. It is no dishonour to die by your hand, your men have fought well."

Mage Festra had crept forward and now gently pushed Tarzis aside directing his words with practised precision.

"Sir Alwyn, your brave commandos are wounded and exhausted, we outnumber you ten to one, you cannot win this fight," he crooned, projecting his voice in a manner designed to cloud an enemy's mind. "Your fight is over, you have done all you could. Go now, go home to your families, go home in peace." There was not a single movement among the Wands warriors.

"I would honour your request, Mage Festra, but although I feel the power of your persuasion, I can sense the falsehood in your foul words. May I propose an alternative? Let us meet in single combat, and call this our reckoning day? If I win then you will cease your plundering and go home. If you win my commando shall be passed into the hands of your captain, an honourable man. But never will I hand my people into your keeping, you vile, scab-backed spider!" This was delivered with a shout and a bolt of lightning from the Knight's staff struck the ground at the mage's feet.

Mage Festra stumbled backwards, the spell broken. Tarzis jumped forward and grabbed the scrawny mage and flung him roughly to the ground.

"You miserable scoundrel!" he yelled and swung his booted foot at the mage. "This parley does not involve you! Get thee behind!" The mage scuttled away to hide behind several rows of Cindermen.

"Alwyn, forgive me, that scoundrel mage has no manners. Please, let us continue and discuss our rules of engagement."

Sir Alwyn nodded for Tarzis to continue.

"Firstly, I see that you have placed your missiles aside and will use no weapon but the quarterstaff. We shall honour this by leaving our bows on the ground behind us." He turned to face his company behind him and called loudly, "Let it be known to all that today we fight with the soldier's traditional weapons, sword, spear and quarterstaff."

"Secondly, I see that you have placed your personal belongings in a pile. I shall ensure that each item is respectfully taken to the nearest village. From there they will be returned to your castle and thus to your families."

Once again Sir Alwyn nodded.

"Thirdly, we shall burn your bodies on the funeral pyre as is your people's custom."

Sir Alwyn looked around at his commando and they nodded their appreciation.

"It is with gratitude that we have this agreement," replied Sir Alwyn. "You honour us with your words and your deeds, Captain Tarzis. I wish things were otherwise between our people, but the evil that drives this war will have it no other way."

Sir Alwyn stood for a moment before turning to his commando lined up behind him. The Wands Knight raised his staff to point towards the glow of the dying sun. The Wands warriors stood, their bare chests gleaming like polished bronze, the battle scars on each warrior's oiled body showing evidence of their courage and fortitude. Each wore their clan's woven kilts, their bare feet planted firmly on the ground. In their hands they held their staff in the attack position, ready for their leader to begin the haka - their battle cry.

At the moment Sir Alwyn began, each Wands warrior lifted their staff into the air to suddenly slam its butt into the ground.

"*Hai!*" They screamed so loudly that it startled the Cindermen into a shocked silence.

"*The enemy invades our Kingdom!*" cried Sir Alwyn, waving his arm and pointing to the Cindermen lined before them.

"*Dishonourable foe!*" came the barked reply from the commando as each punched their fist in the direction of their enemy and stamped their feet into the ground.

"*They threaten our wives and children!*" Sir Alwyn cried with inflamed passion.

"*We must fight! Fight! Fight!*" came the chorused reply as each warrior slapped his thigh and then cracked his staff against that of his partner on each side.

"*We will defend our homes and our families!*" The Wands Knight continued.

"*With our hearts and our hands!*" The warriors slapped their chests while stepping forward and stamping the ground with their feet.

This was followed by a barking cry of, "*Hai! Hai! Hai!*"

Each emphatic yell was accompanied by a foot slammed onto the hard, dry earth, three steps closer to their foe. With their kilts slapping against their bare thighs, the ground quaked at each footfall.

Finally, there came a Crack! Crack! Crack! as each warrior slapped his staff against their partner's before slamming its butt to the ground once more.

The warrior's haka echoed off the rocky gully walls, then there was silence.

~

"What's this then?" muttered Sander softly as Sir Alwyn began the haka.

"I don't know, I've nay seen anything like it," answered Harald, just as puzzled as his friend.

"They trying to frighten us then, eh? Naked savages don't frighten me." Sander's words of bravado sounded hollow even to himself. There was something about the Wands' bronzed bodies and the fierce cry of their haka that made the hairs at the back of his neck stand up.

"They're laughing at us! They don't care if they die," said Pax, fellow warrior of their tribe.

"What's wrong with them? They're glowing like it's sunrise," grunted Quinn looking side-ways at his friends.

"They're like a cornered mountain lion facing death squarely in the eye. They're brave, a week of dying and now just eight left. It's a tragedy, this is." Jarack's face paled as the Wands warriors stepped forward and slammed the butt of their staff into the ground to end their haka. The ground shook and their shouted cries echoed back and forth around the rock-walled gully.

For a moment the two leaders remained still, eyes locked, neither wishing to begin the slaughter that they knew would come. The silence was finally broken when Sir Alwyn lifted his staff to the sky and with a

182

shouted command sent a bright flame of gold and orange to light the staff tips of the warriors behind him. Each of his warriors felt a sudden burst of Flame, right at the centre of their being. They shuddered as though a thunderbolt empowered their muscles and sinews. Suddenly, as one, they crouched low, ready to leap forward in attack.

It was at this moment that Mage Festra moved, fearing that his men would flee in terror. Stealthily stepping up behind the Cindermen leader, he smashed his mage's staff into Captain Tarzis' temple knocking the big man to the ground. Drawing upon the power of his voice, Mage Festra reached into the depths of all sixty Cindermen warrior's hearts and screeched his command:

"Kill them! Kill them all!"

With no will to do otherwise, the Cindermen leapt forward, their weapons raised to smite the foe before them.

~

In the deepening twilight, Captain Tarzis approached the mage, a livid purple bruise bulged at his temple.

"Festra, you filthy coward, I'll see you punished if it be the last thing I do." He spat in the dust at the mage's feet.

Mage Festra barely glanced at him. "Of course you will," he replied in sneering contempt. "Now fetch me a strong man, Tarzis, I need someone to carry me back to our camp," he commanded.

Captain Tarzis glared, spat once more, then walked away to arrange the funeral pyres for friend and foe alike.

"Boy! You there!" called the mage in a commanding voice, "carry me, I wish to leave this foul place."

The solid youth ran to the mage and bowed low in fear. With his strong arms he easily lifted the mage and placed him on his back.

"Why, sir, there be no weight in you at all," he muttered in surprise.

The mage's voice sounded like a squeak in the dark. "I've exhausted my powers in defeating the Wands hero. It's left me with nothing but this shell you carry. Walk gently, boy, for I am fatigued to the bone."

It was as the youth lifted him that a small parcel fell from the mage's cloak. The object, wrapped in aged deerskin, fell and was hidden by the long grass.

The two funeral pyres were almost ready when Captain Tarzis called his nephew to him.

"Harald, I'm leaving you and your scouts to keep the funeral pyres burning. Stay here till dawn and feed the fires, then meet us back at the village, east, towards the coast. I will take our men there tonight. I wish to leave this place of shame."

It was just as the remaining few Cindermen were withdrawing that Sander called his friend to him.

"Harald! Look, here be the Wands Knight, and he's alive," he whispered so as not to alert the others.

Harald walked quickly to where Sander stood pulling at the bodies that lay covering the knight.

"He is too, what should we do?" he whispered softly.

"I say we leave him, if he lives, he lives. I want no part in killing the Wands hero. I saw him fighting Mage Festra, fire against fire. He was magnificent." Sander scowled as he recalled how, like the others, he was powerless to defy the mage's command to kill. The shame was fresh in his mind remembering the raw blood lust that had risen within him.

Harald held his gaze on the knight for a moment as he rubbed at the stubble on his youthful chin.

"Call the gang over, this is serious," he finally said.

Sander softly called to his village friends. Jarack, Pax and Quinn ran to join him but soon stopped their chatter when they noticed the solemn face of their leader.

"Who is he?" asked Jarack, trying to recognise the body in the darkness.

"Look," said Quinn leaning over the knight's body. "He breathes."

They looked curiously at the body on the ground then recognition dawned on them.

"It's Sir Alwyn, he was... he was so brave... but, but I saw him go down, stabbed, over and over, yet he lives," whispered Jarack.

"Did ye notice how he didn't strike none of us? He just fought Festra, pity he didn't kill that filthy scoundrel."

"His staff was aflame all that time too, right to the end when he fell."

"He knocked me over, he did. He just pointed his finger at me, and I went flying backwards onto me rump. I didn't even feel nothin' neither."

"Aye, me too. I tried to get to him but he just flicked me away, like a fly, but..."

"The only way Festra got him to his knees was because he wouldn't strike us down, poor sod. He could have killed us all but he wouldn't... I wonder why?"

"I wish he was one of us."

Harald decided on his course of action. "Don't let anyone come near here. Pretend you're doing your job. I'll speak with my uncle and see what he says, that's the way of our clan."

Harald ran towards the sound of the warriors preparing to depart. He caught Captain Tarzis by the arm, and, nodding conspiratorially, led him aside.

"Uncle, I've found the Wands Knight, Sir Alwyn, he's alive."

Captain Tarzis balked for a moment then, looking about to make sure no one could overhear their conversation, he said, "Of that I'm glad." He pulled at his beard as he considered his options. "Right, I want you to hide Sir Alwyn in the bushes, but be careful not to harm him, make him comfortable."

Harald nodded. "But what should we do with him, we can't leave him there?"

"Yes, yes, of course. Make sure you have done your duty to the fallen, then at first light, carry Sir Alwyn to the village beyond the hills, to the north. Go to the tavern there, ask for Lesaria, she's the matron who runs the place. She has trade with the Wands and Pentacles. Tell her that I sent you, she'll know what to do."

With a nod, Harald ran back to his friends with the news.

By the time the youths had finished attending the fires it was almost dawn and they were exhausted. Harald now gathered his friends to him.

"Right, we'll have a few hours sleep then we'll take Sir Alwyn to the tavern."

Jarack looked around at the growing dawn light. "Harald, you know that we saw Elf Ranger footprints yesterday, if they find us here, asleep, they'll kill us."

The band of Cindermen youths turned their exhausted eyes to their young leader.

"Aye, I saw them too. We'll just have to be careful, and fast. The sooner we deliver Sir Alwyn the better. Now get some sleep, I'll stand first watch."

It was while they were sleeping that the danger Jarack feared almost came to fruition. Two Elf Rangers had indeed crossed the tracks of the fleeing Wands patrol and were only now discovering the tragedy of their Wands comrades.

Carwen, the Lone Wolf, had refused to be left behind when Pandjar and a small band of Elf Rangers left to assist Sir Alwyn's embattled patrol.

"Pandjar," she whispered. "Five Cindermen warriors, what shall we do?"

"I see them... but look, two funeral pyres. I wonder if any of the Wands commando survived." He peered through the parted leaves then decided to wait for full light to show the tragedy hidden in the darkness before acting.

With full light, it was apparent that the small band of Cindermen were but youths. As Pandjar and the Lone Wolf watched, they saw the youths lift someone from the ground and place him gently on a make-shift stretcher.

"Who do you think that is?" whispered Pandjar, his hands seeking his bow. Putting his hand to the ground to steady himself he felt something odd and glanced down. Returning his gaze to the scene playing out before him, he absently placed the object into his haversack.

'A grimoire? That's a strange object to find on a battlefield,' he thought to himself.

"I think it's one of the Wands patrol," Carwen replied.

As the boys drew closer, the colour of the Knight's hair and his dress made it quite clear who was in the stretcher.

"They have Alwyn prisoner," Carwen announced as she quickly knocked an arrow to her bow.

"Not on our watch they don't," rejoined Pandjar as the two Rangers stepped in front of the group setting out along the narrow footpad that led towards the tavern.

"Halt! Leave your hands where they be seen. The arrow of this fair maiden will kill the first to raise a weapon," announced Pandjar in a commanding voice that startled the five youths. Sander, who was still half asleep, all but dropped his hold on the stretcher, the Wands Knight almost slipping from the youth's grasp.

"Hold tight, Sander! Now's naught the time to drop thy end." Turning to the elf, Harald responded with a firm face and forced confidence to disguise his fear. "Well met, Rangers, we be taking Sir Alwyn to the tavern north of here, Lesaria, be the tavern keeper's name. We'd not be sending a brave warrior like Sir Alwyn to the mage's camp for torture, nay, not that."

Carwen eased her arrow back from its ready position, to finally drop her arm. As the boys eased the wounded knight to the ground, she stepped lightly over to examine him.

"He's afire, Pandjar. We'd better help the boys get Alwyn to the tavern before he burns up."

Harald stood back to give the slender elven woman access on the narrow track, he now spoke. "It was our intention to do that, miss. If you don't mind helping us, we're sore fatigued from our night's cremating, and the knight be mighty heavy."

Neither Pandjar nor Carwen could find malice in the youth's voice. After studying the five young men Pandjar nodded and took up one end of the stretcher freeing two of the boys from their task.

He called softly, "Lone Wolf will walk behind to keep an eye on everyone. Lad, you, the one who has all the words, you take the lead. Make sure everyone stays in sight. Any silliness and someone will die, and none of us wish for that to happen."

At their midday break, Carwen boiled the herbs she had collected on their journey and made a poultice for the knight's wounds. The youths cooked some of their food and shared it with their elf companions.

"Pandjar, where be your friends, the other Elf Rangers? I don't like the idea of resting here thinking they might drop in and slit our throats." Harald wasn't one for small talk, '*if you have something to say, then say it*', was his motto.

Carwen laughed lightly as she fed the feverish knight a brew of medicinal herbs. Pandjar grunted, he was busy rubbing a healing balm into the knight's wounds.

It was Carwen who answered in her pleasant Mystic Isle accent which the adolescents found so delightful to their ears.

"We have them about. You've shown no malice to harm the Wands Knight and have struggled valiantly to rescue him. If there is malice on our behalf it is to kill your mage, that is all." Her voice was soft, like a song, its melody hung softly in the air to caress the youth's ears long after she had stopped speaking.

Jarack elbowed his friend in the ribs and lifted his chin to point at the pretty elven girl. "She's gorgeous, ain't she," he whispered.

"She's a devil, that's what she is," whispered Sander in reply. "Did you see how she dropped her bow and then palmed her knife when they stopped us? She's more dangerous than you think, cousin."

Pax had overheard their conversation. "Elven lass be sweet, she helped us carry that stretcher too. If she would kill Festra I'll dump me lassie girl at home and marry her." The youths giggled softly causing Harald to glare at them.

After the food was consumed, Pandjar drew a jar of honey mead from his haversack and passed it around. "Here, this'll put hairs on yer chests, lads, it'll make men of thee." It was a goodwill gesture and helped ease the tension of Harald's questions. But Harald wasn't satisfied.

"Lone Wolf... miss, why do they call you that?" he asked politely, taking a second tipple from the elf's jar of mead.

"I was gifted this name from someone who wished to kill me. And that is all you need to know. We're soon to part company at the tavern yonder, so remember me as one who seeks honour above all else, and may you hold that same honour in thy heart. If someone ever asks if you have ever met an elven warrior from the Mystic Isle, you can proudly announce, *'yes, and her name is Lone Wolf, a fire-friend.'*"

The group arrived at the tavern and delivered their burden late that afternoon. Turning on their heels the Cindermen youths said their shy goodbyes to the two Elf Rangers.

Within the hour, Sir Alwyn was hastily dispatched along secret paths through the Forest of Smoke and Fire by the small band of Elf Rangers. They had secretly scouted ahead of the Cindermen youths. On their arrival at the castle, the story of his rescue swept through the Wands Kingdom. Although the Cindermen of the Wildlands were their enemy, the Wands people found their hearts had softened, but only a little.

It wasn't until a few days later that Pandjar happened upon the book lying in his haversack.

"Carwen, what is this? I found it on the ground at the blind gully."

The Lone Wolf opened its leather cover and examined its tight, barely decipherable scribbles. With a sudden indrawn breath, she froze.

"This," she said softly. "Is the Grimoire of Draig, a book of dragon spells. We need to give this to our magicians, they would know what to do with it. This is more dangerous than all the magic in the Tarot Empire."

~

# Follin's Meditation - 7 of Wands

*Follin was worried, he had felt the conflict in the blind gully and the many souls who had departed for the Shadowlands. He needed to seek out Sir Alwyn to find out if he had survived. In his mind's eye, he saw the Knight being taken to a tavern on the edge of the Forest of Smoke and Fire. There he sensed Pandjar and Carwen with him, but there were strangers - caring youths he didn't recognise. He quickly mind-talked with the Wands Royals who confirmed his findings. Page Blade was on another patrol in the foothills of the Hindamar Mountains and expressed his delight that his brother was safe.*

*Now able to relax, Follin examined the image that showed a single warrior pushing back against a number of enemy staffs swinging towards him.*

*'Is this another image of courage or of triumph or perhaps of conflict?' thought Follin lying in his bed that night. He had felt a jolt of pain hit him in the chest when the Wands patrol went to meet the Cindermen, he didn't want to explore this particular image at all, it brought back the pain of loss.*

*'I must talk to this fellow, he looks resolute.' Follin stepped into the image and addressed the young man.*

*"Sir, may I stand beside you?" he offered.*

*The young man glanced quickly at Follin and nodded.*

*Follin took a stance beside the youth, recognising him as the cadet officer, Ewan. Since Follin's contest with Senior Instructor Rhianna, he had been invited to demonstrate his Dolphin style to the trainees on a regular basis.*

"Ewan, isn't it?" he asked, not allowing his eyes to wander from the staff being swung at him.

"Aye, I know thee, Master Follin it is," the youth replied.

"May I ask what is happening here?"

"Are ye blind?" grunted Ewan. "Pardon my manners, sir, but if these Cindermen get past me they will be into the castle, our families and friends will be at their mercy. You and I are the last line of defence. Look to thy front, sir!"

'I see no castle,' observed Follin. Suddenly he realised that Ewan was dead, but was still fighting. The youth had yet to complete his walk to the Shadowlands. Looking around he could see others in the same situation, fighting, wrestling with their enemy.

"We're in the right, sir, we didn't start this fight, we had a peace-pact and they broke it. Now we're here to defend our homes and families." The youth had pushed a force of Cindermen back and stood to rest on his staff for a moment.

"Aye, I see that Ewan, but I think things are more than they appear." Follin cast about in his mind at how he could guide these warriors, Wands and Cindermen alike, to the Shadowlands. It would be a crime, in his eyes, if he allowed this horror to continue for eternity.

"What? The enemy is there, right in front of you! Are ye a dolt?" Ewan was frightened and in a raging panic.

This was a good opportunity to use the change point he had worked on since his arrival. Find leverage then apply the right amount of force. At the alignment of the change point, Follin pulsed his Flame and knocked everyone around him to the ground. Then, lifting his arm to the sky, he brought the Shadowlands to them. Within each heart he filled a longing for home, for family. With grim satisfaction, Follin saw faces and voices of the warrior's loved ones reaching through the rainbow mist.

The warriors stopped their violent protests and looked, quizzically, at the misty cloud that had crept towards them.

"Ma? Da?" cried a voice, then others too called as they recognised friends and family members who had passed into the Shadowlands before them.

One by one they stepped into the mist and disappeared. All that was left was the chatter of their greetings and the echo of their laughter.

"Nicely done, Follin. I've not seen that performed so deftly in my entire life. In fact, I've never been able to do it myself without a great deal of persuasion and argument." It was the voice of Mage Hermes now standing beside him.

"I feel sad though, I trained with one only a few weeks ago," said Follin.

"This leads me to your lesson... which is?" replied the Magician.

"I think the lesson is quite simple, fight for what is right, the moral high ground, as Ewan said. The Wands people are quite direct, they don't play games with the mind. These Wands lessons are attuned to conflict of some sort, not like the Swords images which are downright unpleasant with all that internal mental torment."

"Son," said the Magician kindly. "I too shall be led away soon enough to the Shadowlands, or perhaps someplace that the Star Lady has in mind. Hera and I have yet to decide where we will go. Have no thought for those whom you assisted this night, they are with loved ones. It is those left behind who need our kindness now."

Follin nodded, he understood, but it was sad that his friends, those youths that had not fully lived and loved, that he felt sorry for.

'Alas,' he thought. 'I can change that which is within my power to change, but I must seek peace of mind to accept that which I have no control over.' It was a saying he heard many a time in the Kingdoms and he had adopted it as his own.

The Magician continued. "Your lesson this night is to stand up and fight when fighting is necessary. But sometimes, as you did with the lost souls of battle, it is more appropriate to lead than to fight."

~

# Eight of Wands

*action, spontaneous reaction, once you release your arrow you cannot call it back, window of opportunity.*

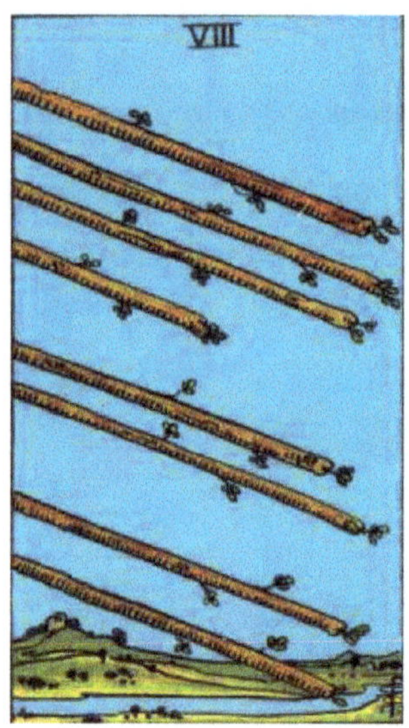

It was most fortunate that Eve was doing her rounds in the hospital when Sir Alwyn was rushed in. His Wands fortitude helped him endure the time it took to be transported from Lesaria's tavern to Dragon Mountain Castle.

"So, Mistress Eve, is there a possibility of saving my arm? I think I may still have need of it." The Wands Knight may have sounded cheerful, but he was far from it. His arm had blown up with blood poisoning and he was in great pain.

It had been a rough journey. Pandjar and Carwen had done what they could on the short trip with the Cindermen youths, but once they arrived at the tavern they finally saw the extent of the Knight's injuries. The wounds from the Cindermen's sword and spear thrusts had introduced a host of dreaded septicemic bacteria. Too heavy for the two elves to carry alone, they had enlisted the aid of their patrol members. This small band of Elf Rangers had shadowed Pandjar, Carwen and the band of youths to ensure they arrived at the tavern safely. Together they brought Sir Alwyn along secret pathways to the castle.

"I think so, but first we'll get you cleaned up. And a bath is in order. I could smell your arrival from the morgue itself, and that's way underground," she tried her best to be just as cheerful as her patient, but it was hard. Sir Alwyn had the tell-tale red line running from his armpit to his hand, and the flesh displayed the blue and red pattern of a serious, life-threatening infection.

"Fresh clothing and clean skin, there are few pleasures in life more enjoyable to an old warrior," Alwyn sighed softly as he fought to suppress the pain flaring in his body. "My arm is beating a rhythm of pain like a bass drum, and I am in need of proper sleep. Eve, my dear girl, do what you must, but be mindful, this arm holds the sword that protects the Wands Kingdom." The Knight swallowed the opioid draught that Eve had prepared and was soon asleep. She would now be able to delve deep within his body and soul to engage his life force and bring it forward to assist in his healing.

Gathered around her was a team of student healers from the Cups Kingdom. Each had their particular healing style and methods. Some used massage and the healing touch, some used herbals, while others counselled the patient's soul. Of them all, the bone manipulators and massage specialists were much preferred by the warriors after a week or two on horseback or foot patrol.

"Careful, Priestess Eve, that was quite a strong draught you gave him," stated one of the herbalists in the group.

"Nay, a man that size needs a man-sized draught. Sir Alwyn is in considerable pain and what we are soon to do may be too much even for his Wands' heart to withstand," replied one of the permanent staff allocated to the emergency wing.

"If we tried to release the pus from his wounds without the anaesthetic effect of the poppy, it would be unbearable. This is an unusual case and there will be a test at the end of the week, so watch closely." Eve, ever the parent, ever the teacher, relished her new role as head of the Royal Wands Hospital.

"Firstly, I'll touch Sir Alwyn and probe his physical body. I'll talk my way through this so that you can follow. When I've finished, I'll invite you to sense what you can."

Eve positioned herself at the foot of Sir Alwyn's bed and took hold of his bare ankles. As she settled her mind, she felt drawn into the Knight's body.

"Right, I am there. I'll now calm my mind and become one with my patient." Eve quickly settled into her healing routine and began her commentary. "I'm now exploring his wounds... yes, they are deep but healing, this is a good sign. I can now sense each of his body systems," Eve sighed. "Hmm, not so good, his lymphatic system is heavily overloaded." After a minute of silence, she continued. "I am satisfied he has no critical wounds, rather, the blood poisoning is trying to overwhelm his system and has already impacted his spleen, liver and kidneys."

Eve opened her eyes and saw that her students were preparing to perform their own symptomatic assessment. One by one they performed as they had been trained to do over many years of residency in the Cups training hospitals.

"Take your time, this is not a healing assignment, we are performing a systematic analysis of his symptoms only. Without knowing what is wrong we may do more harm than good." Eve knew that she did not need to remind everyone of the process of symptom analysis. This was what she drilled into her students every day: do your best to thoroughly understand your patient's condition.

When the students completed their assessments, Eve called for her resident master healers. They too followed the same process of systematic analysis before they began to ease the infection in the Knight's arm. Once they started, Eve ordered her students to observe how the master healers engaged the Knight's life force, gently guiding it towards a state of health.

"Priestess Eve, we know that you're one of the greatest healers in the Kingdom, so, why don't you heal Sir Alwyn yourself? He is perhaps the most important person in the Kingdom," asked one of the students watching the Knight sleeping softly after his healing session.

"I could have practised my healing skill on Sir Alwyn, yes, certainly. Like you, I've trained in the Cups hospitals for many years," replied Eve casually. "There are times to do and times to hand to those who are better skilled than you. I knew that the healers rostered on today were more skilled than I at treating cases of battle trauma, sword wounds and blood poisoning. In the past I have sewn up nasty wounds, I've patched holes left by a Wildlander lance, and I've pulled arrowheads from the chest using all of the tools we have at our disposal. Yes, I've done it all. But when it comes to pride, as a healer, I must have none. This was a job for the best and they were here, on shift today. This is a lesson for you all: know your limitations and don't overestimate your skill level. Sometimes it is best to hand the job to those who can do better."

"Priestess Eve," called another of the students. "I see that your style of healing is different to our Cups water style."

"I'm a bit like a mongrel dog, put together from a variety of healing systems." Eve put her hand over her mouth and giggled lightly. "I've got Mystic Isle, Tarot Empire, Wildlander and even some Elven blood. I learned healing from my parents and grandparents, we are called 'cunning folk' on our isle," Eve replied.

"I noticed that you did more than sense Sir Alwyn's life force, what was it that you did?" asked the same woman.

"Well..." Eve paused and a guilty smile passed across her face. "I didn't think anyone would notice, but I have an assistant, an earth elemental, Molly. She was invited to join me by High Priestess Hera and The Hierophant many years ago. Molly told me not to worry about Sir Alwyn, she had touched his soul and put his body into a calm and restful state. Molly said that Carwen and Pandjar had done just enough to stop the infection from spreading. Now that his heart is in the Wands

Kingdom, he will heal quickly."

Heads turned and a buzz filled the room. Eve ignored the many questions they asked about Molly. She called over her shoulder that she would speak of this matter during their afternoon lessons.

Her day had been eventful, to say the least. Sir Alwyn's arrival had put everyone in a spin and now she was exhausted. Her hands-on interaction with Sir Alwyn was not just with Molly, the King and Queen of Wands also contributed to healing their son. With the student's question, Eve had to acknowledge that she had been in a panic worrying that the Wands Knight would die.

~

The seriousness of Sir Alwyn's injuries, and the story of his hastily put together patrol's massacre at the hands of Mage Festra and the Cindermen, hit the people of the Wands Kingdom hard. It was accepted that life on the frontier would be challenging, total war meant that everyone was trained to the best of their ability to withstand hardship and to fight to the end if need be. But when something as horrific as a massacre of an entire patrol occurred everyone felt the need to take a step back and support the families who lost their loved ones. The patrol members consisted of retired war heroes; some barely out of their cadetship, like Ewan. Captain Nilyard was the longest-serving captain in the military, and also Sir Alwyn's right-hand man. Their loss hit the Kingdom hard.

Pandjar, Carwen and their Elf Ranger companions, were surrounded by old friends and as many others as could fit into the popular warrior's tavern. Over the centuries The Old Smokey Inn had borne witness to the heavy hearts of those who had survived tragedy in the Kingdom. Today it was quiet except for Pandjar's voice relating the story told to him by the Cindermen youths of the Battle of the Blind Gully.

"We've seen the last of the wallets and belongings distributed to the lad's families, those Cindermen kept their word, as we knew they would. For that, we honour them. But that vile creature, Mage Festra, Mage Armitar's protege, must be stopped. If we can find that maggoty grub, we will squash him..." He was interrupted by cries of outrage and demands for revenge from the old warriors and cadet youths.

Page Blade was also at the inn seeking to resolve the guilt he felt at not being by his Knight's side during the battle. Many times in the past, the Page had seen the mood of grief turn into violence and didn't want his friends to drink themselves silly, either. Recognising the brooding mood of the mob, he called for the fiddler and piper who were sitting quietly watching from their corner.

"This is time to celebrate," he cried, lifting his mug of ale into the air for all to see. "To celebrate our comrade's feat of arms. Heroes all, to hold off a superior force, running, fighting and carrying the injuries of battle. Fiddler, a song please, a drinking song for our departed friends. But first our recessional, '*lest we forget*'!"

The crowd stopped their jostling and rough words to repeat the traditional lamentation to those who had fallen in battle.

"*Lest we forget*," they repeated respectfully.[1]

Blade led the ritual as the men and women spoke it clearly and proudly along with him. "*They shall grow not old, as we that are left grow old. Age shall not weary them, nor the years condemn. At the going down of the sun and in the morning, we will remember them.*"[2]

"*We will remember them,*" came the final salutation from the solemn gathering.

At a nod from Blade, the fiddler and piper took up the popular ale makers song, 'John Barleycorn', and encouraged everyone to join.

"Aye, 'John Barleycorn' [3] will help settle the rage in everyone's soul," grunted Nangkari as he lifted his mug of ale and took a long swallow. "If there is one thing humans do well, besides tobacco, potatoes and ale, it's singing."

Follin's eyes were wet. He recalled the times he had accompanied his father to the tavern at Saoirse village on their walks to the fisherman's wharves. Many a time he would sit on his father's lap in the warm tavern on a cold winter's day to sing to John Barleycorn.

"This song brings back memories, I hope I don't cry all the way through it." Surprising himself he fell right into the rousing chorus and sang as lustily as the others in the tavern.


*Sing, ri-fol-lol, the diddle all the dee, right fal-lee-ro-dee.*

*The huntsman can't hunt the fox, nor so loudly blow his horn.*

*And the tinker he can't mend his kettle or pots, without a little barleycorn.*

*Sing, ri-fol-lol, the diddle all the dee, right fal-lee-ro-dee.*

*They worked their will upon John Barleycorn, but he lives to tell the tale.*

*We pour him into an old brown jug, and we call him home-brewed ale.*

*Sing, ri-fol-lol, the diddle all the dee, right fal-lee-ro-dee.*

By sunset, the party had paid homage to their fallen comrades and finally sung themselves out of their bitter, morose mood. Slowly the men drifted towards their homes. Some leaned on the shoulders of their mates, others still singing as they wove their way back to their loved ones. It was this camaraderie that Blade had anticipated. He knew that instead of precipitating a riot with calls for a full-scale attack on the Cindermen villages, his beloved kinsmen would go home to sleep off their grief. They would face tomorrow with sore heads and pride for their brave, departed friends.

~

Follin was in his alchemy study with his father discussing their coming foray into the Hindamar Mountains. This was for his initiation as Magician of the Tarot Empire. He would be honoured by the presence of the earth elementals in the same cave that Master Pew took him for his initiation as an apprentice bladesmith.

"I know this area a little, Da. We could make it a holiday like we did when I was little. We'll need a wagon to take our supplies to the Pentacles castle. Then we need to organise carriers and perhaps a donkey or two. And a guide, maybe the Mountaineers could send a few of their commandos to help..." Follin's mind was ticking off a list of the things they would need.

"Follin," said his father. "I think Sir Darwyn is going to take us there in his chariot."

As soon as he heard Sir Darwyn mentioned, Follin stopped his rattling and leapt from his chair.

"That's great!" he rejoiced. "I've not seen him for years. He's been so busy with The Emperor these days saving the Empire... I've got to tell Ziggy and Eve!" He began to head towards the door when his father placed his hand on his shoulder.

"Son, slow down, let's just sit for a moment and put our feet back on the ground and pull our heads out of the clouds," Sao said, laughing lightly. He hadn't seen his old friend for many years either. "It's time to get back to your lesson. You were telling me that you used the Flame against the Fox elves, and again when you were sparring with Senior Instructor Rhianna. You said that you sent a pulse of energy that knocked her over, how interesting."

Follin's father thus began his lesson. "As you know, fire breathing can be initiated by a specific technique called 'bellows breathing'. Imagine your dragon forge that you built in the mountains is your abdomen, and the bellows is your breath." Mage Sao paused while Follin visualised the dragon forge he crafted under Master Pew's directions.

"Yes, I see that," mused Follin.

"Bellows breathing is done in sets. Start with one breath, rest a little, then a set of two, rest, then a set of three. These initial breaths ignite the Flame in the furnace. Then you create the cauldron sitting within. That's where you create the pearl of fire once you become accustomed," Sao paused. "Hold the fire in your navel chakra, the furnace, when you rest, don't let it move out just yet. With practice, your in-breath becomes a set of three tight, short breaths. Then rest as you slowly release what is left in your lungs. So, three quick breaths in and one slow breath out." The Mage Saoirse demonstrated the breathing process and Follin followed.

"It's easy, I've been doing this for years, Da."

"Yes, I can see that," noted his father dryly. "A few tips then, practice holding your fire deep in your cauldron. This is where you boil your life force into the pearl, which is about the size of a pea. Once it is set you can send that pearl of energy anywhere around your body."

"Da, I've done that too, remember. But no one's shown me where to send it. I've not had a plan, it just happens instinctively."

The mage sat for a while, pondering how to explain the complexity of the pearl.

"Yes, yes, I know you've used it to heal Carwen's wound to the neck. That was masterful and very difficult. I understand that you act on instinct, taught to you by the High Priestess and The Empress. I never had their mentorship, so I had to learn most of this by myself. I was fortunate that my shaman mentor taught me the bellows breath. It helped me astral travel, but it also made me wild, I went a bit crazy. This is why I rarely, if ever, use the Flame. It has burned me, and I have aged way too fast. Unfortunately, I never had the cauldron explained to me properly by my mentors. The cauldron helps tame the wildfire the Flame can cause. This is essential because the Flame can destroy the novice who doesn't have years of solid training behind them."

"Da, I honed self-control during my time with the elves."

"Son, elves don't use elemental energy as we do. In fact, we use it much better than they can."

"Yes, Da, I know, but they have other skills that we don't. Ziggy taught me how to focus, a bit like what The Empress taught. He emphasised the importance of centring my energy at my navel and how to use it in developing my fighting style. That's how I pulsed the Flame at Rhianna and the Fox elf. I used heart energy for Rhianna, but for the Fox warrior it was all Flame, each driven by pure instinct."

Mage Saoirse nodded slowly. "Son, I'm proud of you. Soon it will be your initiation, but you must be ready for the ordeal. When Sir Darwyn arrives, we'll go into the Hindamar Mountains... and don't forget your journals and magicians tools."

~

# Follin's Meditation - 8 of Wands

*That evening Follin began his next meditation. The image was simple, eight wands flying through the air, perhaps aimed at a target or... he wasn't quite sure.*

*'I'll go into the image and find out,' he said to himself as he settled into his warm bed that night.*

*As he slipped deeper into trance, Follin found himself on a hillside looking across the River of Smoke And Fire. He could hear the sound of laughter and turned to see a group of Wands youths in their mid-teens jostling each other, having fun.*

*As soon as they saw him, they stopped their playfulness and stood stiffly at attention, arms by their sides, a sign of respect.*

*"Master Follin, we are honoured," announced the lad standing closest to Follin. "We were seeing who could cast their staff the furthest. Would you please be our adjudicator?"*

*"Of course. All right, everyone claim your staff and line up for me to inspect you," he announced with an authority that came easily to him these days.*

*The youths rushed to do his bidding. Everyone in the Wands castle and surrounding villages knew of Follin's reputation. They quickly formed a line and stood at attention.*

*"Who is your captain?" Follin asked.*

*"Sir, it is I, Damen, I'm the leader of my clan's cadets," the youth proudly announced, his flaming red hair stood at all angles, making Follin smile.*

"Good, would you please do me the honour and introduce me to your troops?" Follin knew that the youths of the Wands Kingdom took every opportunity to practice their skills for the safety of their people.

One by one the youths were introduced as Follin walked down the line. He made sure to carefully inspect each trainee and note that they were properly dressed for war play. He commented on the bruises and wounds on their bodies, each a prized possession that spoke of their toughness and acts of bravery.

Follin recalled the time when he witnessed Captain Bleecher parade a troop of castle guards in the Pentacles Kingdom. He had noted how the captain's comments made the men feel proud and worthy. If that was the standard he had to meet, then he would try his hardest to make that same effort with these Wands youths.

"Cadet Officer Damen, you lead a squad of fine warriors. I see that some have injuries, I expect they received them doing acts of bravery beyond the call of duty."

The youths tried not to smile, and Damen's eyes widened, realising that he was the captain of heroes.

"Sir, indeed our training is hard. We're now using swords, real swords. That cut on Jute's arm was from yesterday's lesson. He wasn't quite fast enough..."

"But he didn't wince or cry out, I bet," said Follin quickly, turning what could have been an unpleasant moment for Jute.

"Oh no, sir, Jute's really brave, he sure is. When the Wildlanders attacked our village last year, he took up his staff and knocked one to the ground and held him there until our troops arrived," replied Damen *just as quickly.*

*Follin nodded at Jute and patted the youth's shoulder in honour of his courage. "Right, squad, prepare for an inspection of your weapons. Wipe it clean of grass and dirt, quickly now!"*

*Starting at the end of the line he inspected each staff commenting on the style of the weapon's craftsmanship, its balance, weight, length, suitability for the individual and the quality of its make. He knew that the cadets were required to provide their own fighting weapons, and these were not toys. These were the cadet's personal weapons, no doubt crafted by themselves under the watchful eyes of a weapon-maker from their village.*

*As he was inspecting the troop, he noticed that Sox had arrived to walk beside him. The cadets noticed too and their chests filled with pride. Not only was their hero, Mage Follin inspecting them, but his legendary fae dog, Sox, stood beside him. What a tale to tell their friends.*

*"It seems to me that all of you have crafted top-of-the-line quarterstaff worthy of even the best Fearless Commando. Not only are your weapons of solid construction but it tells me that you are ready to protect your loved ones in times of peril. There is one more thing I must do. My fae dog, Sox, who fought and defeated that evil Mage Armitar in the Shadowlands, is here to run his own inspection." Follin looked at Sox and mind-spoke his command.*

*Sox barked sharply then trotted to the beginning of the line. Slowly he walked past each youth, sniffing the weapons of each in turn. At the end of the line, he barked once more before resuming his place beside his master.*

*Follin turned to Damen and lifted the corner of one eye.*

*"Cadet Officer Damen?" he didn't have to say any more.*

*"Squad," Damen paused for a moment. "Attention!" he ordered and eight pairs of feet firmly stamped into the ground, the butt of their staff slammed down beside their feet. Follin raised his eyebrow at the captain again.*

*"Squad, stand at ease!" Eight pairs of feet moved and the butts of their staff remained still as the boy's arms moved their weapon to their front and side.*

*"Thank you, Cadet Officer Damen. I'm now going to watch your troop's casting. I see that you already have a target. You will each take your turn and cast your staff like a spear." Follin stopped and turned to Damen. "That was the game you were playing, was it not?"*

*Damen smiled and nodded. "Yes, Sir!"*

*"Cadet Officer Damen, you shall proceed," ordered Follin, keeping his face as calm as possible, trying his hardest not to break into a giggle. Playing soldier was so much fun, he'd never had this opportunity before and he relished it.*

*"Squad, form line from the right. When you are ready you will cast in turn," came Damen's command.*

*As each cadet cast his weapon Follin would escort them, with Sox and the captain, to inspect their result.*

*The evening air was growing cold, twilight approached, and Follin saw the troops growing restless. It was time to let the youths return to their homes.*

"Cadet Officer Damen, call the squad together, please," ordered Follin.

"Squad..." Damen waited for them to line up then barked, "Squad, attention!" At the sound of feet and staff slamming into the ground, Follin stepped forward.

"Not only am I proud of what I have seen you do today, but so too is Sox. He has watched you perform feats of skill even I struggled with when I was a trainee. I'm from the Mystic Isle where elves kill the unaware and Wildlanders invade the unprepared. My life, like yours, has been hard. We have each had to learn how to defend those we love. You fill me with confidence in the knowledge that my children will be safe with you to protect them."

One of the girls put up her hand to speak. At a nod from Follin she said, "Master, thank you, this has been the best day ever," she announced shyly.

At that, Follin stepped forward and shook them each by the hand and encouraged them to pet Sox as he walked past. At his signal, Damen dismissed his platoon and Follin woke up in his bed.

'What was that all about?' he asked himself.

At the end of his bed came a familiar voice, "That was well done," announced The Hierophant. "And what a pleasure it is to see you again, Follin, it's been a while. Hermes is busy undertaking a particularly arduous rejuvenation program in preparation for your initiation. He asked me to drop in for your final meditations. Now, did you catch the lesson of the image of the eight of Wands?"

"This is a wonderful surprise, Master Hierophant, but I'm afraid I can't see the link. Is it speed and a need for accuracy?" Follin replied, still waking up.

"These images can be confusing," replied The Hierophant. "Now let me see what I can say about this Wands image. A Wand is energy. If used correctly it becomes a focal point for the magician to make changes in the world. You used the intent of the eight of Wands to direct confidence and encouragement to those impressionable youths. The message is simple, like a staff, a spear or an arrow, once a word is cast, it cannot be recalled. Your words will echo throughout the youth's lives, each will be able to recall this day forever. It will turn a sad mood into one of expectation of better things to come.

"Yes, the image shows speed, but this must be seen in terms of the act itself. Your kind word or kind act can turn a situation around from failure to success; an argument into a conversation; a moment of shame into a moment of pride. Magic is in what we do, your intent today was to give an example of how to lead, and Damen, who will one day become a Captain of the Wands commando, will copy your example long into the future."

Follin nodded, unconvinced. "I still don't quite understand. The image is of a flying quarterstaff, how can it represent a word... Oh, I get it! There was a poem I heard once in the Swords Kingdom, it was by one of their sages, it goes like this: 'The moving finger writes; and, having writ, moves on; not all thy piety nor wit shall lure it back to cancel half a line; nor all thy tears wash out a word of it...' or something like that."[4]

"What a beautiful poem." The Hierophant paused for a moment. "It reminds us that, like the written word of your poem, once the staff is *cast it cannot be recalled. Do you recall the name of the sage who wrote those lines? I must take my dear old friend Hermes, to visit this scholar before our magician's shuffle off this mortal coil."*

~

# Nine of Wands

*be prepared, battle-weary, success, batten down the hatches, survivors.*

"Follin?" called Eve, standing at the open front door ushering their elf friends inside.

"What?" came a faint reply from the alchemy study.

"You've got visitors."

"Oh yeah, send them in, thanks." Follin invited his guests to sit and join him in a cup of hot tea and some freshly made toast he had made only minutes earlier. The cups and plates had to compete with a pile of papers and books lying on his workbench.

"What's that you've got there, Pandjar? It looks like a book wrapped in waterproofed leather," Follin said as he accepted the parcel from the elf's hands.

"It most certainly is, but be careful opening it," Carwen warned.

Follin pulled his chair up closer to the study fire and chewed on his toast smothered in honey. The three visitors sat in the battered old chairs that Follin had gathered from some of the empty rooms in the castle. Helping themselves to their morning tea they waited for their friend's reaction.

"It looks old... and... well, well, well, it looks like a mage's grimoire, and..." he paused to carefully put his cup of tea on the table so that he could study the book in more detail. "It's a grimoire, and it looks to be spells of the draig." Follin stopped trying to eat his toast while balancing the book on his knee. He dare not risk dripping honey all over this extremely rare book of spells. "This is incredible, it's written in the draig tongue, a book of dragon spells." He turned to the elves and looked at each in turn trying to figure out the mystery of this incredible find. "Where did you get it?"

"Aye, the Grimoire of Draig it is," replied Pandjar. "Carwen and I found it at the gully where Alwyn and his commando fought. We think it was dropped by Mage Festra during the battle. See, it's not damaged by the weather, so it hadn't been sitting on the ground for any length of time."

"My, my, these books of magic are impossible to get hold of. The High Priestess calls them the Book of Shadows. They contain a magician's spells and meditations, how to cast them and their outcomes, like a journal. But this one, wow, this is rare indeed," said Follin.

Ziggy stood, rubbing his chin as he paced back and forth in front of the fire. "But where did it originally come from? If it's not written in the Wildlander tongue I can only imagine that either Festra or Armitar stole it from a mage of great power. We're certain that this book contains the spells cast on Hera and the Sanctuary."

"My father said that the only way to learn a dragon's spells is from a sleeping dragon," offered Follin. Although he didn't read the draig script, he leafed through the pages of the grimoire to examine the diagrams and images.

"What are you talking about?" asked Pandjar, leaning towards the fire to warm his hands.

"Da's shaman mentor told him that the only way a human can learn dragon magic was to breathe the dragon's breath while it slept. That must be done while it snores so it can't hear you sneaking up on it," answered Follin, not looking up from the grimoire.

"What?" Eve entered the room having heard but part of the conversation. "So, if you sleep with a dragon and wait until it snores, then breathe what it exhales, you gain its spells? There's no way anyone can do that." Eve had spent enough time with Nangkari to know a few things about dragons, or so she thought. She glanced at the cover of the grimoire before leaving. It was her turn to pick up the children from school. As she left, she made certain to walk calmly, hiding the burning desire to have the grimoire for her own.

"Dragons are not inclined to be visited by humans," stated Ziggy. "Humans are slow and clumsy and at one time were considered a delicacy. This is not the only place where you can find a dragon, they live all over the world. Perhaps the spells in this grimoire were stolen from an old or ill dragon from across the seas?"

"Aye," added Carwen. "There were once dragons on the Mystic Isle, I saw them. They didn't take too kindly to us elves because we were too clever for them to catch, and we had poisoned arrows. We couldn't kill them, but our arrows were enough to make them think twice about bothering us."

"So, what do we do with this grimoire?" Follin asked, lifting the book from his lap.

"We do have a Dragon Mage next door. Your father should be able to solve our dilemma. I'll go and get him." Ziggy grabbed his coat and raced next door to collect Mage Saoirse.

"Ah-ha, so this is where Armitar's draig grimoire ended up," Sao announced sitting comfortably in front of the fire. "I heard whispers of this grimoire many years ago while in the Outlands. This may be proof that the rogue mages of the Wildlands used it to work their magic on the High Priestess and the Sanctuary. This is a dangerous book, there is no doubt about it, it needs to be destroyed."

"No, Da, not until I speak with Mage Hermes. Besides, I want to try and decipher some of it, there might be something useful inside," Follin quickly responded.

Sao nodded slowly, thinking. "Yes, that is one course of action. I would suggest, however, that we invite Nangkari's advice on this matter. Make sure to bake some potatoes then show him the grimoire. I don't know how he'll react, but to withhold this book from him would be entirely disrespectful - and mighty unwise."

Follin considered his father's suggestion. "Yes, that's a much better idea, I agree." He handed the grimoire back to Pandjar for safekeeping. "What do you think? After all, you found it." Pandjar looked at his companions and nodded in agreement.

The following afternoon, they sat together with Nangkari in Follin's study. He held the grimoire in his hands, turning it over and over as he considered his response.

"You can see that it is written in the draig tongue," announced Nangkari as he placed the book on the table. "Whoever did this was very clever and very brave. If he had been caught, or information of this burglary leaked, he or she would have been hunted down by every dragon in the region and killed. I admire courage but am saddened that this book has led to such tragedy for the people of this world. We're no longer the beasts we were thousands of years ago, these spells should have died along with our desire for human flesh."

At that moment Eve entered the room with refreshments, stating that Nangkari's potatoes were still in the oven and wouldn't be too long. Immediately she felt a thrill run up her spine when she spied the book of dragon spells sitting on the table.

"I see you've had a look at our grimoire, Nangkari," said an excited Eve, who was more inclined towards reading than Follin ever was. "Can you tell us anything about it? Like, who wrote it? And which of its spells should the magicians of the Tarot Empire use?" Her questions came thick and fast leaving Follin squirming uncomfortably in his chair.

"Eve," said Carwen, noting how Follin reacted to Eve's questions.

"That is the Grimoire of Draig, written in the dragon tongue. I suspect that it is most unwise for the High Priestess-in-waiting to touch it. Nangkari is still pondering what to..."

"Oh, Carwen, that's silly elven superstition," interrupted Eve, her eyes wide with an almost ecstatic desire. "I've trained in the magic arts for many years now, dear girl. Besides, my grandmother was of the Mystic Isle wicca line, she taught me spell casting. I've never been spooked by the calling of spirits, not once. If I can't survive a peek at a grimoire then no one can." Eve leaned across Nangkari and grasped the book from the table. With practised ease, she flicked through its pages. "Look, the text is indecipherable anyway, how could anyone even read this?" she said as she paused to stare at one particular spell that leapt out at her.

Nangkari tamped the ash from his pipe into the fire and looked steadily at Eve.

"That book, Eve, is not for human eyes," he said without inflection, as he did when he wanted to convey something of importance.

"Of course it is, Nangkari. This was written by a human hand. Look, the signature states that the author comes from the tribes of Hapistasia, or something... it's smudged and hard to read though. But inside, look, it's clearly well written by a scribe with perfect writing style. I've seen draig grimoires in the Swords libraries written in a similar hand." As she examined the grimoire, the spells seemed to take on a life of their own. Images formed in front of her, and whispered words crept into her mind. All the while, Nangkari sat quietly observing the future

High Priestess.

The others sat patiently, waiting for Eve to finish examining the grimoire, respecting her educated authority on the written word. Nonetheless, they were uncomfortable, wondering what might be inside the grimoire, and what effect it might have on those who peeked inside with a hunger such as Eve displayed.

At last, Carwen stood and put her hand on Eve's shoulder.

"Enough, Eve. Nangkari warned that this grimoire was dangerous. I suggest that you take heed and put it back on the table," she said softly, but firmly.

As though awakening from a trance, Eve looked around and noticed that everyone was silent, staring at her. None displayed the excitement that she felt. Awkwardly she apologised and placed the grimoire back on the table.

Follin quickly seized the grimoire and, turning to Nangkari, asked, "What do you suggest we do with it?"

"I'll show you what to do with it," answered the dragon with a depth of emotion that Follin had not heard before. "The past is the past and it is best that the evil of those days disappears, just as the dragons who crafted these spells have disappeared." Grasping the book from Follin's hands he threw it into the flames of the fire.

Like a demon-spawned tornado, bright, angry flames reached upwards to snatch the book as it flew through the air towards the fire. With a flash of light, it ignited violently, turning to ash before it even touched the red hot coals. Finally, with a hair-raising scream, the ashes too disappeared leaving nothing but a sense of loss and sadness in their hearts.

"Phew, I'm glad that's gone," grunted Mage Saoirse, brushing his hands down his chest and arms as though they were covered in soot. "I never liked those old grimoires anyway. They are way too morbid, creating the illusion of power only to leave a trail of grief in their wake."

Eve couldn't take her eyes from the fire, watching the flames leaping as though thrilled to have destroyed such a heinous object.

"I'll get some more tea." Eve swayed a little as she stepped from the study and put out her hand to steady herself against the door as it closed. *Why did I lie about not being able to read draig?'* she asked herself.

"Can someone please explain how dragon magic is so different to ours?" asked Follin after Eve had left the room.

"It's too complicated to explain, Follin, just accept that dragon magic is too powerful for this new world of men." Nangkari had his pipe in his hands and busied himself packing it with Ziggy's precious weed as he spoke. "It comes from a time when worlds were created, we could do as we wished in those times. But alas, we finally decided to settle down to enjoy what Pan had created. Over time we forgot our violent and destructive ways. That should have been the end of it, but it wasn't. I hope there are no copies of this Grimoire of Draig, but that is a forlorn hope indeed." The old dragon puffed several times on his pipe and blew smoke into the air. Out of the formless cloud, shady dragons appeared, lifting slowly to dance around the ceiling.

Satisfied, the dragon continued. "In my time I have seen all kinds of stupidity. But I have to admit that humans win the stupidity competition. It is just as well they are not birthed with magic as the elves have been. Only those humans worthy, through dedicated practise and selfless service, gain access to high magic. This, fortunately, helps to screen out most of the hapless, power-hungry dolts."

The other smokers in the group had taken the opportunity to refill their pipes. After some minutes Nangkari spoke. "Sao, when are you taking Follin into the mountains for his initiations?" he asked.

Mage Saoirse looked up from the fire. "Huh? Oh, I'm waiting for Sir Darwyn to arrive with his chariot. We're going to fly there in style."

"Harrumph!" grunted the dragon. Turning to Follin he asked, "Are you prepared for your initiations to become the Tarot Empire's Magician?"

"Da has explained some of what I might be called upon to do." Follin was interrupted by the call of his wife. "It seems the potatoes are ready. Let's relocate to the dining room and the fire there. And, Nangkari, I have a feeling that Aidan and Fiana will probably have some questions for you about the grimoire... just warning you," he added, noticing the dragon getting ready for another '*Harrumph*!'.

~

For the rest of the day, Eve felt peculiar. She kept seeing one particular spell, the one she was certain had caused Hera's memory loss and the Sanctuary's near demise. Inside her head, she heard whispered lines from the spell, they would not stop. Even though she tried to think of something else the spell was constantly there.

*'Curse that grimoire! What am I going to do, I can't stop it?'* As the afternoon wore on she felt that she was becoming possessed by the

spell itself.

The more she mumbled the spell the more she felt a growing presence in the room. It started as a coldness quite different to the cold of winter. It had a winter's breath with an evil presence that clutched at her heart while clawing deep into her mind.

In a sudden explosion of panic, Eve raced through the front door and across the snow-covered lawns towards the castle walls. Climbing to the top, she leaned out over the battlements wanting to scream, to cast the spell from her mind.

"M'lady!" cried Puddlehop in alarm, running to grasp Eve by the arm. He had, only moments before, been warming those gnarled, arthritic hands by the fire of his watchtower. "M'lady, don't do that, ye might fall." He put his arm around Eve's waist and slowly eased her back onto the stone walkway.

"That's right, aye. Now walk with me. That's good, but don't look down." He kept up a patter of conversation to distract the priestess healer that everyone in the castle knew and admired.

Entering the shelter of Watchtower Nine, Eve stumbled as she desperately tried to clear her mind.

"Where am I?" she muttered, her voice slightly slurred. Suddenly a gust of wind caught her cowled hood and threw it back. The icy blast cut into her face, and she woke as though from a nightmare with a loud gasp.

"M'lady, you're safe, you're with old Puddlehop now. We're in Watchtower Nine, not far from your'n the Master Magician's chambers. I saw ye running up the stairs and, well, it's cold enough to freeze the nits in yer hair." He kept up his chatter noting that Eve was beginning to come back to a semblance of herself.

"Oh, yes..." Eve looked at her rescuer. "It's you, Puddlehop. Yes, of course, I know you. Your granddaughter sometimes helps me with the twins... but what am I doing out here?" She looked around trying to sort out the puzzle in her mind. As an afterthought, she put her hands out to feel the warmth of the fire in the watchtower fireplace.

"You been trancing, M'lady. I seen that look in Master Follin's eyes 'afore too. He does it when he's sparring. I've seen him go into trance, that's when he knocks everyone down with his sword 'n quarterstaff. I'd want him on my side when we meet the Wildlanders, that's fer sure."

The warmth of the fire seemed to do Eve some good, she could feel her beating heart begin to slow and the panic in her chest ease.

"Thank you, Puddlehop, I have no idea what I'm doing way out here. I feel so confused. Would you mind if I stayed here, with you? Maybe I could keep you company for a while?"

Puddlehop smiled, his broken teeth made his face appear crooked. Some people thought him simple, but the truth was that he was a kind and honourable old soldier, nothing more nothing less.

"Of course, M'lady, guard duty be lonesome at times, boring too. 'Tis not very often I get the company of a pretty lady on a cold night like this." Puddlehop grinned shyly and dropped his head so Eve wouldn't see his red face. "Sorry M'lady, that was downright rude of me."

If Eve hadn't been so frightened of the darkness that seemed to grow beyond the glow of the fire, she would have teased her protector.

But there was something out there, beyond the firelight, and she would not tempt fate by dropping her guard. If she had evoked a demon by mouthing the draig spell, then it was up to her to do something about it.

~

"Eve?" came a voice from the kitchen. "We need to run through what you need to bring to your initiation... Eve?" Temperance had arrived for Eve's regular training session. The angel busily cleared the twins' toys to form a space in Follin's vacant alchemy room. This was where Eve would practice her circle rituals and the various spells that utilise the magician's wand and dagger. Temperance was planning on a lesson in necromancy. She wanted Eve to entice a benevolent wraith to enter her sacred circle, then request answers to questions related to the past and future.

"Eve? Are the children with Follin and your parents? Eve? Follin? Anyone?" called Temperance becoming a little concerned. Strangely she could not even locate Eve's psychic trace, it had disappeared.

"Oh, no!" she groaned, sensing the darkness that had enveloped Eve - the same darkness she had felt when Hera was trapped by the draig spell. "Please no, not again." Temperance sat heavily in the lounge chair and dropped her face into her hands.

~

"M'lady, please, don't go outside, not just yet. There's something out there and I don't like it one bit," whispered Puddlehop. He had drawn his sword and had one hand on Eve's arm keeping himself between her and the door. "I'll not let anything harm thee, Priestess Eve. Oh no, nothing will get past me. Stay by the fire, I sense it is a'feared of fire." He didn't turn to look at Eve, he had no time to. In a sudden flash of movement, he stepped onto the stone walkway of the battlement and swung his sword with all his force at the demon.

"BEGONE! Get thee behind, demon of the night!" he cried as he swung left and right but there was nothing there to fight but shadows.

Eve felt herself going into shock. Her head spun and she wished that she was back in her chambers preparing for Temperance's arrival. She would be here soon... soon... Temperance... Hera... the Sanctuary demon!

With a flash of insight, Eve cried, "Get inside! Quickly, Puddlehop, hurry, hurry!" She cried with such force that the courageous old guard almost fell over himself trying to get back inside his watchtower and the welcome safety of the bright flames of the fire.

"It be a demon, indeed, but I canna see it to fight it, M'lady."

"Hand me your sword, hurry now," Eve commanded. Taking the weapon from the shaking guardsman's hand she said, "Stand right up against me, behind me, that's it. Follow me as I move, and don't say anything. This creature will be in through that door in a heartbeat if I don't do this right." She began to scratch a wide circle around herself and the guard.

"Hold! Which direction is East, quickly now!" Eve commanded, her mind buzzing with the strain of remembering the sequence she must follow.

"I, ah, it be," Puddlehop was shaking so much he almost stepped out of the priestess's circle. Then he pointed towards the doorway and yelled, "There! The sun rises through yon door." His voice raced upwards in pitch, for, in the doorway, stood a black shadow twice as tall as himself. A figure of evil that fought to enter but was held back by the roughly drawn magic circle in the tower's centre.

Pointing her sword at the doorway, Eve made sure to level her intent in the space between the demon wrestling with her rapidly fading circle of protection, and herself. With the sword point she inscribed the pentagram and cried, "I summon, stir and call ye up, Knights of the four Kingdoms!" Fighting to contain the panic growing within her chest she continued, "To guard this circle and to protect all therein. Sir William, Swords Knight of Air, I call upon ye to seal this point."

Turning to the south, Eve pointed the sword, quickly drew the pentagram and gasped, "Sir Alwyn, Wands Knight of Fire, I call upon ye to seal this point."

Spinning quickly, panting so rapidly that her voice was but a whisper, she commanded, "Sir Rohan, Cups Knight of Water, I call upon ye to seal this point."

'*Almost there,*' she thought, but suddenly, with a powerful lunge, the demon forced its way into the cramped room. Its screams rent the air as it tried to cross the boundary separating them. Eve slashed at the figure caught in the spitting, flashing fire threads of her magical circle with her sword.

Orienting herself to the north she finally called in a powerful voice, growing louder as she commanded, "Sir Dale, Pentacles Knight of Earth, I call upon ye to seal this point!"

Suddenly there came a crack of thunder as a bolt of lightning hit the doorway to lance across the floor of the sentry tower. The four elemental Knights stood as giant guardians, their swords drawn, their faces hard. Three Knights were in their radiant glory, but Sir Alwyn, still recovering from his wounds, was barely able to hold his position against the demon's violent assault.

In the glow of the watchtower's fire, Puddlehop and Eve watched as the demon formed into a ball of darkness to dodge the lightning bolt's flaming tongues. At that moment they saw such evil that they almost broke and ran from the scant safety of the circle.

"Evil filth, I see thee! Get thee gone from here!" cried Eve reaching for the power she knew dwelt deep within her being. Lifting her head she let out a frightened sob as, with a growing panic she screamed, "Champions of the mystic's circle, stand beside me in my time of need!"

The Knights stood firm, their attention focused solely on the demon, not one had the time nor energy to spare for reply. The draig demon was more powerful than any force they had experienced.

Casting her mind within, she sought once more for her power. In that instant, she felt her Cups centre, the resting place of her healing force, the water element... element, elemental...

"Molly!" she screamed. With a surge of hope in her heart, she heard her elemental's voice in reply, then she heard Sox barking furiously.

"Molly! Sox! Help us!" she cried as the demon's fetid breath tried to envelop her and the brave Puddlehop.

Without warning the demon screamed in delight as it battered the exhausted Sir Alwyn aside. Leaping into the circle itself the demon knocked Eve and Puddlehop so violently that they were sent beyond the circle's safety. But, for some reason, the demon could not exit the circle to steal its victim's life force.

Suddenly, with the intensity of a tornado, a firm voice commanded, "Evil demon of the Draig! I know thee! Ye will be gone from this sacred space!"

At that moment the two humans thought their lives had ended, but the demon exploded into flame, and, with a scream that almost deafened them, it disappeared. The room billowed with smoke and the smell of brimstone hung in the air. As she lay in dazed confusion against the wall of the sentry tower, Eve heard a friendly voice.

"Well, my girl, you certainly know how to put on a performance don't you," tittered the Angel Temperance grasping Eve's quaking hand as she helped her to rise.

"How? You...?" but Eve was too drained to complete the thought and collapsed into the angel's arms.

~

Eve slept all that night and half the next day. Molly remained beside her, afraid to leave her side even for a moment. In the study sat the same group who were present the day before. Follin was with his father and his elven friends, closest to the fire sat Nangkari, his pipe in his hands waiting for Sao to finish with Ziggy's fast-dwindling supply of Water Elf tobacco leaf.

"So you knew?" asked Mage Saoirse as he tamped the loose threads of tobacco into his pipe's blackened bowl.

"Of course I knew. Do you think a dragon could be outsmarted by a human?" replied the dragon with a snort.

"I wish you had warned us, Nangkari. I could at least have sent Sox or Molly to watch over Eve." Follin was angry that Nangkari had allowed Eve to put herself, and everyone else in danger. None of the group was in a good mood apart from the dragon.

"Think about it, Follin, can you imagine your wife ever trying something like that again?" asked Nangkari, reading Follin's mind.

"That's not the point." Follin was thinking of how terrified Eve must have been with the very same demon that almost destroyed the Tarot Empire, trying to kill her.

"But that is the point, young man. Eve will very shortly become the High Priestess of the Tarot Kingdom, that same Kingdom I live in, these elves and so too your children. Do we want our High Priestess to evoke another malevolent demon into our world? What if Eve had no time to call up the guardians of the four Kingdoms? As it was, Sir Alwyn's injuries almost caused the demon to succeed. What if our Knights had failed to pin the demon in place for those few moments that allowed Temperance to destroy it? What if Molly and Sox failed to hear Eve's call and came too late to lend their strength? What would have happened then?"

Follin remained silent, his frustration unabated.

Nangkari continued. "Yes, I saw Eve's future the moment she touched the Grimoire of Draig. I also knew that she would handle herself well in her battle with the demon. It was she who initiated the demon's destruction. You may not realise it, but Eve's banishing spell stopped the creature in its tracks. But that demon was draig-made, it forced its way into the circle despite the best efforts of your brave Knights. At that moment, Eve acted instinctively and immobilised the demon. This is why Sox, Molly and Temperance were able to destroy it completely and utterly. Eve introduced something exotic, a magic that was unique to herself, into her circle. It was something the draig-spawn had not encountered before and thus could not cast aside." He looked at his wide-eyed audience. "There is more than magic in that girl, she has power beyond our reckoning."

Ziggy stared at Nangkari sharply. "But if you knew, why didn't you warn Eve?" The tension in the room had begun to ease, but it ramped back up with Ziggy's question. The Elf Ranger leaned back in his chair to puff at his pipe awaiting the dragon's reply.

Nangkari considered his answer. "If I told Eve that I knew she could read draig script, what would that have solved? Nothing. She would still have that spell rolling around in her mind until it unravelled into a formal spell regardless. They are draig spells, and they have power. That particular spell has the power to worm its way into the mind until it is released - and I did warn her. I told Eve that the grimoire was not for her, did I not?"

He waited but no one answered, so he went on. "Eve has a wonderful disposition but her curiosity is like the ocean, it knows no end. I warned her, she did not listen. Do you think that she will listen the next time someone of knowledge gives her sound advice? As it was, she clearly lived up to her reputation as a spirited and powerful magician. She will prove to be a formidable High Priestess indeed."

Ziggy looked up and slowly nodded in agreement. "Perhaps, but your indulgence could have endangered the welfare of the twins, and our children with them, not to mention it nearly cost Puddlehop's life. He didn't deserve that, he's done his part for the Kingdom. He's fought his battles and deserves a better retirement than being scared out of his wits."

Nangkari smiled knowingly at his friends, "Be not a'feared for Puddlehop, Ziggy, he is a survivor, just like Eve."

~

# Follin's Meditation - 9 of Wands

*The image for Follin's meditation that night was of a battle-weary man leaning on his quarterstaff. Lined up as though creating a barrier behind him, were eight more staff. Interestingly this scene was inside the Old Smokey Inn.*

*'He looks so tired, it's like he doesn't even have time to sit down and rest,' thought Follin, easing himself into a deeper trance to drop out of his body to stand near the man.*

*"Dear sir," Follin began but stopped, it was Puddlehop himself.*

*"Aye, it be me. I saw yer missus earlier, our Priestess healer is a mighty fine warrior too. Fought off a demon, she did. She took me sword and fought him, scratched her magic circle on the sandstone floor of Tower Nine and all. Now we know we're safe in that tower no matter what might happen."*

*"I heard, Puddlehop, but I wish I had been there to help. I was with the children and had no idea anything was amiss until Molly and Sox just disappeared in a flash and then we heard the blast of lightning from the angel Temperance. It certainly put the wind up us, I can tell you."*

*The aged warrior leaned heavily on his quarterstaff and smiled brightly. "I was sorely distressed too, lad. I saw that demon, he looked me right in the eye and he came at me. Yer wife, I mean Priestess Eve, stood betwixt the monster and meself. She called down the powerful Sentinels from the four Kingdoms and cursed that demon with her spells. A mighty battle it was, sir. Fire and brimstone, lightning bolts and bursts of flame. I can still smell the stench of that demon when I think of it."*

Follin could not help but smile, indeed, old Puddlehop would never have to buy another ale. He was the proud custodian of the story of the famous battle between the Empire's Priestess and the draig demon.

"I wish I was there, Puddlehop, I truly do. I would have given him what-for." Follin felt himself growl as he spoke. He was still angry at Nangkari for allowing Eve to read the grimoire and endanger his family.

"Indeed, I've seen thee fighting and sparring with the Masters Tombei and Sir Alwyn. In all the times I've watched I've not seen them put a touch upon thee. And, what's more lad, I heard of your fight in the Hindamars, nasty place in the winter. You took on a dozen Fox elves I hear, 'n not a hair on thy head was touched yet all of them became yer prisoner. I've lived a long life but I count me luckiest days to be these since your family arrived. Them twins, my goodness, me granddaughter says they're a handful," Puddlehop laughed delightedly. "She says they hide where she canna find them. Sox and Molly make them disappear at bath time too, they does."

Follin smiled as he listened to this delightful old man. Eventually he broke into deep, body shuddering laughter. To think that someone else had trouble with his children made him feel that he wasn't the only one with problems that day. He hadn't laughed like that for a long time. He and Puddlehop stood there gasping for air as they laughed till they sat down at the table and ordered a jug of ale so that they could make a toast to family and friends.

"Lad, yer a good one, you and yer missus. Them kids of yours are the joy of the Kingdom, all our children are. It's what we live fer, what we die fer. I'm a proud old soldier who will stand by his watchtower 'til *he's relieved, and not a second before. I have a duty to see that my family, yours, and my neighbour's family, are safe. I'm ready fer anything that comes my way, I am. Aye, see them staffs behind me, them's the staff of those warriors who came 'afore me, they form the solid core of our Kingdom. They be my ancestors, and perhaps yers too." The old man stopped speaking to drink from his mug of ale.*

*"Lad," he continued. "Remember, be always ready. When M'lady took on the fight with the demon she knew what to do straight away. She might not have had the weapons or her magician's tools, but she stepped up to the mark. Oh aye, she was brave, it made me proud to stand beside her. That's what we do in this Kingdom, we stand-to-arms when the trumpet calls and the enemy are charging through our gate."*

~

# Ten of Wands

*dogged determination in the struggle to succeed, pride in accomplishment, inner strength, willpower, desire neither reward nor praise, I will complete my task.*

### Follin's initiation

It was the day of the Spring Equinox when the party arrived at the same cave where Follin camped with Master Pew and Justin for his bladesmithing apprenticeship. Follin examined the campsite to see if there were any signs that Justin or Master Pew had visited since. All he saw though, were faint footprints of the little people, the earth elementals he had met previously. There was nothing else but the windswept cave floor and a pile of undisturbed ash in the old campfire.

Outside it was snowing, the wind had dropped but the cold was as unpleasant as it was in the castle.

Sir Darwyn kneeled on the earthen floor of the cave trying to strike a spark from his flint to light their fire. The Emperor, The Hierophant, Mage Hermes, Ziggy, Mage Saoirse and the four Kings of the Tarot Kingdoms, looked on despairingly.

"I would not believe this if I hadn't seen it with my own eyes," Ziggy announced with a grunt of disbelief. "Here we are, freezing our coddiwomples off, surrounded by ice, and our Charioteer cannot strike a spark. Unbelievable."

Follin, ready with a handful of tinder for Sir Darwyn, looked at the gathering and broke out in laughter. "Ha! I bet that was for my benefit, Ziggy," he said. "OK, stand back everyone, let me have a go."

Sir Darwyn stopped the clicking and clacking of flint upon his iron knife and motioned for Follin to proceed.

"Lad, please, strike the fire so we can all get warm and boil the kettle," announced The Hierophant. "There is no joy in camping out in the depths of the Hindamar Mountains without a hot cup of tea or a brew of coffee."

Follin was fiercely determined to demonstrate his competency to command the Wands' Flame in this, his first challenge. He centred his life force at his navel, sucked in several rapid inhalations and forced the Flame into his hands. Crouching over the fire, he calmly breathed into his navel for a minute before he moved. Then, forming the dry moss and thin twigs into a ball, he prepared to create fire, just as he had done in his rescue of Carwen from the Fox elves.

Kneeling on the cave floor, Follin pulsed energy from his hands into the centre of the ball of tinder. There came a grunt from his lips and the tinder burst into flame. Gently he propped the flaming ball into the centre of the campfire and carefully added dry twigs until the fire began to roar with life.

After a month-long, high level meditation regime specific for Follin's initiation, the rejuvenated Mage Hermes leaned over and patted his apprentice on the back.

"Well done, I couldn't do it the first time you know. Oh deary me, I felt such a failure. I was so nervous that I nearly passed out."

That evening, they sat around the campfire to discuss the problems The Emperor encountered in trying to win the hearts of the Wildlanders in the north. "It is fortunate that we have Londar, the Browncaps archer from the Hindamar Highlands. He has been a genuine blessing. He talks sense to the tribes we visit, and they respect him. For the first time in a thousand years, I have a good feeling about our success in bringing peace to our frontiers. But, enough of business, it's time to get some hot tea and warm food into our bellies."

At the end of their meal, The Emperor called, "Follin, did your father remind you to bring your grimoire and magician's tools?"

"Yes, yes he did. I've got my journal and tools wrapped in canvas over there."

"Well, go and get them," The Emperor instructed.

A magician's journal contains his thoughts, dreams, astral experiences, experiments, and secrets, for the period of his apprenticeship, and beyond.

"I've written some personal things in these pages, and, well, some of it is about me and Eve," Follin muttered uncomfortably.

"Be at ease, Follin," offered Mage Hermes. "My journals held some very personal poems from a love-struck youth to a beautiful Cups lass. Every magician worth his salt carries his grimoire everywhere and studiously records every adventure, including those of love," he said with a knowing smile.

Picking up his magician's tools Follin prepared to give a description of what they were and how he came to make them.

"I made these with my own hands," he said as he placed the canvas wrap on the ground to display his magician's tools.

"This is my dagger, I made it in Justin's forge. It's a real beauty, a proper black handled athame. It will cut my magic circle when I need to. I've inlaid the blade with a silver image of Nangkari flying over Dragon Mountain. And this, this is the cup I fired in a wild dragon forge that I built in the castle keep one evening. It took a dozen or so attempts too. There's a pile of broken and deformed cups lying outside my window to remind me never to give up. But look at it, isn't it beautiful?"

Carved into its surface was a scene of his closest friends and mentors: The Hierophant was relaxing at his campfire drinking tea, seated next to him was Ziggy with his pipe in his hand, while Sir Darwyn was talking with the Strength Lady, a lion at her side.

As he spoke, he handed his tools, one by one, to The Emperor who inspected each carefully, then passed them around the group.

"This is my Pentacle. Argyll gave me the timber and showed me how to carve it. It's of a heavy wood that he said wouldn't break if I dropped it. It took a lot of work to get that fine sheen, and then I carved the Kings and Queens of each Kingdom around the edges. On the other side you'll see a carving of me with my family, Sox and Molly, sitting on our favourite Cups beach. I'm proud of my carving, it's the only artistic talent I have." He held his Pentacle in the firelight and indeed, it all but glowed of its own.

"And this is my staff. Argyll and I went into the forest where I was drawn to a young yew tree, untouched by blade of man. It took ages to make. Argyll told me to scrape the bark off, then, as it seasoned, I had to keep it oiled. He stored it in his work shed for three months so that his elemental could work on it." Carved into its centre was a scene of The Emperor and The Empress sitting beside the Sanctuary's pool. At each end of the staff were scenes from Follin's battles. On one end was himself, Ziggy and Sox surrounded by Wildlanders and the rogue mages, and at the other was Follin defending the wounded Carwen from three Fox elves. Hidden among the trees in the background could be seen Pan looking on.

He swung the traditional weapon of the Wands Kingdom, the quarterstaff, around his head making a whipping sound. "It's mighty tough, and flexible too, a grand weapon to protect my beloved Tarot Empire."

Handing the quarterstaff to The Emperor to inspect, Follin took up his wand. It appeared a delicate piece of timber in hands so used to wielding weapons. It was from the same yew tree as his quarterstaff, carefully polished to a bright sheen.

"Can you see how I've carved the Knights of each of the Kingdoms sitting around the campfire? Mage Hermes, if you look closely, you'll see your reflection in the flames, look, here, next to Hera..." When Hermes found his image, he was delighted. It caused the others to lean in closer to see for themselves.

"Yes, yes! I see it, how clever, such delicate lines too. I believe that thing is a caterpillar crawling on Hera's neck, is it not?"

"It most certainly is. I consider what you did to rescue our Sanctuary your highest accomplishment." Follin put his arm around the thin shoulders of his mentor and held him close.

"My magician's tools remind me to face life's challenges with wisdom, courage, and to patiently allow the Tao to illuminate the path I must take."

"Well, this is just wonderful," exclaimed The Hierophant. "I've made your favourite's list. That is a high honour, my friend, though I had my doubts about our young Magician's wisdom back then."

"I saw a young man with the gift of self-discipline and sensitivity but scarred by the bullies from his childhood. I am honoured to have been of service to you, Follin. To be carved into your magician's tools, well, that takes my breath away," stated the Charioteer, firmly clasping his friend in a warm embrace.

After the inspection of the tools of magic, The Emperor announced, "Follin, it is time. Are you ready to begin your initiations?"

~

### Pentacles - Earth

Mage Hermes had previously informed Follin that one of the goals of his magician's initiation was to satisfy the four elemental Kings who had facilitated his learning during his sojourn through the Tarot Empire. His first test was by the King of Pentacles - and Follin couldn't wait to get started.

"A magician must have multiple talents that he can manifest in the physical world," began the King of Pentacles. "This evening you will meet with the elementals that form the backbone of the Pentacles Kingdom. You have met them before, with Master Pew. It is expected that your earth initiation will produce something of tangible value which you will bring back and present to us."

Follin nodded his head slowly, this sounded easy, he thought.

"Ha!" cried Hermes, reading his apprentice's mind. "You think this is going to be a walk in the park, but remember, pride comes before a fall." Mage Hermes was almost back to his old jovial self. It was obvious to all that the mage's rigorous regenerative meditation program enabled him to participate in Follin's initiation.

"I am confident," stated Follin. "I know, but these earthling elementals are like friends to me. When I was here with Master Pew they showed me wondrous things, but I'll take your words to heart."

"It is time," announced the King of Pentacles drawing a circle to include the campfire and they gathered around it. He then performed the Ritual of the Pentagram.

"We have plenty of firewood, and plenty of water for our tea, so none of us will die of the cold or dehydration," announced the King as he sat on his pile of soft blankets. Noting that Follin looked confused, he added, "You may be gone for quite a while, Follin. Your quest might take many days to complete, and you wouldn't want to come back to find us all withered corpses?"

Follin tried to smile but he couldn't. *'What,'* he thought, *'could take days?'* When he did his initiation with Master Pew it took a single evening. As he was processing this, the King began to hum a tune, a tune that Follin immediately recognised. Forgetting his misgivings, he began to hum along with everyone else.

The King gently changed its rhythm and pitch. Following the King's lead, Follin soon fell into a light trance. As he did so a tiny figure appeared and, walking around the circle, he bowed low to the Kings, The Emperor, the archetypes and the elf in turn. It was the same wrinkled old man that had appeared in the cave when Follin was with Master Pew and Justin. As the old man danced beside the campfire, he was joined by other earth elementals, small human-like creatures with similar features and dress. Putting voice to the King's tune they started to sing and dance.

Their combined energy assisted Follin to half float half walk to the back of the cave, to the same rock wall he had entered in his previous visit to the cave more than ten years earlier.

*'I remember this,'* he said to himself in a dreamy, sing-song voice. With a rush of enthusiasm, he ran forward to embrace the rock wall and immediately entered a world of silence and a wonderful, tactile serenity.

*'I am the rock, I am granite, basalt, quartz and shale. I am the element of earth which notes the evolving nature of the soil, the creatures that are sustained by it, and the seasons that change it...'*

'But,' said the voice of the earth elemental. *'A master of the earth must transform just as the earth does. He must align with the seasons and adhere to the rhythms of the creatures it nurtures at its breast. What will you present to the King that demonstrates your command of the physical qualities of the earth?'*

Follin thought for a moment before replying. *'There is coal in the Forest of Smoke and Fire. May I go there to create a diamond as evidence of my competency?'*

*'That is a most difficult task that takes millions of our planet's cycles, yet you may try,'* advised the elemental. Suddenly Follin found himself standing on the crest of a lightly forested hill. Not far away he could see smoke rising from a burning coal seam.

By grounding his feet deep into the earth, he found the raw coal, untouched by fire. With only minor effort, he melded with the ground and sank deep into the soil to touch the coal seam with his hands. Centring himself he sent a pulse of power to grasp a handful of the black rock.

*'Let's see if I can live up to my promise.'*

In his discussions with Mage Hermes of his upcoming Pentacles trial, Follin had said that he wanted to present a diamond of his own making to The Emperor and Empress.

"Aye, lad, it's been done before. I heard of a mage who once created a diamond," Mage Hermes had said. "But the magician who did it was a power to behold. He attempted this feat in his prime, you are but a novice."

His father, Mage Saoirse, nodded in agreement adding, "I've seen this done on my travels. A great shaman once demonstrated his power by crushing a lump of coal to produce several tiny diamonds. He too was in his prime, a powerful shaman can do almost anything using the power he draws from the earth."

"But what if I combine earth with fire? That's what I did with the dragon furnace with Master Pew. Surely that would help, wouldn't it?" Follin had asked hopefully.

"Perhaps," offered Hermes.

Follin ceased his reflections and focused on the lump of coal in his hand and drew deeply into his core self. The Flame was there, and it glowed just as it had during his fight with the Fox elves. As his power grew stronger, Follin sensed the Pentacles change point combine with that of the Wands. The earth elemental moved closer to watch, fascinated by what Follin was attempting.

With a sudden CRACK! Follin found himself back in the cave. As he opened his hand, a fine drizzle of coal dust spilled to the floor. Sitting in the middle of his palm were four bright diamonds, each the size of a small chestnut and of perfect form.

"Well, the lad has done it and in such a short time too," announced the King of Pentacles as he examined the two diamonds Follin handed to him. "A thing of beauty that the Queen and I shall treasure forever."

The Emperor was similarly impressed with his gift. "The day I met you I knew that we had chosen wisely. You arrived at our castle gates a naive fool, yet today you are our equal in wisdom and spirit. I am sure The Empress will also be delighted with your gift."

~

**Swords - Air**

The following morning Follin awoke with some trepidation to face his next trial, Air was his weakest element. On the one hand, he might be asked to give a speech or be asked to debate a topic with the King of Swords. On the other hand, he might be asked to do something easier, like fly a kite. If only it was as easy as creating diamonds, he thought.

As soon as they had broken their fast, the King of Swords announced, "Your initiation requires you to perform an act that demonstrates command of your mind. As you know, the path of magic is a dangerous one, a path littered with corpses. Few mages of the Tarot Empire live beyond their initiation." When he saw the puzzled look on Follin's face, he explained further. "Over the centuries we decided that our mages should be integrated into our communities for their safety. The Pentacles mages created trade guilds to assist in this transition. They became chefs, horticulturalists, herbalists, craftsmen and women, adopting powerful elementals to help them in their work. The Cups mages became healers as this is their natural talent. The Wands mages had a most perilous role of protecting their community on the Wildlander frontiers. Alas, there aren't any Wands mages left. Your father, Mage Saoirse, was only recently inducted as a Fire Mage but has sworn never to use fire magic as a weapon. Wisely, the Wands Royalty had decided to share their fire magic directly with their community, and we believe that this has worked out well. The Swords mages chose the art of negotiation for treaties and trade deals, most took the path of scholarship and wordsmithing. As you know, the art of flying is exceedingly dangerous, fortunately, very few of our mages are tempted to try their hand at mastering the wing."

The Emperor added, "A magician's life is perilous and often very short. Are you still willing to continue with this initiation?"

Follin did not hesitate in answering. "Yes, of course."

The King of Swords nodded. "Then, let us proceed. Your task is to step onto a narrow tree bridge that lies across the ravine not far from here. Once there you, who have the training of our Bowmen, will loose a single arrow at your target."

"I can do that with my eyes closed," grinned Follin. Suddenly realising that he had spoken his thoughts out loud he let slip a soft, "Oops."

The Swords King looked firmly at Follin and shook his head. "That is exactly your stumbling block, Follin. Didn't your mentors teach you to engage your brain before you open your mouth?"

"Yes, Sire, that has been one of my faults for as long as I can remember and I'm still working on it." Follin didn't know what else he could say.

The Emperor chuckled softly and winked at The Hierophant who nodded his head in acknowledgement.

The group escorted Follin through the softly falling snow to the ravine. The King of Swords pointed to the fallen tree and the target, a red cloth placed on a stick some hundred metres away.

It wasn't as easy as Follin thought. There was a light wind driving small flakes of snow but it was not a problem. His fingers though, were at risk of stiffening in the cold air. With effort, he strung his Bowman's bow, selected an arrow that was well balanced, straight, the feathers firm and finely trimmed. He knew that in this cold air the bowstring could snap so he took the warmed grease from his pocket and rubbed it into the string.

"Ziggy, what do you think? Ninety metres? Wind drift... a little to the left?" he asked his friend.

Ziggy studied the target and the tree across the deep ravine. "That's about right, but I'd be careful on that tree. The ice there might cause you to slip, and that is a long way down, elf-wise."

Follin carefully studied the tree bridging the ravine, took out his knife and scraped the ice as best he could from its top edge where he planned to stand. Stepping onto the fallen tree he firmly placed his feet in position, took his time to centre his breathing and knocked his arrow to the bowstring. But right at that moment, a small blackbird flew towards his face causing him to almost lose his footing and fall.

Steadying himself once more he drew back on his bow but the bird had returned and flew right at his eyes. Follin immediately ducked his head and, with great trepidation, stepped off the slippery tree trunk onto firm ground. The sweat forming on his brow quickly turned to ice.

"You'd better hurry, the cold is getting worse and your string and bow are starting to stiffen," said Ziggy, struggling to hold the smile from his face.

"I'm trying, but that darn bird wants to knock me off this tree-trunk and fall to the bottom of this ravine," moaned Follin, having lost the confidence he felt in the warmth of the cave.

"Then do something about it," called Sir Darwyn with a grunt of exasperation.

Once more, Follin stepped carefully onto the tree trunk sliding his feet along to force the fresh snow to fall off and improve his grip.

"You need to do something soon, Follin," called the King of Swords, "the snow is getting heavier."

*'That darn bird, I need to control the bird first.'* Follin slowed his breathing and sought the mind of the blackbird flying incessantly at his face. *'I've done this before with the Wildlanders, and I can do it again.'* Sinking his breath deep into his navel chakra, he sensed the bird's Swords change point.

"Got it!" grunted Follin and the bird immediately disappeared just as it turned for a third attempt to force him off the tree bridge. Without waiting another second he drew the arrow to his cheek and released it at his target.

"Perfect!" cried Ziggy grasping Follin's arm and helping him off the bridge. "I was a little worried we would be standing out here in the snow for hours waiting for you to make up your mind."

The ice on Follin's face began to melt as the tension in his muscles eased. But his heart was racing, and his hands began to shake as he looked down the narrow ravine.

"Did I really do that?" he asked softly, realising just how perilous a position he had been in.

"Congratulations, this deceptively simple task was harder than you expected, yet you executed it with precision," said Hermes. "You were so consumed by The Hierophant's little birdy that you forgot your fear."

"I was half expecting you to fail this test, Follin," announced the

King of Swords. "Controlling your mind has always been a challenge."

The Hierophant stepped over to Follin and asked, "Did you enjoy my little blackbird?"

"No! It nearly got me killed. But I was wondering, blackbirds don't live up here in the freezing mountains, how did you do it?"

"That, my friend, is a secret. Command of the creatures is something I've studied over many centuries."

"But where is the blackbird now? I hope I didn't harm it."

"It's back where it came from, safe in the Cups forest with its mate. I doubt it even remembers this little adventure."

Follin was prepared for the second part of his Air initiation, but instead, the group headed straight to the campfire for lunch. Turning to see where Follin had gone, Mage Hermes noticed that he was standing at the cave mouth waiting.

"Master, what about the rest of my Swords initiation?" Follin asked. "Doesn't the King want to test my negotiation skills?"

"So that's why you're still standing out here in the cold. Let me put your mind to rest. When the King heard how you managed the Fox elves, and then Pandjar and Ziggy, he knew that you had no need of further testing." Mage Hermes put his hand out to lean on Follin's shoulder. "Now help this old, washed-up magician back to the warmth of the campfire and some food."

~

**Cups - Water**

"I've decided that there is no use testing your water breathing abilities, Follin, you mastered that in your Quest of Life," announced the

King of Cups. "Instead, your challenge is to melt the ice beneath your feet and pour it into this bucket. Once you've done that, refreeze it. Your task, specifically, is to melt the ice with your heart chakra and then freeze it using passive water energy alone. That means you can't engage the Wands Flame that you have been so studiously practising."

Mage Hermes strolled over to stand beside his uneasy apprentice. "Gentleman, would anyone care to place a bet that he can't do it?" No one took the magician up on his challenge. They knew that Follin's power over the elements was beyond most mages thrice his age and experience.

"Lad, go ahead, show them what you can do," he commanded his apprentice.

Follin silently took the bucket from the King's hand, sat on the soft snow and removed his mountain boots. These were the same he had taken from Karadar, the Elf Ranger, in his rescue of the Lone Wolf.

Turning to the King of Cups, Follin said, "This is not going to be easy, Sire. I expected some sort of watery Quest of Life adventure. Travelling to another dimension would have been a lot easier. This, well, I shall do my best not to disappoint you."

Placing his mind in his navel chakra, he guided the passive water energy to flow downwards to just below his feet. Gently tapping into his chakra again, Follin felt the warm, liquid energy spill into his heart. With several measured breaths, he sensed the energy build of its own accord until his heart chakra burst into a radiant fount of love and joy. It was a soft, gentle glow that spread easily to encompass his entire body.

Carefully, he shifted his awareness and, with only a little effort, he eased the energy of love and joy sitting in his heart into the ice. Within seconds he felt it begin to melt and his feet slowly slid into a puddle of water.

Drawing the water out of the hole he placed the bucket on the ground and began the process of reversing his flow of energy. This was difficult, he had not done anything like this before, but his instincts immediately took over. Follin shifted his breath to draw the freezing cold of the ice around him into his hands. This was an extremely dangerous procedure. He needed the icy energy to bypass his organs, otherwise they would freeze. Even the archetypes and the Kings of the elements would have difficulty rescuing him from such a fate.

Acting entirely on instinct, he used the passive water meditation process from the Quest of Life, to guide the ice energy at his feet to flow just beyond the outer layers of his skin. It formed at a point several inches beyond his outstretched hands. The freezing energy of the ice wanted to enter his body and permeate every cell, but he dispelled the urge to let it have its way.

At the critical moment, Follin intended the ice energy to turn the bucket's contents into a frozen lump of ice. Standing back with a smile of satisfaction, Follin handed the bucket to the King of Cups. Becoming aware of the frozen perspiration on his body he staggered and almost fell.

"Steady, elf-wise, I've got you," said Ziggy softly as he led Follin back to their campfire to thaw out. "That was a dangerous challenge. The King of Cups knew that this would be an impossible feat even for an advanced magician. Well, elf-wise, I believe that you've just done the impossible."

The group gathered around Follin at the campfire and slapped him on the back in congratulations.

"That," said the King of Cups, "was superbly done. I have been watching you for many years now, Follin, and even though you had mastered the Cups lessons during your time with us, I was uncertain as to whether you had the flexibility required to take on the role as Magician of the Tarot Empire. You have erased my hesitancy to recommend you."

"Thank you, Sire, but I'm sorry, I really need to rest now." Follin reached down to take his blanket, and, with Ziggy's support, walked to the back of the cave and was soon fast asleep.

~

**Wands - Fire**

The pile of soft blankets, generously provided by Sir Darwyn, made the hard, rocky cave floor like a feather bed. In the early hours of the following morning, though, Follin was woken by the sound of someone calling his name.

"Follin!"

"Huh?" mumbled Follin sitting up.

"Follin!" came the voice again.

'*Who is that?*' he thought. Struggling to wake up, Follin saw a figure standing at the cave entrance, silhouetted by the light of the full moon.

"Come, it is time to meet thy destiny," the voice announced.

As he stood to dress, Follin could just make out the figure a little more clearly. It was a warrior, dressed in what appeared to be light armour. On his head was a horned helmet, and he wore a mask that covered his face.

A wave of energy surged into Follin's mind and body and he quickly grasped his newly made Wands staff. In a few strides, he faced the figure at the cave entrance.

"Who are you?" he demanded.

"I am destiny," the man replied, lifting his own quarterstaff above his shoulder adopting the standard attack posture.

"I don't usually spar with strangers, but if you're here to harm my friends then I won't hold back," warned Follin, his voice sounding loud in the chill air.

The warrior's answer was a sudden, vicious assault to Follin's upper body with a series of rapid thrusts and blows, each expertly parried and blocked. Recognising the mastery of his assailant, Follin took the fight to him and launched a series of powerful blows and jabs with his staff. The warrior easily avoided each thrust, and, for every blow, he swung his own weapon in a return attack.

At each strike and thrust, the fight became more vicious and the blows came faster and faster, blurring like a dragonfly's wings in the moonlight.

Taking a step back to disconnect from his opponent, Follin called, "Sir, you fight well, your style is familiar."

"You know it well enough," replied the horned warrior drawing his sword. "But may I suggest you take up your sword? I believe that the stick in your hand will soon break at the edge of my blade if you don't."

Follin propped his staff against the cave entrance and ran inside to take up his sword. The familiar power imbued by Master Pew and his elementals raced into his arms and chest making Follin feel invincible.

"I may not destroy your sword, for it is crafted by a Master Bladesmith and his elementals, but I will destroy the man who wields it."

With that pronouncement, the horned warrior attacked with such ferocity that Follin was barely able to hold out against him. He parried, blocked and at every opportunity tried to force an opening to attack his opponent. Follin knew that his sword could not be broken, but despite his best efforts, he was unable to force his opponent back. He was pushed and turned in all directions by the horned warrior's ferocious assaults.

Follin had relied on his Dolphin style to keep his opponent at bay, but it was not enough. In desperation, he felt for the Flame at his navel centre, but each time he prepared to pulse a blast of energy at the warrior, he was compelled to pull back and defend. His skilled offence was cramped, and he could not find a flaw in the warrior's defence.

"If you wish to fight with fire, so too will I," said the warrior as though reading Follin's mind.

Taking advantage of the momentary break in his opponent's concentration, Follin sent a blast of fire energy at the warrior. Instead of being forced backwards, the warrior spun the flame in a circle around his body, then sent it spiralling back at Follin. The horned warrior's flame, however, was twice as fierce.

"I was trained in the martial arts by captains of the Elven Rangers;

in the Force of the Flame by Nangkari, last of the Tarot Empire dragons; and in swordplay by the Knights of the four Kingdoms, but still I can't beat you. WHO ARE YOU?" cried Follin in anguish as he managed to dodge the fire that threatened to overwhelm him. But as he spoke he was smashed to the ground by a crushing palm strike to the chest.

"You know who I am," came the warrior's answer as he took off his helmet to reveal his face. "Prepare to die, Follin, fool of the Mystic Isle, apprentice Magician to the Tarot Empire. Three days shall you lie fallow, after which you will be reborn. Fail this test and your rebirth will be in the Shadowlands."

Follin felt a flush of confusion at the face he saw beneath the helmet. Then, gritting his teeth he fixed his feet firmly into the snow to grip the earth beneath him. He was exhausted but his spirit was unbroken. As he tried to stand upright, he suddenly bent over in pain, dropping his sword. The horned warrior's palm strike had caused a debilitating injury to his ribs.

"Argh!" grunted Follin in pain. "I have been bested and for no reason. I demand to know why you wish to kill me."

The stranger walked up to Follin, bowed low and announced, "During your sojourn in death you will learn the answer to your question. Now, it is my honour to fulfil your destiny."

In surreal slow motion, Follin watched as the warrior lifted his sword high and, with a powerful stroke, cut him in two. In a detached state, he saw the warrior's sword slice through his body. Follin grimaced, expecting it to hurt, but it didn't. Nothing mattered now, this was where he belonged, in the astral planes, free of the encumbrances of the physical world.

All of a sudden Follin was alone, the warrior had disappeared. He continued to stand in the snow, untouched by the silent falling snowflakes. *'I suppose I should put myself back together and see what is going on in the cave. Surely everyone must have heard the noise and are wondering where I've gone.'*

Looking down, instead of seeing his broken body, there remained nothing but a patch of blood-stained snow. In a state of mild confusion, Follin walked into the cave, but everyone was still asleep.

*'What should I do now?'* he asked himself, but no answer came, so he walked out of the cave, and kept walking.

~

At dawn, Sir Darwyn awoke to bring the campfire to life. Soon after, Ziggy sat up and wandered over to join him, rubbing his hands in front of the roaring flames.

"Where's Follin? It looks like he's been gone for some time, his bed is cold."

The Hierophant heard and joined them. He had his cup in his hand waiting for Sir Darwyn to finish making a pot of tea.

"He's undertaking the final test of his initiation, Ziggy," The Hierophant said matter-of-factly.

"Oh? But I thought we were to do that after breakfast?"

"Nay, the King of Wands said that he didn't need to test him. He recognised that Follin was a master of the Flame already. It was decided that we should go ahead with the final stage of his initiation as the Tarot Empire's Magician."

Ziggy felt he had missed something important but didn't know what.

By the time breakfast was ready everyone was awake. Strangely, none offered to explain what had happened to Follin, so Ziggy asked.

"Your Majesties, if you don't mind me asking, where is Follin?"

"Oh, yes, how rude of us," answered The Emperor. "I forgot to tell you. Last night we decided that Follin should move to his final task, to create the Elixir of Life."

"May I ask what that task might be?"

Hermes took up the explanation. "This final test is for the apprentice magician to achieve enlightenment through specific alchemical processes. It is best explained by your favourite tavern song, *John Barleycorn*. When the barley grain is ripe it is harvested and threshed. This forms the first stage of alchemy, the deconstruction of the raw material in preparation for its next phase. One might say that this initial phase is the death of the Self.

"Secondly, the barley grain is soaked and germinated to produce malt. The malt is necessary for producing alcohol and helps contribute to its unique flavours. This stage describes the growing wisdom and awareness of the initiate through reflection and meditation.

"The final stage is distillation when these delicate flavours, oils and essences are purified and collected. This is when the essence of the individual forms what is called the Elixir of Life. It is also known as the Attainment of Enlightenment."

"Hmm, so Follin is using alchemy to create this Elixir of Life?"

"Correct, but right now, Follin is dead and we have to wait to see if he can find his way back. If he returns to us, then he has passed this final test and will be the Tarot Empire's new Magician," said Hermes, knowing that Ziggy knew little of human magic.

"What? Dead? But, but will he come back?" stammered Ziggy, managing to catch the gasp of grief before it broke from his lips.

"I really don't know." Mage Hermes lowered his head and turned his face back to the campfire, deliberately avoiding his elf friend's shocked stare.

Ziggy nodded woodenly, then suddenly stood and walked to the cave entrance where he noticed Follin's quarterstaff leaning against the cave's entrance. Just beyond he saw a patch of bloodied snow and the scuff marks of a fierce fight. Collapsing to his knees, he cried for the loss of his dear friend.

"Elf-wise, why didn't you call me?" he sobbed. "You were there when I needed you... but I've failed you when you needed me."

~

Follin felt more bemused than confused at the travellers who drifted past him. Strangely, none stopped when he called to them.

*'What is this place? Everything is so strange.'*

As he wandered in the gloom trying to orient himself, he spied a small chapel. Glancing inside he saw that it contained a single sarcophagus. Staring at its marble top he felt a sudden urge to rest. The solution was right in front of him, so he climbed onto the cold, stone lid and closed his eyes.

*'Perhaps I'm dreaming, and I'll soon wake up.'*

On closing his eyes, Follin saw a projection of his life, from birth to his battle with the horned warrior. Each joyful and traumatic experience was re-enacted, and he felt every emotion with singular clarity.

Lying on the sarcophagus, Follin contemplated his memories as they arose in his mind. He sought to pinpoint each emotional theme that had caused him pain. Those themes that gave him joy were similarly processed. At last, he awoke feeling different, buoyant.

*'That's strange, I feel bright and clear inside,'* he said to himself. *'It's like I've had a bath after training all day and now I'm clean.'*

He slid off the sarcophagus and walked outside to continue watching the parade of souls moving like a tide towards a rainbow mist in the distance.

Despite his newfound sense of freedom, he soon felt lonely, and a black despair overtook him. Once again, he took to calling to those who walked by, asking if they knew where he was - but none turned nor answered his queries.

After what appeared to be an eternity, one of those shadows, a handsome man dressed in fine robes, heard Follin's greeting and stumbled towards him. At first sight, Follin thought him of royalty, but the gentleman's dress hid a dishevelled, putrescent body. The man's eyes were sunk deep in their sockets, and his pallid face lay devoid of emotion.

"What do you want of me?" whispered Mage Armitar unaware of whom he was greeting, his speech weak from lack of use. He quickly found his 'voice' once he recognised that standing before him was Follin, apprentice magician of the Tarot Empire. "Young man," he now spoke in a sonorous, commanding voice. "I have been searching for you ever since I learned that you had been cast into this desolate place." Noticing that Follin had yet to recognise him, Armitar straightened his back and changed his posture to one of friendly familiarity.

"I see that you are forlorn and lost, it is fortunate that I found you. Sir, I know that you have been cast aside by those who wish to steal what is rightfully yours. I can help you claim your true destiny, if you will allow me," he declared. "I have the power to give you what you are destined to take as your right."

Without waiting for Follin to reply, the mage continued. "I know that you desire another as your wife, Olivia. Is she not attractive and desirable?" An apparition appeared before Follin, it was poorly formed yet a hint of Olivia's beauty tugged at his heart.

"I, I don't know who she is, but yes, she is pretty," Follin stammered, confused yet interested in hearing more of what the man had to say. Anything that would help explain what he was doing there would be of value.

"Young man, you can have any woman you want, and more. The power I command is far superior to that of the people you served. I know how wickedly they treated you. Alas, they have played you for a fool long enough!" Armitar was empowered by Follin's naivety and weakness to see through the enchantment of his voice. "Listen to me! Allow me to help you snatch destiny from the grasp of the mindless sop who rules by crushing gentle souls like you and Olivia. Claim the throne for yourself and free your lover and your people!" Armitar's voice was comforting and sensible.

"Is this why I am here, to claim my throne and rescue my lover?" Follin asked.

The mage grew in confidence as he saw how easily Follin's desire could be aroused with so little effort.

Just as Follin was weakening, caught up in the mage's spell, he heard a sound. It was strangely familiar, a barely discernible *'yap'* that triggered a memory. Something, there was something he needed to remember, but what was it?

"I have the power to take you from this barren wasteland and make you wealthy, powerful, a ruler of empires. With me beside your throne, we shall rule the earth!"

As though waking from sleep, Follin suddenly saw through the man's royal disguise. *'This is that vile scoundrel, Mage Armitar!'*

"All you need do is permit me to take you back to the land you left behind. It is so easy, a simple nod of the head is all it requires. Give me your consent and all of what I promise is yours." The Mage smiled broadly knowing that he was but a heartbeat from success.

*'How easy it is to fool a fool,'* he thought. *'A single nod is all I need to cede me your powers. I can then return to the world of the living where none will be able to stand against me, not even the Tarot Archetypes.'*

Once again there came a sharp *'yap'* and Follin turned his head to listen, but it had gone.

*'Armitar, you cunning swine, what are you planning to do to me?'* Another *'yap'* and Follin's mind exploded in understanding. *'It's Sox, he's telling me something! It's the mage, he has a weakness! He's stranded*

*here and can't return to the world of the living.'* Again, Sox's bark stirred a greater understanding in his master's mind. *'If I give my consent he'll seize my magic, then I'll be stuck here forever!'*

"Armitar, you scoundrel, you shall stay in the realm of shadows for eternity!" With a roar of anger, Follin sent a bolt of energy into Armitar's being. The rogue mage screamed, a high-pitched squeal that echoed in the gloom. In a state of mindless panic, the mage turned and raced towards the rainbow mists and was gone.

The moment passed leaving Follin empty of emotion and his sense of clarity quickly began to fade. It was at that moment that the Star Lady appeared.

"Oh, hello!" Follin cried seeing someone he thought he recognised, but then he was unsure if he knew her or not.

"So, you wish to leave? But first, tell me, what led you here in the first place?" the Star Lady asked.

"I don't know. I was somewhere and then I was here. This is such a strange place, no one stops to talk, they just keep walking when I call to them. I met a man, a robber, he tried to trick me so I cast him into the rainbow mist. It's that mist you can see over there, I've been watching people walk into it and disappear. It looks peaceful, maybe I should go there too?" Follin put his head in his hands and rocked back and forth.

"What is your name?" the Star Lady commanded bringing Follin back to the moment.

"I, I'm... I know that..." Follin fought hard to remember. "I... I had a name, I'm sure of it!" Follin moaned loudly before replying. "I was a fool! Everyone called me a fool... but no, that's not my name... it was... Follin, yes, that's it, Follin, I'm Follin the fool, I remember now." He looked around and noticed the Star Lady begin to glow.

"And I have a wife, Eve, and I have children, Aidan and Fiana, and I have friends... The horned warrior killed me, didn't he? That's why I'm here." Then it all came rushing back to him. "I died in the fight which means it's my time to walk into the rainbow mist like all these others."

"Follin," the Star Lady whispered in reply. "Remember, there was something the horned warrior said to you."

Follin thought for a moment. "Yes, he told me that I would lie fallow for three days before being reborn. How could I forget that?"

"And what do you think his words meant?"

Follin replied. "He said that I would lie fallow, that's like the Four of Swords image. You know, the image of the knight lying on the sarcophagus in the church? He lies there to process his life, to seek personal forgiveness and healing before returning to his loved ones. Well, I've already done that."

"Yes, I know you did, and so?"

"What's the use of remembering all those things, I'm dead."

"Remember the horned warrior's words, the clues are there."

"That horned man was such a good fighter, he anticipated my every move. His fighting style was as good as mine, his command of the Flame was superb."

"What happened next?"

"He sliced me in two, then I stood up and put my body back together, and then I found myself here. I think that's it, it's all a bit confusing."

"Then why haven't you walked into the rainbow mist like everyone else?"

Follin thought for a moment. "Because I had to dispatch that villain, Mage Armitar, beyond the Shadowlands, that's why!" said Follin forcefully. "No, that's not why. It's because I want to go back to my family and friends," he replied.

Suddenly, Follin slapped his forehead with the palm of his hand. "The horned warrior's three days are the three stages of alchemy. That's it!" Follin said with a laugh that caused several of the wraiths to turn and look.

"Your first task was to demonstrate command of the four elements - Earth, Air, Water and Fire, which you have done. You have just completed the second task, the alchemical Attainment of Enlightenment; and finally, you must gain the Alchemist's Elixir of Life to be reborn. To complete your initiation you must answer this simple question: *what do you really want from life*?" asked the Star Lady as the light above her head glowed so brightly that it consumed them both.

"I was born a nobody, a fool, but I met some kindly people who picked me up when I fell down. They are the ones who inspired me, who gave me the confidence to be who I am today. Star Lady, I'm ready to be reborn."

~

Ziggy woke with a start, someone was outside the cave, he was certain of it. The sun had yet to break above the mountain peaks to the east to begin the fourth day of his silent vigil. The predawn glow created an eerie atmosphere as he stepped forward.

He scanned the area and saw, shuffling towards him, a shadowy figure.

"Follin?" he called softly, slowly walking forwards.

"Follin?" he called a little louder. The figure looked up from within its hood and stopped.

"Follin? Yes, yes, that's who I am," the figure whispered looking around as though waking from a deep sleep. Pointing to the patch of blood-spattered snow he asked, "Is this where I died?"

"I fear it was. I came outside and saw your sword lying beside, beside..." Ziggy had to stop speaking before he was overwhelmed with the memory of that moment.

"I fought the horned warrior, Ziggy. He took his helmet off and I saw myself. Pan had created a copy of me."

"Why would Pan do that?"

"It was required that he send me to fulfil my destiny. I had my elemental-made sword and could not be defeated, so I had to defeat myself. My clone knew what I was going to do before I did. I used the Flame but he just spun it around and threw it back at me," Follin added becoming more animated. "He knocked me down and broke my ribs with a palm strike. That's when I knew that I had lost the fight."

They turned at the sound of footsteps crunching on the snow.

"Follin!" cried Sir Darwyn, reaching to pull his friend into his embrace. "I see you found your way back to us!"

"Yes, Darwyn, I was lost for a time, but now I am back." Follin looked at his two friends and felt such warmth in his heart.

"Good! Now let me have the honour of preparing your breakfast: barley and oat porridge. You must be starved!" announced the Charioteer leading his friend towards the warmth and his companions inside the cave.

~

**Eve's initiation**

The Empress had arranged for Sir Darwyn to bring Eve to the Sanctuary in time for the Spring Equinox, which fell on a Full Moon. But there was an issue that still hung over Eve's head like a blade which The Empress wanted resolved before the initiation began. With her was High Priestess Hera, and the two archetypes who had assisted in securing the Sanctuary: the angels Temperance, and the Star Lady. Standing quietly behind them were the Queens of the four Kingdoms.

"Eve, we still haven't discussed your experience with the Grimoire of Draig, and the spell you uttered which could have destroyed our Tarot Empire." The Empress opened the wound that Eve had desperately wanted to remain closed.

"I'm so very ashamed and so sorry, Empress. It got stuck in my head and I couldn't stop it. I just wish I hadn't seen that grimoire," she uttered in a soft voice.

"You wish?" queried the Star Lady. "That reminds me of a saying we had on our home world: '*If wishes were fruits, everyone would plant orchards*'. You were lucky, Eve, that demon was a hellhound that, to quote one of our famous poets: '*doth hunt us all to death*'[(5)]. If Temperance, Molly and Sox hadn't heard your cry for help... well, you can finish that sentence yourself."

The Empress studied Eve for a moment before speaking. "It was only by chance that the Grimoire of Draig fell from Mage Festra's pocket that day and was found by two Elf Rangers. The rest of the story you know. No one could have predicted that you would be caught by the very same spell that trapped Hera and almost cost us all our lives."

"Your experience, as unpleasant as it was, gave us the opportunity to test your mettle," Temperance added in a more conciliatory tone. "We believe that your confrontation with the demon demonstrated that you are more than suitable to become our next High Priestess."

"We understand that you had things well under control." The Queen of Wands continued. "You had prepared your circle and called forth the four elemental sentinels correctly. In a situation where you were under threat of destruction, you did extremely well. When you were thrown from the circle the demon became trapped within. We don't know how you did it, but you did. With the demon pinned within the circle by your personal power and that of our Knights, Sox, Molly and Temperance were able to destroy it."

"Your actions confirm that you have the power to command magic even beyond my own," whispered Hera. "This is something I was unable to do when I was tricked by that very same draig spell, but the demon is now thankfully gone." Eve saw that her mentor was fatigued, her presence only a fraction of what it was even a year ago. The High Priestess sighed and turned to her companions. "We have discussed this to its conclusion, let us now get on with Eve's initiation."

The Queens of the four Kingdoms assembled with the archetypes, looked at each other and nodded their agreement. They recognised that Hera was fragile and the sooner Eve's initiation trials began the better. A very relieved Eve took up her grimoire and handed it to The Empress.

"Your Book of Shadows is exquisite," announced The Empress holding the beautifully decorated journal containing Eve's experiences as priestess and healer. Indeed, her grimoire was magnificent, with pressed flowers and scented herbs spaced among its pages and coloured ribbons woven through the leather cover, front and back. Its binding was covered in runes drawn in delicate lines, inked with different colours to highlight those she identified with the most. Each page was decorated with drawings of what she saw in her dreams and meditations.

"I've not seen one as grand as this," agreed the Star Lady.

"And I see that your tools of magic are just as beautifully crafted," announced The Empress, leaning over Hera's table to examine Eve's tools carefully arrayed ready for examination. She first lifted Eve's athame, the black-handled Dagger, and held it to the light. A trail of small runes could be seen carved into its handle. Its blade displayed symbols of magic inlaid with silver. When she finished examining each tool The Empress passed them on to her companions.

Eve's Chalice was of gold, decorated with runes of magic that floated on a river surrounded by trees, flowers and animals. On the river bank sat the four Queens of the Tarot Empire.

"I had the help of our friend, Justin. He helped me craft the chalice and then advised me on how to carve the decorations. Both Follin and I are blessed with talented and generous friends."

Eve's Pentacle was carved from a single piece of timber. It was adorned with a twisting grapevine, complete with small grapes and vine leaves made of gold wire lightly hammered into its arms. The vine led the eye around the pentacle but there was no beginning nor end. Turning it over revealed a scene of Hera, The Empress, Temperance and the Star Lady beside the Sanctuary pond covered in lotus flowers. Hidden among the flowers were delicately carved symbols of magic.

"I wanted to decorate my magician's tools with nature. I took my time, working on them when I could. I wanted to see what I could do to make them attractive as well as functional. I'm really pleased with how they've turned out," announced Eve, proudly.

Finally, The Empress picked up Eve's Wand. It was larger than most wands and of extreme strength. Along its length could be seen Eve and her family standing outside their Cups cottage. As she turned the wand around she could see the carved images of her mother, father, sister and her grandparents sitting among the flowering herbs of the Mystic Isle.

"I asked Argyll if he could help me find a suitable piece of timber for my wand," explained Eve. "He showed me this piece of hazel that he sensed held a powerful energy. I could feel how it would promote love and creativity, which is just how I wanted my wand to express itself. Argyll's elemental generously assisted me in crafting it into a wand of power. It was ready to be turned into something special, and I think I've achieved that."

Although Hera's health had seriously deteriorated, she didn't want to miss the initiation of the next High Priestess. She rested her hand on Eve's shoulder and said softly, "Priestess of the Tarot Empire, I am so proud of what you have done and the woman you have become. It fills me with joy to see you on this special day. Especially so knowing that when I am gone the people I love so much will be held safely in your gentle hands."

By evening their examination of Eve's priestess tools was complete, and the group escorted Eve to the pool at the centre of the Sanctuary. Under the rays of the full moon, the pond surface glowed with a luminescence that she had not noticed before. Her mentors looked up at the night sky and nodded to each other - it was time.

Pointing at the moon's glowing orb reflected on the pool's surface, The Empress announced, "The moon is soon to reach midheaven. It is time for you to meet Cerridwen, the Moon Goddess, who will act as your benefactor this evening."

"I don't quite understand, your Majesty. I've seen the Sanctuary pool many times during the full moon, and I've heard you all speak of Cerridwen. So please tell me, how will she help me tonight?" Eve asked, glancing at the moon's reflection in the pool.

"As you know, we call Pan, the Horned God, a masculine god. You have met him. Now is your time to connect with Pan's correspondence in the feminine form, the Goddess Cerridwen. The secret of life derives from Cerridwen's gift, the gift of the sacred Cauldron which lies within a woman's womb. Your initiation begins with the drawing down of the moon and to visit Cerridwen in her lunar home. Once there you will know what we mean," answered The Empress. "Now please, stand here beside the pool, see how the moon is reflected back to you on the pool's surface? Close your eyes and follow the Star Lady's directions which will guide you to the Moon Goddess. The High Priestess must be as one with her, for, as your benefactor, she is your strength, as Pan is for Follin." The Empress stepped back, and the group formed around Eve.

The Star Lady whispered in Eve's ear, inviting her to see the moon's stairway reflected on the pool's surface in her mind's eye. The radiance of the moon was so bright that it scattered her thoughts.

In this bedazzled state, Eve heard the Star Lady intoning the Charge of the Goddess: "Listen to the words of the Great Mother, Cerridwen. Also called Hecate, and Isis, she of ten thousand names, by other Priestesses of this land."[5]

The Star Lady stopped speaking and a different voice took on the ritual. "*Let my worship be within the heart that rejoiceth, for behold: all acts of love and pleasure are my rituals.*" Eve felt an ecstatic happiness growing in her chest as she realised that the voice was that of the Moon Goddess, Cerridwen. "*And therefore, let there be beauty and strength, power and compassion, honour and humility, mirth and reverence within you. Whenever you have need of anything, once in the month when the moon is full, then shall ye assemble in some secret place and adore the spirit of me, Cerridwen, who am Queen of Wicca.*"

Visualising the moon's reflection on the pool's surface, Eve saw a moonbeam that was like a stairway to the heavens above. A moment later she heard Hera's voice: "To become High Priestess you must become acquainted with Cerridwen's Cauldron which is the secret of the Sanctuary, our portal to the universe. Mastery of the Sanctuary's portal lies in your ability to unite your navel chakra with your womb. This commands the magic of life, something no male can ever understand."

Eve felt her breath shift exactly as Hera described and her womb filled with light and warmth. This sensation was strangely familiar - she had felt this before.

"Eve, your Cauldron awoke when you were learning the centred breath with me many years ago. Your twins were immersed in its power for nine months which explains why they are exceptional. Cerridwen's Cauldron is the secret of the High Priestess which she uses to open the portal of the Sanctuary," explained Hera.

"Eve, it is time, step upon the moonbeam," announced The Empress in a gentle voice.

*'I can do this,'* Eve said to herself and, to her surprise, she felt her womb unite with her navel chakra to form the Cauldron. At that moment her feet touched the firm ground of the lunar landscape. *'Hey, it's beautiful here, just like the Sanctuary. There's the pool and there's the little cottage where we have our morning tea, and...'* she suddenly stopped her internal dialogue as a most beautiful woman stepped into her field of view. Strangely the woman had three faces.

"Eve, my sister, don't be put-off by my appearance. In celebration of you forming my Cauldron, I wanted to show you the three phases of the moon and therefore of womanhood," Cerridwen said. "You see me as Maiden, Mother and Crone, in my truest form. And now it is time for me to welcome you to my home, please visit whenever you wish."

"I am humbled that you greet me as sister, Cerridwen." Eve took the goddess' outstretched hand and together they walked to the table set with food and drink.

"Look around you, Eve," Cerridwen commanded. Standing beside the goddess now appeared Eve's mentors, Hera, The Empress, Temperance and the Star Lady. They embraced Eve and congratulated her.

"But... the pool, it did something to me didn't it?" stammered Eve a little overwhelmed.

"The pool is our portal to other planes of existence. It allowed us to escape from our own planet before it was destroyed," answered the Star Lady. "By engaging your Cauldron as you stepped upon the moon's stairway you were transported to Cerridwen's lunar Sanctuary. You will learn to unite your Cauldron with the pool  to form a portal. Then you can travel anywhere you wish. Now please, come with me."

Cerridwen took Eve's hand and together they stepped into the pool which transported them to dazzling alternative universes and distant planets. Her final trip was to the planet of her Tarot ancestors. It saddened her that such a beautiful planet could so easily be transformed into an inhospitable wasteland.

"What was it like before?" she asked Cerridwen.

"Close your eyes and see," replied the Moon Goddess. Closing her eyes Eve saw a planet covered in lush and vibrant forests, grassy plains, and jungles. There were hills, mountains, rivers, and oceans much like Earth, a vibrant, beautiful place.

"It's like what we have here in the Empire."

Cerridwen nodded in agreement. "It was so beautiful, but the people of Earth wrestle with the same issues that plagued the Tarot ancestors: greed, ignorance, apathy and self-interest. Wise and just people must remain vigilant to ensure that only good is permitted to flourish on this planet. A task, I am afraid, that appears almost impossible at times."

When they finally returned to the Goddess' Sanctuary, Eve's mentors escorted her through Cerridwen's portal back to the Tarot Empire.

"Well, Eve, you have shown no difficulty in accessing and commanding your Cauldron. This is the secret of the Sanctuary's pool which we hold close to our hearts," said Hera, her voice much stronger from her visit with the Moon Goddess.

"I had no idea, really, that I could use the Full Moon Ritual of drawing down the moon as a means to travel either. I've got some practice to do, haven't I?" Eve giggled, she was still on a high from her adventures with Cerridwen.

"My dear girl, are you ready to accept your role as the Tarot Empire's new High Priestess?" Hera asked. When Eve nodded her head, Hera continued. "Then let us begin your formal anointment, for I am weary."

~

# Follin's Meditation - 10 of Wands

It was the end of a busy week when Follin slid into his warm bed and pulled out the last image of his sojourn through the Wands Kingdom. The image showed a man carrying ten quarterstaff over his shoulder. They appeared cumbersome, but the man was determined to complete his journey and not let any of them fall.

'I'll ask this fellow what he is doing and what his plans for the future are,' thought Follin as he entered the image.

"Kind sir, that's quite a load you have there. What are you going to do with them?" Follin noticed that the man was neither young nor old, perhaps just past his prime.

"Why, hello," the man replied as he stopped to rest his bundle with their butts on the ground, careful not to let any of them fall. "I didn't see you standing there, I was totally focused on getting to the village yonder. I have an order to fill and I plan on completing it this day." He breathed deeply to catch his breath. "A fellow must be prepared to accept his responsibility when he takes on the task as quartermaster of the Wands Kingdom."

"I've seen you preparing the weapons, training mats, targets, and everything else the trainees need. Every morning you're there to make sure the cadets have their equipment. I'm sorry that I've never introduced myself to you, that was rude of me," said Follin.

The man shook his head and laughed. "Nay, lad, that's of no consequence. I have a job to do and that's that. I seek neither reward nor praise. I'm Wands born and bred, we each have a task set for us and we see it through to the end. I've watched thee, oh aye, I have. You're the magician who has a peculiar gift. You have the Flame, but it has a twist I've not seen in this Kingdom before. I've seen you knock Sir Alwyn and Master Tombei off their high-horse many a time, they canna touch you. And laugh! My goodness, me and my assistants would gather and watch, but mind thee, we never let on. Oh no, that would be bad manners indeed.

"Our families live in a safe and happy Kingdom, and that is worth an early start and late finish. I canna give my children that level of security out in the farmlands to the south, nor on the coast. Nay, we have our fill of respect, that be enough."

"I see you limping a little, may I help?"

"That? It's just an old battle wound. I'm but one of many who can no longer run about in the mountains chasing Bluebeards and Browncaps. But I can put an edge to a spear point, or hone a sword so it cuts like a razor. Hand me a broken harness or a pair of leather sandals, and I'll mend it. But today, I've got Master Argyll's quarterstaff to deliver and deliver I must." He hefted the weapons back onto his shoulder to resume his journey towards the village.

"May I walk with you?" offered Follin.

"Certainly, and I have some advice for thee, if I may? Our Wands fire breeds optimism, and it is this fire that inspires us to keep going towards what we believe is right. We draw upon our inner strength and willpower, shouldering our responsibility like these staff here, and carry it to completion. Your final lesson is to never give up, no matter how heavy the burden. If your burden is guilt or grief, then find a way to *resolve and come to terms with it, then find the will to carry on."*

*"Thank you, your words will help illuminate my path when I become the Magician of the Tarot Empire."*

*The man stopped walking for a moment, put out his hand and said, "It is my pleasure to meet you properly, Mage Follin. Let us shake hands in friendship, and then I must deliver these quarterstaff before my arms fall off."*

~

# Epilogue - endings are beginnings

Follin and Eve's ordination as Magician's of the Tarot Empire was a simple affair. Taking the hand of his wife as he opened the ceremony The Emperor said, "It is with delight, in perfect love and perfect trust, that we install our new Magician and High Priestess to their offices in the Tarot Empire," he said in a clear, powerful voice.

"But," added The Empress, "we recognise their youth, their ongoing studies of the magic of the Tarot Empire, and the fact that Aidan and Fiana are young and need their parents with them. It has been decided by the combined voices of our community, that our

Magicians shall continue in their parenting roles, fulfilling their official duties as needed. At this stage, Temperance, the Star Lady and I will remain as guardians of the Sanctuary and advisors to Eve. This is something that we normally would not do as we have our own responsibilities. However, these are challenging times. We would also like to consider ourselves accessories to Aidan and Fiana's upbringing. To add to your tasks, Eve, as a healer of incredible talent and knowledge, it is our wish that you remain as head of hospitals in the Wands Kingdom." Eve responded with a delighted smile.

"Follin," announced The Emperor. "You will continue to be supported by The Hierophant, Sir Darwyn, and your Elf Ranger friends, Ziggy, Pandjar and Carwen." When he saw Follin's look of joy he added, "For an elf to want to be your attendant shows that you are much loved," he added.

Hera held the official crown of the Tarot Empire's High Priestess up in the air for all to see as she passed it to The Empress. It was a beautiful garland, woven from the vines found growing in the Empire's Sanctuary. Flowers bedecked the weave of vine leaves to form a slight peak which was topped with a bright diamond. This was one of the two diamonds that Follin had created during his initiation and presented to The Emperor and Empress.

"Priestess Eve, please present yourself to our community as High Priestess, by accepting this crown of office." The Empress carefully placed the crown on Eve's bowed head. There was an abrupt outburst of clapping and shouts of congratulations as Eve raised her head to thank her mentors and those present.

Turning to Follin, The Empress announced. "Master Follin, a mage in all but name these past few years, it is our honour to anoint you with your crown of office. It pleases me to also announce that your designations include those bestowed by the King and Queen of the Wands Kingdom, and Nangkari, last dragon of the Tarot Empire. Please come forward." The Emperor lifted a simple archers wrist band and a pair of gloves from the table beside him and handed it to his wife.

"It has been our tradition to give our Magician something practical, a gift that he will use every day. On Mage Hermes' ordination, we gave him the gift of parchment and writing materials in recognition of his studious disposition. We have noted, Follin, how you have dedicated yourself to becoming an expert in the weapons of each Kingdom. To this effect, we present to you an archer's wrist guard, and these soft leather gloves," announced The Empress.

As Follin waited, The Emperor indicated that he wanted to say a few words.

"This wrist guard will protect you from the slap of the bowstring when you release your one hundred arrows every morning. These gloves are for your sword and quarterstaff training, made by Master Lexis of the Pentacles Kingdom." He stepped back and allowed The Empress to complete the ceremony.

"Master Follin, please present yourself to our community as Fire Mage of the Wands Kingdom, Dragon Mage of the Nangkari lineage, and Magician to the Tarot Empire, by accepting these gifts of office."

With a broad grin, he lifted his gloves and wrist guard above his head which was greeted with shouts of congratulations and applause.

"Our outgoing magicians, Hera and Mage Hermes would now like to offer their own gifts to Follin and Eve," announced The Emperor.

The former Magician of the Tarot Empire appeared smaller than the giant figure that had come to Follin's rescue at the very start of his Fool's Journey.

"Mage Follin," Hermes held a bundle of notes wrapped in thin, ink-stained leather. "You have been as a son to me. You have given me more joy in my later years than I could ever have hoped for. These are my journals, a compendium of my experiences and musings from my long association with magic and life. I have called this collection the 'Corpus Hermeticum'. As you can see, I've not had the time nor energy to complete them, but I know that you will add and revise them as you see fit. Please accept this as an old man's treasure that he wishes to pass on to future generations of magicians."

Follin stood uncomfortably, this was a gift beyond his wildest dreams.

"Thank you, I am honoured and humbled to be the custodian of your wisdom." He couldn't think of anything more to say so he sat down.

"Wait, Follin, I have these as well." Hermes reached behind his seat to bring out another bundle, much bulkier than the first. "In my hands, I hold the secrets of thousands of years of esoteric study. These are the grimoires of long-forgotten mages and magicians of the Tarot Empire. Some were written by our very first Magician. He left this, the Emerald Tablet, though 'scroll' would be a more appropriate description as the original tablet was lost."

Follin stood once more to accept the gifts, and, with Hermes encouragement, let the Emerald Tablet scroll fall open. It contained only a few verses of script.

Follin read out loud, "*Tis true without lying, certain and most true. That which is below is like that which is above, and that which is above is like that which is below.*" Smiling affectionately at his mentor he said, "Master Hermes, we've discussed this truth from the Emerald Tablet many times."

"We did? Oh dear, I must have forgotten." Hermes shook his head, slightly embarrassed at his forgetfulness before turning to walk slowly back to his seat.

The Emperor called Hera to step forward. The priestess' beauty and power was the most resplendent that Follin had seen in many years. When Follin tapped into her aura, he sensed that the other archetypes had contributed their own life force to allow her to maintain her physical presence for this special day.

"Eve," Hera said softly. "I have few material objects in my cottage, but I do have the most precious of gifts that I know you will appreciate, my personal Book of Shadows. I'd also like you to accept the tools of magic that I have relied upon as High Priestess: my Wand, Dagger, Chalice and Pentacle."

On receiving her gifts, Eve pressed her face into her free hand and began to cry.

"I'm, I'm going to miss you!" she stammered as she hugged her mentor. "My life had met its end before I met Follin, and through him, I met you and Master Hermes. Everyone here has had a hand in giving me opportunities that I never dreamed possible. I shall honour your Book of Shadows every day..." she started to cry again and had to stop speaking.

"I ask but one boon from you," announced Hera. "Would you kindly decorate my grimoire as you have done yours? I don't have the artistic talent that you do, and it would make me happy to know my gift is something of beauty as well as practical."

Eve smiled through her tears and hugged her mentor. "Your gifts are more than I deserve. I shall certainly decorate your grimoire, it will be a pleasure, Priestess Hera."

The Emperor waited for a moment before calling for everyone's attention one last time.

"There remains but one more question to be asked of Follin, and that is, '*What is the Elixir of Life?*'"

It was a question Follin wasn't expecting, yet it was something he could answer from his recent experiences.

"The Elixir of Life is the essential substance of the magician. We create and refine it in our energy body by combining the four elements of Earth, Air, Water and Fire. In many ways it has its own wisdom and acts without conscious thought. That's what happened when I met Mage Armitar in the Shadowlands. Sox's barking triggered an awareness of his corrupted soul and my essential self reacted and I blasted him."

"Excellent! I wish I was there to witness it," announced The Hierophant quite unable to prevent his exuberance from taking over.

The Empress let out a snorted chuckle before lifting the goblet of wine sitting on the table beside her. Tipping some of her wine onto the ground she announced, "With this libation of wine in honour of the Gods and Goddesses of this planet, we seal this moment in time."

With the ceremony complete, the party moved from the Sanctuary to the Emperor's castle itself where food and drinks were arrayed. Among the archetypes and the royal families of each Kingdom, there were many guests including those who stood by Follin and Eve's side in their sojourn through the Kingdoms.

"Page Arthur!" cried Follin running to greet his friend. Next to Arthur was Londar, Pages Jon and Blade, seated with them were Argyll and Justin. Justin and Argyll's children were happily playing with Aidan and Fiana - closely supervised by Molly and Sox, of course.

"Is that seared garlic scallops I see on your plate, Arthur? I don't believe it! Surely, not after the night you spent sitting on the privy in the village of Weathersea?"

"My dear Follin, what do you take me for, a dolt?" laughed Arthur scooping another scallop into his mouth. "Yes, I know, I know, but I can't leave them on the plate, they look so lonely. Alas, my body is strong but..." Follin interrupted before he could finish.

"Let me complete that sentence for you, Arthur. '*My body is strong, but my will is weak!*' There, I still remember exactly what you said back at Weathersea." The friends embraced and sat to relive their many adventures together.

Standing by himself outside the circle of well-wishers was Follin's closest friend, Ziggy. He quietly waited for Follin to notice him.

"Elf-wise," he said as they embraced. "I'm so glad that you and Eve have now fulfilled your destiny. But, you know, I thought you were dead when I saw the blood outside the cave."

"Thanks, Ziggy, yes, it was a difficult time for us both."

Ziggy paused for a moment before adding, "I wish someone had warned me. It wasn't fair that you were left to face a God all by yourself."

"It was meant to be, Ziggy. I had to die to my old life, reconcile my place in this world, and then come back from death with steadfast resolve. This is an ancient ritual that all mystics must face on their path to enlightenment." Follin placed his hand on Ziggy's shoulder. "But all the same, I wish you were there with me, like when we stood against those Wildlanders to rescue Sorcha and your children."

"Well, I'm now your official guardian, along with Carwen and Pandjar. I'm glad Sir Darwyn agreed to join us, though you'll have to share him with everyone else now that his chariot is fixed. The Hierophant has already made plans to improve your alchemist's study too. Something about building a proper coffee roaster so that he can have fresh coffee when he visits."

Follin wanted to laugh but then, without warning, he was overcome with emotion, he was so lucky to have such wonderful friends. Ever since that day when he ran away from home, he was fated to undertake this adventure. Stepping off the cliff near his home village of Saoirse, he expected to die on the rocks among the waves. Instead, his feet touched the rainbow bridge. Thus, he entered the magical realm of the Tarot Empire under the kind mentorship of Mage Hermes and many other of the Tarot archetypes.

Eve was delighted to see her old friends too, Page Alice and her cousins, Pages Kahmia, Asha and Natalie. Friends came and went as the party continued well into the evening. They arranged to join her at the Wands Kingdom on a regular basis, to catch up on events and to form stronger bonds. They knew that Eve would need all the help she could get, and as they agreed, friendship was the strongest magic of all.

~

The next morning everyone gathered at the Sanctuary portal to give the retiring magicians their blessings. Waiting by the pool was the Star Lady with Hermes and Hera standing beside her. The two magicians were ready to embark on their final adventure.

"You are certain that this is what you wish?" asked The Emperor, taking each of the departing magicians by the hand.

"Yes, we are quite certain," answered Hera in a thin, barely perceptible voice.

"Hermes, you are certain?"

"Of course," was Hermes' gruff reply.

"Then I place you in the gentle hands of your guide, the Star Lady, who will escort you on the next stage of your journey," announced The Emperor.

The Star Lady stood tall and serene. "It is with a heavy heart, and much delight, that we take our leave of Hermes and Hera, who have selflessly served our Empire for many centuries. Much have they sacrificed to keep us safe."

Eve began crying and Follin put his arm around her, his own tears dripping down his cheeks.

"I shall now accompany Hermes and Hera, returning them to their home village on the Isle of Runda, the island of secrets. There they will be attended by the elementals, those who have remained hidden from the eyes of man." Turning to Hermes and Hera she said, "These elemental beings have kept their secrets well and will transition you into an elemental form that will enable you, in time, to become one with them." The Star Lady turned to escort them towards the pool, but The Empress stopped them with a wave of her hand before they could proceed.

"My dear friends, let me wish you good fortune as well. May you always feel the breeze fresh from the Hindamar Mountains on your face; may the fragrances of the Sanctuary gardens fill your step with anticipation each morning; and may you remember the joys of dreaming on a moonbeam with your companions of the Tao. We anticipate your return, in whatever form you take, once you have completed your sojourn with the elementals of Runda Isle," she said, fighting back her tears.

"Harrumph!" grunted Hermes, sounding just like his dragon friend. "You make it sound like we're going to our death instead of our rebirth. Come on Hera, let's get cracking before they convince us to go to the Shadowlands instead."

Hera smiled, something Follin had rarely seen from her. To Follin and Eve, she said in mind-talk, "*Expect us of an evening, twilight is our time. When Aidan and Fiana are ready, we will make ourselves available to them too.*"

Without another word, the retiring magicians stepped into the Sanctuary's pool and were gone.

That evening in the castle, it was a more solemn gathering. Follin and Eve had tried to keep their eyes on Aidan and Fiana but it was impossible. Fortunately, the twins were constantly attended by Sox and Molly, and rightly so, each day they seemed to find a dangerous new adventure to embark on.

When it was time for bed the twins ran up to their parents.

"Da?" said Fiana. "Grandpa said that you know about astrology and the planets, can you teach us?"

Follin was pleased, his children would finally learn something of magic that wouldn't get them into trouble.

"Of course, maybe Ma and Grandpa can help me," he replied with some degree of relief.

"Great!" announced an enthusiastic Aidan. "And, and, and that means Fiana and I can visit the planets through Ma's portal!"

Follin turned to Eve and gave a pained, defeated smile.

"Son," he sighed. "If you and Fiana want to visit the planets to invoke their magic, you'll have to wait until you've passed your initiations."

"But Da, what if Sox and Molly come with us?"

Follin looked to Sox for support but the fae dog quickly crouched on the floor and placed his paw over his eyes. Turning to Molly he saw that she had hidden behind Eve's legs.

Shaking her head in resignation, Eve groaned. "Oh dear, is this the price we pay for having children with special gifts? My first day on the job and I'm already going grey."

**THE END**

<<<<>>>>

*This concludes:*

***The Fool's Journey through the Tarot series, by Noel Eastwood.***

*~*

*This series is also available as audiobooks from honest online booksellers and Noel's website, brilliantly narrated by professional voice actor, Jonathan Johns.*

*~*

*For books and audiobooks by Noel Eastwood, please visit his website and subscribe to his free newsletter: www.plutoscave.com*

<<<<>>>>

# Astrological Correspondences with the Tarot Wands

**Fire signs – Aries, Leo, Sagittarius**

Fire dominated people are enthusiastic about everything they do. They have plenty of physical energy and drive, often in glaring contrast with the other elements. There is an emphasis on creativity and charisma which can inspire others to follow their lead. The Fire person prefers to experience things in a physical, passionate and energetic way, they are the adventurers of the zodiac.

The element of Fire is like a flame which warms, provides joy and pleasure to those around them. Sometimes that flame can burn - themselves and others. The emphasis is on creativity, inspiration, adventure and they certainly seek attention and acceptance – and they can act out like the drama queen. It is the element of warriors, adventurers, artists, celebrities, romanticists, psychics and leaders.

Their negative qualities include aggressiveness beyond normal bounds, selfishness and greed, outrageous behaviour which can put others at risk, egotism, and the physical and mental domination of others.

Aries is decisive and adventurous.

Leo leads with courage and nobility.

Sagittarius is the wise counsellor providing advice before and during their adventures.

You calculate this elemental dominance by examining the sign and house placement of the luminaries (Sun and Moon), Ascendant and Midheaven, personal planets, conjunctions between inner and outer planets, and the type of aspect patterns they form in the chart.

Fire keywords: charisma, leadership, assertiveness, aggression, romance, passion, warriors, adventurers, courage, positive and optimistic, dominating, bullying, daring and they always have to be right.

# Keywords – Wands Meanings

Wands are the adventurers of the tarot deck, their qualities include: creativity, imagination, friendship, artistic, irresponsible, talented, music, adventure, danger, risk taking, attention seeking, rites of passage, charismatic, reckless, daring, poetry, storytelling, honour, loyalty, courage, strength, respect, loyalty, motivation, meaningfulness, driven, fired, impulsive, hyperactive, spiritual, romantic, heart chakra, chi, inspired, passionate.

**Ace of Wands** - the beginning of an honourable adventure

**Two of Wands** - to hold the world in your hand, choice, honour, responsibility to make wise decisions, the change point.

**Three of Wands** - wanderer, travel, trade, the mystic's journey, strategic thinking, responsible decisions.

**Four of Wands** - celebration, united purpose, structure, stability, family, community effort.

**Five of Wands** - competition, inspired chaos, play, conflict, rivalry, argument, commitment, standing strong against adversity.

**Six of Wands** - victory, triumph, pride, attention seeking, accomplishment, recognition for job well-done, respect the dead and honour the living.

**Seven of Wands** - confrontation, defense, moral high ground, readiness, courage, I will retreat no more, enemy at our gates.

**Eight of Wands** - action, spontaneous instant reaction, once you release your arrow you cannot call it back, window of opportunity.

**Nine of Wands** - be prepared, battle-weary, success, batten down the hatches, survivors.

**Ten of Wands** - dogged determination in the struggle to succeed, pride in accomplishment despite opposition, inner strength, willpower, desire neither reward or praise, I will complete my task.

**Page of Wands** – youthful, fun-loving, inspired, driven, reckless, impulsive, enthusiastic, rash, first in line for any daring or dangerous adventure.

**Knight of Wands** – tempered enthusiasm, honourable, respectful, brave, knowledgeable, at the forefront of activities that require courage and leadership.

**Queen of Wands** – exhibits a mature and balanced approach to living life to the full, enthusiasm, charisma, loyalty, master of the feminine qualities of the Fire element.

**King of Wands** – subtly redirects the wild and impulsive fire qualities in his people, wisdom tempered by life experiences, charismatic, respectful, master of the masculine qualities of the Fire element.

# Character list:

Follin – the Tarot Fool, hero of the series

Eve – Follin's wife, healer, Priestess

Aidan – Follin and Eve's son 7 years old

Fiana - Follin and Eve's daughter (twin to Aidan) 7 years old

Mage Saoirse – Follin's father, Fire Mage, Dragon Mage

Katlyn - Follin's Mother

Theresa – Follin's younger sister

Tombei – Wands' Master of the sword, Theresa's husband

Tanika and Atsu - Theresa and Tombei's daughter and son

Sox – Follin's fae dog

Molly – Eve's earth elemental

Argyll – wood carver

Justin - Bladesmith

**Wands characters**

Nangkari - one-eyed dragon

King and Queen of Wands

Sir Alwyn – Knight of Wands

Asha and Blade - Wands Pages

Captain Nilyard - Wands Captain of the Home Guard

Ewan + Mahina - siblings, Fearless Commandos

Helminia - school captain and commander of cadets

Rhianna - Senior Instructor of the cadet officers

Puddlehop - Tower Nine guard – retired warrior

Cerridwen – female moon goddess

Pan – male god of the earth

Kwadinsa – stag Pandjar saved from the lions

**Elves – Wood Elves, Elf Rangers, Fox Elves**

Ziggy – Wood Elf and Elf Ranger, brother to Pandjar, brother to Kerrytan and Naroo

Sorcha – Ziggy's wife, Water Elf

Tamotan - Ziggy and Sorcha's son

Lily - Ziggy and Sorcha's daughter

Pandjar – Wood Elf, and Elf Ranger, adopted brother to Ziggy, Kerrytan and Naroo, Carwen's partner

Princess Carwen – the Lone Wolf, Pandjar's partner, of the Wolf Clan from the Mystic Isle

Kerrytan – deceased brother to Ziggy and Naroo, brother to Pandjar

Prince Gravus - prince of the Fox Elf Clan, from the Mystic Isle, husband to Carwen

Captain Gilbert - Prince Gravus' captain of his personal guards

Fox elves - Simon, Listan, Velkar

**Wildlanders - Cindermen and Bluebeards Clan**

Tarzis – captain of the Cindermen

Harald, Sander, Jarack, Pax, Quinn – Cindermen youths, scouts

Mage Festra – evil mage, apprentice of Mage Armitar

Ostick – leader of the Hindamar Highlands' Bluebeards

**Tarot Archetypes**

The Emperor and The Empress

The Hierophant

Temperance

The Star lady

Hermes – the Magician

Hera – the High Priestess

Charioteer - Sir Darwyn

# About the Author

Noel Eastwood is a retired psychologist with over forty years professional experience in psychology, counselling and education. Now a full-time author, Noel shares his lifelong passions of Taoist Alchemy, Jungian psychotherapy, meditation, tai chi, astrology and tarot. A gifted storyteller, his fiction and nonfiction works blend ancient wisdom and contemporary themes. His unique blend of hands-on experience and knowledge, rollicking good storytelling and the wisdom of esoterica is evident in his writing.

You can visit his website and subscribe to his free newsletters on the many diverse topics above - **www.plutoscave.com**

# Footnotes

1) Chapter 8 – *Recessional,* Rudyard Kipling (1897).

2) Chapter 8 - *For the Fallen*, Laurence Binyon. Source: The London Times (1914).

3) Chapter 8 - *John Barleycorn* - traditional English ballad.

4) Chapter 8 - *The Rubaiyat of Omar Khayyam* – translated by Edward Fitzgerald (1859).

5) Chapter 10 - *Shakespeare* – Richard III.

6) Chapter 10 – *Charge of the Goddess* - adapted from Doreen Valiente Foundation, under Creative Commons license.

# Books and Audiobooks

# by Noel Eastwood

**Pluto's Cave**